Lured by Lust

Clara picked up the plate of strawberries. She would treat herself to just one or two, she thought, her mouth tingling in anticipation.

'Clara!'

'The voice sounded so harsh behind her that the heel of her boot slipped between two of the floor tiles. In the surprise of it all she dropped the plate and watched as red juice seeped over the floor.

Swivelling round she saw Jason standing in the doorway. 'That was a silly thing to do, wasn't it?' His voice was edged with danger. As she reached for a cloth he came up behind her and she felt his body pressed up close behind her back.

'You're a very bad girl, Clara,' said Jason. He gripped her waist and led her to the kitchen table. He sat down on the chair and, with the other hand, pulled up her dress and lowered her onto his lap. 'Bad, bad girl,' he repeated, as he brought his hand down on her arse.

'What if someone comes in?' she wailed.

'Shut up and be punished,' he said.

In the middle of it all, against the hot swollen core of her, he brought his hand down on her pussy. With each stroke she felt herself nearing her climax and now it was she who urged, 'Harder, harder.'

Lured by Lust
Tania Picarda

BLACK LACE

Black Lace books contain sexual fantasies.
In real life, always practise safe sex.

This edition published in 2007 by
Black Lace
Thames Wharf Studios
Rainville Rd
London W6 9HA

Originally published 2000

A catalogue record for this book is available from the British Library.

www.black-lace-books.com

Typeset by SetSystems Ltd, Saffron Walden, Essex
Printed and bound by CPI Bookmarque Ltd, Croydon. CR0 4TD

The paper used in this book is a natural, recyclable product made
from wood grown in sustainable forests. The manufacturing process
conforms to the regulations of the country of origin.

ISBN 978 0 352 33533 3 [UK]
ISBN 978 0 352 34176 1 [USA]

Distributed in the USA by Holtzbrinck Publishers, LLC, 175 Fifth Avenue,
New York, NY 10010, USA

Chapter One

Wiping the beads of sweat from her brow, Clara Fox sighed with agitation. She was waiting for Eric to arrive at the gallery, an artist she had spoken to often on the telephone but never met in the flesh. She had finished hanging his paintings moments before and now, exhausted, she surveyed her handiwork. Her eyes were drawn to his canvases, huge and overpowering, and their bright surfaces glistened in front of her eyes. Something about their shimmering colours and floating faces and bodies was disconcerting.

She shifted restlessly in her chair, cursing the lack of air-conditioning. It was high summer, and even clad only in a tight skirt, hold-up stockings, a black push-up bra and a white linen shirt she felt the heat, which made her agitated and unable to concentrate.

Any minute now she should start setting up the gallery for the private view. Languorously she flicked on her computer to check her e-mails. She dipped her fingers between her breasts and in the cleft between them her fingers felt a few pearls of sweat. It was stifling in there – a close, oppressive heat that there was no escape from.

Leaning back she saw the heat haze rising from the pavement outside the gallery window. Her whole body felt closed in, like the gallery, and a heated restlessness was running just beneath the surface of her skin. She got up from behind the counter where she had been sitting in full view of the passers-by, who moved wearily through the harsh midday sun.

Slipping through a door behind her, she was relieved to find that the back room was a little cooler. As her eyes caught sight of the bouquet of flowers stuffed into the bin she prickled with irritation. They had arrived out of the blue that morning, from her ex-boyfriend Paul, whom she had split from more than six months before. She had glanced at the card, 'Let's try and patch things up', and had disposed of them, angered by the way he still had the power to rouse emotion in her.

Paul. There was something about him, something that would always affect her, particularly his voice, a seductive Irish brogue that always got under her skin. A stab of desire unfurled in her stomach as she tried to push him out of her thoughts. It had all gone so horribly wrong in the end and yet she missed his lovemaking; what he had lacked in imagination he had made up for in stamina.

Now the vision of his hard, urgent body pressing against hers flitted into her mind and with some difficulty she pushed it away and turned towards the fridge. It was crammed full of white wine and Champagne for later on. Opening the freezer compartment she basked for a moment in the icy vapour seeping out, which was causing her nipples to harden, then took out an ice tray and carried it over to her desk.

Rapidly she brought up the list of e-mails on her computer and began to read them. Her skin felt tight and sensitive as if the slightest touch would cause meltdown. Damn Paul for making her react like this! They'd lived together for a year but in the end his controlling nature had made her flee him, the flat they'd shared and their future together. She'd tried to forget him, had thrown herself into her work and just recently felt as if she had turned the corner; that was until this morning.

She concentrated on reading her e-mails. It was the usual stuff about shipping deliveries of paintings and routine events that had to do with her job as gallery manager. Manipulating the mouse with her right hand she picked up a cube of ice in her left and began to rub it in the dip of her cleavage. Mmm, that felt good.

The owner of the gallery, Xavier, was downstairs in his office, and was not likely to come up for some time. He had been a fat lot of use yesterday, leaving her to hang the heavy paintings herself. She would have a word with him about that if he ever surfaced. She rubbed the ice along her neck and let it rest at the nape, where its cold wetness tingled against her hot sensitised skin.

Suddenly her attention was caught by one of the e-mails. It was entitled simply, 'Ms X.' Quickly she clicked it open and picked up another ice cube, working it in little circular motions across her temples. She began to read:

Don't you ever feel an ache between your legs sitting behind that counter?

She paused for a moment, the ice dissolving against her overheated skin. Melted ice was streaming down her face and she stuck out the tip of her tongue to catch a drop of water. What on earth was this? An icicle of apprehension passed through her, followed rapidly by a leap of desire.

I've seen you there, sitting behind your white counter with only your lovely head visible, your dark hair a

3

cloud around your face. Almond-shaped eyes with irises the hue of dark cherries, luscious, thickly fringed with lashes.

That was a description of herself, she thought, her breathing becoming more rapid. The e-mail was evidently from some Peeping Tom. Really, she thought crossly, of all the nerve, to write her an anonymous e-mail like that. And yet, despite herself, she couldn't tear her eyes from the screen.

I will address you as Ms X, because that suits me well, suits us both well. Please don't be offended by what you read, I am not some weirdo who gets his kicks out of writing to women anonymously. I have never approached anyone this way before. But I wanted to make my advances to you in a new way, a different way.

Rapidly she skimmed greedily over the rest of the text.

Sometimes, when you are talking to a customer, I observe you standing up, leaning across the counter, smiling that smile that does something very peculiar to every man who comes into contact with you. Well, when I see you, giving out that provocative look, I can't help entertaining the thought that the counter might be just the right height. If I was to stand behind you, I could make love to you. To your right the big glass window, the people going about their business in the street, sometimes glancing in at the pictures lining the walls. The occasional person stopping and peering at the woman bending lasciviously over the counter and the handsome man (believe me, this is the truth, I am not being boastful!) taking her from behind. What would you say to that? Would it turn you on?

4

Clara reddened. She knew what she should do. She should ignore the e-mail. Her first thought was that it was from some crank. But the thought niggled that she must know this man. He had been watching her, that much was clear. He knew what she looked like, that the L-shaped counter she sat behind for much of the day was about waist height, and that the glass window stretched from floor to ceiling to her right. And yet, she reasoned, it was no big deal for someone to have her e-mail address. It was printed on her business card and the gallery's headed paper.

Who are you? Do I know you? she typed. Agitatedly she waited for his reply, a hot flush of anticipation building up inside her.

His e-mail blinked on the screen and she clicked it open.

No, you have never met me, but I have observed you and wondered what goes on in your head, behind that calm exterior. I have also wondered what it might be like if we abandoned ourselves to the scenario I have just outlined. Humour me, play along a little? What have you got to lose?

She knew that she was taking a risk, e-mailing him back like this. He had put her in a compromising position. He knew who she was although she didn't know him at all, only his e-mail address, which gave nothing away. He held the power. And yet, he seemed to be offering her some kind of a challenge, which excited her.

Would I lock the gallery doors or leave them open? she typed, amazed at her own boldness. She wasn't normally this impetuous. What had got into her? Maybe it was a combination of the heat and a restlessness she had been feeling all summer. It didn't help that she had been so tied up with the gallery she had not had time to look for a new man.

After sending the e-mail she waited impatiently for his reply. She crossed and uncrossed her legs, trying to distract herself from the throb at the top of her legs. How on earth did he know that she had got a thrill out of the thought of being watched before? Her imagination overstimulated by his e-mail, she half closed her eyes, letting her mind spin out a torrent of images.

There had been an incident, or had she dreamed it, when a man had stood in the window and given her a look of raw desire, then moved frustratingly out of view. She had wished for him to come in, waited, and when he had not returned she had feverishly rubbed herself to a climax, still sitting behind the counter, ostensibly looking at the catalogue in front of her. That was the nearest she had come to making contact with men these past few months. When she had started at the gallery she knew that it would require a lot of work, but now that she had found several established artists for the gallery, the pressure was off. She could afford to relax. Nevertheless, it was proving difficult to really let her hair down.

The image of the man at the window disappeared from her thoughts, leaving a blank. And then a slow and uneasy sensation began to rise in her. With a lurch of nausea mixed with desire it hit her. Could Paul be trying to contact her indirectly? The thought was a disturbing one. Paul was a novelist who spent most of his time at home staring at a computer, day in, day out. Who knew what six months of fixating on her could drive him to? But if not Paul, then whom? How did Mr X know what she had often thought sitting here? What if he was watching her right now? She opened her eyes and swiftly scanned the street outside. No particular figure stood out in the stream of people on their lunch break. Did she care if he was observing her?

All fear had left her now, replaced by an urgency that was building deep within her. The realisation dawned on her, making her stomach lurch. A complete stranger had read her mind. Re-reading his words now the hairs on the back of her neck were standing on end and the prickly excitement was making her skin clammy. Absent-mindedly, she slipped her hand into the neck of her shirt. She pushed the ice cube over the curve of her breast, which spilled over the constraints of her underwired bra, and pressed the ice cube against first one nipple then the other, gasping at the strength of the sensation.

At last his e-mail came back.

I like your boldness. Not afraid of a challenge, hmm. And so harmless too, because you don't know who I am and I don't know who you are. And we'll never meet, not unless I want to.

Clara bit her lip. She glanced up and took a sharp intake of breath. How long had he been standing there? She slipped her hand out of her blouse and smoothed back her dark mane of hair. Her boss, Xavier, was looking at her quizzically. He was in his mid-forties, with a square jaw and green eyes. His dark hair, which had begun to grey at the temples, was swept back from his face. Now he shot her a quick glance.

'Everything OK for the opening tonight?'

'Yes, everything's under control.' She smiled up at him, distracted. She had meant to discuss her gripe about having to hang the show herself but Mr X's e-mails had made her enter a trancelike state and she was eager to get back to her intimate chat. Sending e-mails was so slow, but, she reasoned, if they went into a chatroom there would not be this tantalising sense of privacy, this peculiar intimacy.

'OK, I'll be back later this afternoon. Eric should be here soon. His plane landed half-an-hour ago.' His mouth creased into a warm smile and his green eyes flashed at her as he pushed open the glass door to the street. She had desired him since she started working at the gallery, but he had made it clear from the outset that he did not mix business with pleasure and she had reluctantly left it at that.

When he had left she sent a message back.

You are very arrogant. But assuming you are as hot as you sound, I'd enjoy the wait. You would walk around the gallery, looking at the pictures, glancing a little in my direction every now and then. I would blush, not knowing why you kept looking. I would get up slowly and lean over the counter. We wouldn't speak. Silently, effortlessly you would come nearer and nearer, until I felt paralysed with excitement. And then you'd reach out and touch me.

She rubbed her silky stockings together, willing him to write back quickly. The front of her shirt was now drenched in sweat and the filmy black bra was clearly outlined.

After waiting for what seemed like forever, Mr X's e-mail popped up. Rapidly she read his message:

Yes, you would be aching for me, but I'd make you wait a fraction longer. I was thinking, wouldn't it be bad for business to close the doors? If we left them open, if a customer came in they'd be given a free show. Where was I, yes, I'd ruche your skirt up, exposing your taut bottom cheeks. What sort of underwear do you like? Ah well, I can imagine, something pretty skimpy, a red G-string and stockings. You do wear stockings?

That's for me to know and you to find out she typed. What on earth was prompting her to reply to this man? She slipped her hand under her skirt and, pushing her panties aside, absent-mindedly began to fondle her clit. She waited with impatience for his reply.

Oh well, be like that. I would hope that they would be topped with red lace, of exquisite quality. A gift from me to you. There wouldn't be much time for preliminaries, partly because you would already be dying for me to push my cock into you, biting your lip with anticipation. I would pull the gusset of your panties aside and simply fill you with my cock, with a strong, hard thrust, the force of it making you gasp through half-open lips and take the weight on your elbows, a ragged cry escaping from the back of your throat.

She could feel what he was describing, a pounding ache deep inside her, but it was frustrating because she could not achieve the satisfaction that he was describing so graphically. She squirmed against the flat of her palm, imagining his cock pressing into her, activating ridges of sensation all along her engorged nerve-endings. She'd never met a man like this, with such a prodigious imagination. And this forwardness was exciting her for the first time in a long while. She pushed two fingers into herself, but it was not enough, she needed precisely what he was describing. She continued to read.

You will bite your lip in anticipation of the next thrust, when filling and stretching you I will pull out and thrust into you again. You notice a woman lingering by the glass, staring at you and the man positioned behind you. You notice that she is not shocked by what she sees, just curious, and her watching you only heightens your excitement, as you are being carried away now by the pleasure, moaning against me. Then she pushes open the door.

Clara pistoned her fingers in and out of herself until she felt the contractions ripple against them. She leaned back in her chair feeling the hot rush of pleasure radiate out from the tops of her thighs and flow upwards over her breasts. Blood flushed her face and the black typeface on the glowing screen swam before her as the sharp stab of pleasure ebbed away.

She had just taken away the edge off her frustration, but now she felt hotter than ever. A few buttons had come undone on her shirt and she pulled it closed. But soon she was cupping her breasts and feeling their heat. She ran her fingers over her voluptuous breasts, her nipples still hard with excitement.

As she placed her fingers over the keyboard she began to feel indignant. He had left her high and dry. She tried to formulate the words, to write exactly how he had made her feel, when she saw a movement at the glass door, which was set into the window. Damn, the last thing she needed was someone who was going to hover around in the gallery asking questions about the pictures. Flustered, she closed down her e-mail file.

The man who had entered the gallery had a confident swagger and was loaded down with luggage. 'Clara,' he said, stretching out a hand. 'Good to see you at last.'

She knew immediately that it was Eric. She had only started managing the gallery six months ago and this was the first exhibition of his that she had organised. She had spoken to him regularly in Copenhagen over the phone, but nothing had prepared her for his impressive physicality. He emanated a sense of rude good health and was dressed casually in chinos and a T-shirt.

'Did you hang the show?' he asked.

'Yes. Do you like it?' It was always a cause of anxiety, hanging a show at the last minute without the artist's approval. But this time she needn't have worried.

'Yes, I love the way you've set it up.'

Eric leaned on the counter and they chatted for a while. She noticed that his eyes, which were an attractive shade of amber, kept skimming her body as they talked. She swallowed, losing her train of thought momentarily. He was undressing her, his gaze boring through her like a lion eyeing its prey.

He carried on the light-hearted banter, telling her that he would only be around today because he had to fly back tomorrow.

When she looked down to check her watch she was surprised that it was already four o'clock. At the same time she noticed that her skirt was still ruched up from her masturbation session and that an expanse of lean thigh and her stocking tops had caught Eric's eye. For a moment neither of them spoke and he held her gaze. His expression had become mischievous. He gave her a broad grin, but made no comment. Despite his apparent unconcern she coloured a little.

As she got up she knocked a pile of papers to the floor and began to smooth down her skirt. What kind of impression was she making on this gorgeous man? She chastised herself and said in what she hoped was an authoritative voice, 'Let's go downstairs and put your luggage away. And is that another picture?' She gestured to the flat package tied with rope.

'Yes, I just finished it and thought that you might like to see it.'

It seemed to take forever to walk along the length of the gallery to the door at the back that led down a flight of stairs. She could sense Eric eyeing her bottom as she started the descent.

Down in the cellar, which was kept dimmed to

protect the pictures, the coolness was a relief. She almost forgot the fevered state that she had been in, not an hour ago, trapped by the sunlight beating in through the plate glass window and aroused by Mr X. She glanced around the room, the walls of which were stacked with racks of pictures standing up vertically in the slots.

'Just put your stuff in a corner, it'll be perfectly safe,' she said.

She reached to take a case out of his hand but as she did so he gripped her wrist firmly and pulled her towards him. It was a brutal movement but it had the effect of making her very turned on. He released her wrist and put down the case. She ran her fingers through her hair nervously.

Without another word he pulled off his T-shirt, revealing a taut chest, lightly tanned and with a patch of dark-gold hair running over his pectorals. He rubbed his hand through his chest hair, back and forth absent-mindedly, and she noticed that his forearms were powerful, and his hand too, full of strength, with square blunt fingers. He looked more like someone who lived the rough, outdoor life, a farm hand, than someone who spent his life in a studio painting pictures.

'It was so hot in the gallery, I just need to cool down for a bit. You look a little bit overheated yourself.' He held her gaze steadily. He was challenging her and in a split second she realised that she could not resist what he was offering. Or had she misunderstood him?

He bent over and lifted up the picture, wrapped in brown paper and tied with a thick piece of rope.

'This is my surprise. A gift for you, for organising this exhibition.'

She watched him as he started to work the knot loose. Although it was a privilege to receive a gift like this, and she knew that Eric was one of the gallery's best-selling artists, right now she couldn't give a damn about his painting.

She was mesmerised by the way the muscles in his forearms bulged as he loosened the knot. How compact and packed with strength he was. An impulse came to her that she wanted to be held by him and crushed in his arms until she was imprisoned. A prisoner of passion. It was an exciting idea but she had never had such an impulse before and it scared her. She pushed it aside.

Finally he loosened the paper and held up the piece. She could make out female body parts here and there in the loosely daubed canvas.

'It's . . . very nice.' Her words came out in a whisper. Surely he must be picking up the vibes she was giving out in her voice hoarse with desire. God, she needed him.

'When do you need to start preparing for the private view?' he asked, his amber eyes flashing her an unmistakable signal.

A violent flush ran through her as she tried to speak. 'Oh, not for another hour or so.'

She was holding his gaze, willing him into activity. For a moment they stood staring at each other, he still twisting the rope in his hands. Then he stepped forward and pressed his mouth roughly against hers. He pushed her legs open and slipped one of his thighs between them, pushing her against the cold stone wall. The scent of his maleness and his hard thigh prising her legs apart made her feel dizzy with desire.

He pulled back. 'That gives us enough time,' he said, looking around. 'Where does that door lead to?'

'Xavier's office.' She was pulling off her shirt, exposing her full breasts in the black half-cups. She felt for the door handle. To her surprise the door opened. Xavier usually kept his office locked. She took in the broad sweep of the desk and the soft leather of the executive chair.

'Well, Miss Fox, let's see how we can pass the time.'

She pulled off her skirt, revealing only the matching high-cut black lace panties and hold-up stockings. She still wore her high-heeled black shoes with the strap around the ankle. He lifted her up and prised her legs open. She felt like a doll being positioned for his pleasure. As his eyes ran over the curve of her bust and skimmed along her long elegant legs she felt a smouldering passion building, desperate for release. When would he touch her, make love to her, put her out of her misery? She squirmed on the desk and gave him an imploring look. His flesh hovered just out of reach.

Now he had stripped off and her eyes were drawn down the flat plane of his stomach to his cock, which protruded from a patch of hair and veered upwards, already fully erect. He pulled her panties down and, again in that brusque manner, scooped her up and lay her face down over his knee. What on earth was he up to? He unclipped her bra and she felt her breasts pressed against his hard thighs, as he sat on the edge of the desk, one hand clasping her waist so that she did not fall. It was on her lips to ask him what he was doing, but he was pressing one exploratory finger into her, followed by another, and the sharp pleasure that he was generating made her lose her train of thought.

She dimly recalled that she hadn't locked the door upstairs. Xavier would be furious. But, she figured, he wouldn't be back for some time. She relaxed against Eric's fingers, which were turning in her tight passage in a corkscrew motion. But before she could lose herself more deeply in the waves of pleasure he was generating, he rapidly withdrew his hand. The bastard! She dug her fingers into the calf of his leg, her sense of frustration causing her to lash out.

She heard him laugh, and felt his hard cock boring into her stomach as she lay across him, making her feel hot at the point of contact. Then she felt a sharp pain as the flat of his palm met the cheeks of her bare bottom.

'Ow!' she cried out.

'That'll teach you to dig your nails into me!' he said and laughed. 'Why, you need to learn some manners, young lady.'

Again his palm made contact with her bottom and then the slaps began to rain down as he held her wriggling on his lap. The spanking he was subjecting her to was hurting, of course, and her bottom cheeks were becoming red and warming up under his ministrations. She had never found herself in such a position before. She hated him for doing it, and yet she realised that it was precisely this humiliating scenario that was making her moan as he spanked her a little harder. She hadn't meant to claw at him. She just wasn't used to waiting for someone to make love to her. If anything, in the past she'd had to slow down men's ardour.

'You like it, hmm?' he asked. 'And your bottom is really very pretty. Pert and small. I watched you once before: you were in a tight skirt. I don't think you were wearing any knickers.'

What was Eric talking about? As far as she knew they had never met before.

'I remember longing to touch you, to lift your skirt up there and then and fondle you.'

A shot of fear went through her. Was he Mr X? But that was impossible. How could he have sent e-mails while on a plane from Copenhagen? It was on the tip of her tongue to ask him when he had seen her. But before she had a chance to give the matter any further thought she felt another sensation. She felt something brush against the sensitive backs of her thighs. Then the rough implement was dragged along the crevice of her bottom. It created a prickly sensation as he rubbed it across her engorged clit; she jumped. It felt like the rope that he had just unknotted from the picture. She saw the rope clearly in her mind. She had noticed its unravelling ends. That must be what he was caressing her with.

Then he began to bring the rope down, very lightly on the crease just below her bottom cheeks. It caused a sharper pain than the spanking, a sting, and she relaxed into the smarting sensations as he marked out the lengths of her thighs with the piece of rope, flicking it across them, leaving reddish horizontal markings. She began to cry out, she felt so aroused, so wired, as if she were about to drown in the hot, all-encompassing sensations emanating from her smarting thighs and heated pussy. Then he dragged the end of the rope over her clit again and immediately she came, crying out and bucking against his hand, which remained there, teasing her opening further with the rope end.

In a daze she felt him pull both her arms up and firmly secure them behind her back. She was weak and spent, every inch of her body alive to the slightest touch. He lifted her body and with his warm hands on her again she felt the quickening pace of her own arousal, laced with an anticipation of what he would do next.

'You understand that I needed to tie you up like that, otherwise you are likely to lash out like a little cat.'

Flinging her over his shoulder he unceremoniously lowered her down so that she was astride him as he sat in the big leather director's chair so that she faced the door. She smarted as she thought what she must look like, her tied hands making her bosom curve up provocatively, her hair a wild tangle around her head. She knew that Xavier might return at any minute and her head began to cloud with anxiety at the consequences. But soon Eric broke her out of her thoughts by reaching one hand around her body and pinching her nipple into a hard point.

She looked down at his cock, glistening with a bead of his arousal at the opening. She longed to ram herself down on it and bring herself to the brink of orgasm, but she was immobilised by his strong arm holding her firmly around the waist.

'Alright, I think you've learned enough for today,' he said softly.

He fondled her other breast for a moment, then placed both his hands around her waist and lifted her so that her pussy was positioned over the head of his cock. Then he lowered her onto it, inch by inch, so that she began to whimper. He had kept this from her for so long and still he was tormenting her. Her insides aflame with sensation she felt his rock-hard cock fill her completely.

Suddenly he changed gear. He put his slightly play-ful act to one side, driven now by his own overwhelm-ing desire to find release. Lightly biting the back of her neck he lifted her halfway off his cock and then began to thrust upwards with force, holding her steady with his powerful arms. He pistoned into her with an urgency and she closed her eyes, immersed in the sensations that were washing over her. It was strange not being able to move, even a centimetre, as he held her steady over his cock.

Then her excitement rapidly reached fever pitch; when she finally felt herself come it was like a dam bursting open. And still he thrust into her, causing a flame of pleasure to burn through her whole body, the relief was so intense. Shuddering against him, she felt his hands tighten their grip on her arms as he burst.

They rested for a second, then when he had pulled out of her she flopped back against her tied hands and his chest and gasped for breath. She felt so weak, like a rag doll, and utterly spent. The orgasm had been so strong, it took a while for the room to cease to be a blur and come into focus. Through half-open eyes she saw another face looking back at her. It was a woman's face. Clara gave a gasp of surprise.

'See anything you like?' said Eric.

The woman stood in the open doorway. 'Yes. Interesting, very interesting.'

Her voice was low and gravelly, tinged with a foreign accent. The diminutive blonde stepped forward. She was wearing a long leather coat, her hair cascading over it in unruly blonde spirals. How long had she been there, thought Clara, and what had she seen? The blonde's eyes were grey-green and feline, and from the look on her face she had seen everything. Her expression was like the cat who had got the cream. Clara wondered what, if anything, the woman was wearing under the coat, which hugged her curvy figure under the soft weathered leather. She looked unflustered and yet she must be sweltering, thought Clara.

'Excuse me, the door was open, so I just wandered in. I came for the private view, of course.'

Eric had untied Clara's hands and now she rubbed the red marks from her wrists. With her body still sapped of energy she pulled on her underwear.

Eric was matter-of-factly pulling on his clothes and gave the blonde woman a broad smile. 'Well, you certainly got your own private view,' he said. 'Oh Clara,' he said absent-mindedly, 'this is Astrid, a friend of mine. She's been living here so long, she's practically a native.'

'Are you from Denmark?'

'No, I'm Swedish actually,' said Astrid, lighting a cigarette and taking a drag.

Clara pulled her shirt over her breasts. Her first reaction had been to be disconcerted, knowing that she had been watched while she and Eric had made love, but then to her surprise, with Astrid's eyes taking in her half-naked body appreciatively, she suddenly felt an electric connection with the other woman, as if she had found a kindred spirit.

As she pulled on her stockings she couldn't help wondering about the uncanny duplication of what had just happened and the fantasy – of being watched by someone – that her anonymous e-mail correspondent had outlined to her. The longing to be watched had swiftly and effortlessly been made real, and it had been an added thrill to be made love to in her boss's office. She was gradually regaining her energy and began to feel an adrenaline high sweep over her as she cautiously returned Astrid's gaze.

It seemed perfectly natural to Clara since corresponding with the mysterious Mr X to stand there talking to Astrid about the gallery. Astrid was far too cool to mention what she had seen and Clara was enjoying chatting to her so much that when she glanced at her watch she realised with a start that the guests were expected in half an hour.

'Eric, Astrid. Do you mind helping me out with the wine? I'm a bit behind schedule.' She figured that it was the least Eric could do.

Eric acquiesced with a shrug and they went upstairs and covered a set of tables with white tablecloths, glasses and wine. When the caterers arrived and began setting out the canapés Clara took the opportunity to change into a classic black shift dress. Then Xavier returned, gave a swift nod in Clara's direction and hurried down to his office with Eric. When they emerged for the beginning of the private view Xavier began to circulate, shaking hands with many of the elegantly turned-out guests.

Astrid had removed the leather coat to reveal a white strapless dress that was of a light, semi-transparent material that wrapped around her tanned, lean figure.

19

Clara thought she looked sensational, her nipples clearly showing through the delicate fabric.

Astrid told her that she and Eric were old friends. Reading between the lines Clara inferred that they were also occasional lovers. While she poured wine and made polite chat a desire grew in her. She couldn't wait for the opening to be over so that she could have an intimate e-mail chat with Mr X. She wondered what he would make of her encounter. She was looking forward to describing it to him in graphic detail. Instinctively she knew that it would arouse him too.

Chapter Two

Clara could barely keep her mind on the job as she moved about, shaking hands and throwing little glances at Eric. She was still dazed by the events of the previous hours. The gallery was crowded with people, but Clara felt little inclination to chat and instead kept herself busy pouring out the wine for the guests. Astrid stayed by her side and was helping her out, for which she was grateful. In a brief lull they exchanged numbers and promised to get together soon.

She watched as Eric stood in the corner with a sophisticated man, who Clara gauged to be around forty, dressed in a casual linen suit, with dark wavy hair swept back from his forehead. But while Eric whispered urgently in his ear, as if imparting some pressing information, the man's smouldering dark eyes surveyed the room.

Clara observed that superficially he was taking in the pictures. But time and time again his wavering gaze came back to rest on her. It was stiflingly close in the gallery now, even though the door was wide open, and his gaze, light as a butterfly resting on a leaf, was making her self-conscious.

Astrid had noticed too. 'Looks like you've got an admirer,' she said.

Clara began to redden. 'Mmm. He is nice. Do you know him?'

'Never seen him before. Shall I get Eric to introduce you?'

Before she could reply, Astrid was already moving confidently through the throng, and had drawn Eric aside. Eric leaned closer to the stranger's ear and said something, which made the stranger throw back his head and laugh and make a more pointed glance at Clara. It was so humiliating to be gossiped about like that, thought Clara, turning her face down to pour out more wine, and yet she couldn't deny that the stranger's gaze was making her feel hot, even inside the flimsy dress. They were coming over.

Eric gave her one of his beaming smiles. 'May I introduce you to my new friend, Mark Chalmers. This is Clara Fox, the manager of the gallery.'

She shook his hand. 'Nice to meet you. Seen anything you like?'

Close up, his gaze was even more mesmerising, drawing her towards him with a magnetic pull. As he smiled, his eyes crinkled at the corners.

'Well, Eric's work is very interesting. I think I'll probably buy a piece.'

'We've already sold quite a few of his works so you'd better get in there quickly,' said Clara.

'Why don't you take a break,' said Astrid pointedly. 'I'll take over.'

'Thanks.'

She moved out from behind the counter and stood next to Mark. Eric was nowhere to be seen.

'I think that Eric's paintings are very unusual,' said Mark. 'With their swirling limbs and faces the subjects hint at our deepest, darkest fantasies. Eric isn't afraid to confront the unknown, I think. He's a risk-taker.'

She smiled, thinking of the risk she had taken in Xavier's office with Eric. She smiled at Xavier who caught her eye from across the room. If only he knew! She had taken a huge gamble, but part of the thrill had been the danger of being caught. She realised now, now that she had had time to reflect on it, how much she relished the idea of knowing that Astrid had been watching, drinking in their lovemaking. Now that the desire had been ignited, she suddenly knew with a certainty that she wanted to repeat the experience, in a public place, amongst a sea of anonymous faces. She would make a point of telling Mr X all about her desires.

'What kind of art do you like?' she asked, as they walked along the length of the gallery, looking at the canvases. It bothered her that even as she chatted to this sophisticated, intelligent man, Mr X was still at the back of her mind.

'Well, I'm quite discerning. I like things that are unusual, that make you think, that are off-the-wall. Like this.' They were standing beside a large canvas painted in broad brushstrokes of red and yellow. 'At first it appears to be a woman lying in a field of flowers, but if you look closely the heads of the tulips are a thousand fiery tongues, licking her body, and where they make contact her skin looks as if it has melted, like candle wax.'

She peered at the picture. She had always thought that they were flowers, now they looked like flames. There was no denying the sexual charge of the picture, but it disconcerted her.

After he had decided that this was the picture that he would purchase, they talked more generally about things, art mainly, and she was impressed by the breadth and wealth of his knowledge. His manner was

23

elegant and understated, and she guessed that he was a wealthy man who collected art for fun. But he revealed almost nothing about his personal circumstances.

As they talked his eyes held hers, hanging onto her every word. It was an altogether different approach to Eric's, much less obvious but no less exciting. Before they parted she had agreed to have dinner with him the following evening.

It was half-past ten when she said goodbye to Astrid and the last stragglers left the gallery. Cooler night air was filtering in through the open door as she took in the floor, strewn with cigarette butts and empty glasses, and began to busy herself with tidying up the debris. She hoped that Xavier would also leave soon. He came in from saying goodbye to Eric and looked surprised to see her rinsing out glasses in the back room as he had booked a cleaner, who was coming in the next morning to tidy up the mess.

Although she was exhausted she was itching for him to leave so that she could type out the day's events to her anonymous correspondent. But Xavier was in a better mood than she had seen him in for some time, exhilarated at how much Eric had sold, and stood talking animatedly for another few drawn-out minutes. Finally he left and she switched on her computer and settled down at her desk. To her delight, when she e-mailed Mr X he responded immediately.

It all came out in a frenzy. Her afternoon with Eric, how he had punished and restrained her. How this new turn of events had not frightened her, but had opened a door to new pleasures.

At the moment the door is only ajar, she typed, but I know what I want now. I'm more sure than I've ever been, that I need to follow my desires and see where they lead me.

Do you want to be seen? Do you want to be pleasured in public and know that people are watching?

Yes, very much so. But it's so frustrating, not knowing if the opportunity will arise. Eric is going back to Denmark.

Is there no one else you know who would be interested in this kind of experimentation?

She thought of Astrid. She was living in London, and hadn't batted an eyelid when she had found Clara astride Eric.

There is a girl, a very hot foxy girl who I met this evening. Astrid. I think she'd be up for anything.

Mmm, very interesting. I'd love to see you two in action one day.

Believe it or not, I've never been with a woman before, although I've thought of it. So that's a possibility.

Any guys?

She thought of Mark, his dark glance, his appreciation of pushing the boundaries. They had made a connection, she was sure of that.

Yes, there is someone who has possibilities. She yawned and stretched in the chair. She didn't want to tell Mr X about Mark just yet. I'm meeting him tomorrow and we'll see what happens.

Are you going to tell him what you want? That you want to be watched?

Yes. But I must go now, Mr Mystery Man. I need my beauty sleep.

You are quite beautiful enough as you are. Goodnight.

She logged off. Wearily she locked the doors, stepped into the empty street and flagged a taxi.

The next day at the gallery Clara was kept busy. News of Eric's exhibition must have spread by word of mouth from those who'd been at the private view, because streams of people kept coming in to look at the pictures. She had already sold two more that morning. Although delighted that his show was a sell out, she would have been relieved for a quiet hour or so to regain her composure and to think about yesterday.

She had had to come in early to let in the cleaners, so that everything would be shipshape before the gallery opened at ten. Now, at half-past one she felt drained. She put her head in her hands for a moment and saw a swirl of faces. First she saw Eric, his amber eyes blazing, then Mark, who, in his understated way, had hinted at something mysterious to come. And Astrid too, vibrant, sexy and confident. She remembered her throaty laugh as she had tossed back her ash-blonde curls. They were all interested in her in one way or another. She was, she guessed, a little overwhelmed, to have become the object of so much attention after such a long drought.

Gazing around the gallery, she breathed a sigh of relief. For once it was empty. The phone rang and when she answered it was Paul.

'Hi there, how are you?' he said. It had been so long since she had spoken to him. Now she felt his voice, rich as melted chocolate, begin to work its magic on her. She took a sharp intake of breath, resolving not to let him get to her.

'How did you find out where I was working?'

'Oh, come on, don't be paranoid. I just asked at your last job. Did you get the flowers?'

'Yes, but I can't say I understand why you sent them.'

'I've thought about things and I realise that I handled things all wrong.'

'I'm sorry Paul, but we gave it our best shot and there really isn't anything else to say.'

'Listen to me Clara, I know it's a cliché but I really have changed.'

'I don't see the point of going into this. I really would appreciate it if you didn't contact me here again.'

'Can't we at least meet and talk about it?'

'No. I'm sorry.' As she put down the phone she realised that her hand was trembling. Why couldn't he see that there was no hope, not a hope in hell, of them getting back together? With Paul there had been no freedom, he'd always needed to know where she was, when she'd be back and would pick a row if she went for drinks with male colleagues. She wouldn't have minded if she'd actually done anything to cause him to feel insecure and jealous, but she hadn't!

She took a few deep breaths to calm herself down. She had to face the fact that although Paul had a peculiar sexual hold on her she could not go back. She needed her own autonomy now, the chance to map out her own destiny.

In an effort to distract herself she began to peruse her e-mails. She was irritated, almost angry, that there was nothing from Mr X. She chastised herself for her reaction. After all, she was an independent woman of thirty-one, and yet from one day to another Mr X had well and truly got under her skin. Well, she was damned if she would let him know that he had got to her. At the moment, he was the one in control. He had seen her, desired her and approached her.

She was, as usual, sitting behind the big white counter. Now she flicked open her mirror and took a good look at herself. Despite her tiredness, her eyes gleamed and her olive skin radiated vitality. She examined herself from several angles, and then on a whim began to pin up her hair so that a few tendrils fell about her face, softening it. She took in the cupid's bow mouth, with the slightly protruding lower lip, the slightly upturned nose and dark limpid eyes. She brushed mascara through her lashes, making her eyes look bigger and more alluring. She did look rather delicious, she thought to herself. Mark would be in for a treat tonight. Snapping shut her compact she began to type an e-mail to Mr X.

I'm back in the gallery as usual. I'm not in the mood for polite chitchat today. But I've got just what you want, Mr X. You don't know what you're missing. I don't need to receive it as a present from you. Right now I'm wearing a matching red bra and panties of a very fine mesh and French lace, very see through. And they unfasten at the side, for convenience, in case I'm in a hurry. If I needed your cock inside me urgently, Mr X, you would just have to undo the catch at the side and they'd fall away. I'm also wearing a suspender belt, of the same scalloped red lace. It looked very sexy on me this morning as I watched myself in the mirror, positioning it against my lightly tanned skin. As I pulled on the suspenders I thought of how much you would have enjoyed the view. They are almost translucent in colour and edged in lace.

She began to feel her nipples harden as she recalled how she had scrutinised her image closely that morning. It had been a long time since she had taken a really good look at herself, taken pleasure in the curves of her body. That morning she had felt a strange new thrill on discovering the raunchy underwear at the back of her cupboard. Mr X's message about what he would like her to wear had prompted the impulse to unearth the saucy red lingerie. She clicked on her mouse to send the e-mail.

While she waited for his e-mail, an image of him began to form in her mind. Mr X appeared as a shadowy figure walking towards her, his face a blur, the features undelineated.

She jumped as the phone on her desk began to ring. Surely it couldn't be Paul again? Suddenly the conviction rushed through her: it was Mr X. She was frozen, watching it as it continued to ring. It had to be Mr X, she was certain of it. Maybe he had just received her e-mail and had decided to break out of his anonymous persona. She steeled herself, lifted the receiver to her ear and waited.

'Clara? How are you today?' The voice was cheerful, effusive. For a second the caller's identity did not register.

She ran her hand through her hair. The mystery was over. Feeling an overwhelming sense of relief, she let a low sigh escape from her lips.

'Mark! I'm very well indeed.' Her heart still pounded from the adrenaline that was rushing through her body. But there was also a sting of regret that it was not Mr X that mingled with her relief. 'It's lucky you bought Eric's picture when you did because this show has already nearly sold out. It's really quite incredible. Of course, I expected his stuff to sell well, but the exhibition runs for another three weeks and I didn't expect everything to go by the second day.'

'Well, I'm very pleased for you.' He paused for a moment and then went on, his well-spoken voice having the same effect that his presence had had, both calming and mesmerising her at the same time. 'Are we still on for tonight?'

'Yes of course. Where are we going?'

'Do you know the Barton Club in Dover Street?' She knew of it, of course, it was a pretty exclusive club. A couple of the gallery's clients had mentioned that they were members. But she had never been inside. She wasn't even sure that she would be able to find it.

'I've heard of it. Would you pick me up at the gallery first and we can go together? How long have you been a member?'

'Oh, I've only recently joined and I've only been once or twice. Suppose I pick you up at six?'

'Yes, I look forward to it.' As she said goodbye she wondered if the Barton would be very posh. Although she loved art and working at the gallery, her salary was not high enough to allow her to join exclusive members' clubs. For a second she felt inadequate, but then, remembering how at ease Mark had made her feel she began to relax. Beneath her jacket she wore a plum-coloured dress, lined with silk, which was making her feel very sexy. She also wore very high-heeled shoes in a dark damson velvet to complement them. Beneath this elegant ensemble only she and Mr X knew that she was wearing the scarlet, see through, somewhat sluttish underwear.

Settling herself back in her chair she knew that time would pass slowly until the evening. Mark was an unknown quantity and she had no idea what would happen. She stretched luxuriously in her chair. Xavier had gone to take Eric to the airport and probably wouldn't be back that day. She stared listlessly at the screen. Mr X had obviously not bothered replying. Or maybe he had other things on his mind.

She grew despondent as a restlessness settled over her, before she noticed the new message winking at her on the screen. It was from him! In her excitement she could not control herself. Running the tip of her tongue over her lips in anticipation she clicked it open.

All dressed up for your date this evening, hmm? He's a lucky guy. You're acting all mysterious not telling me who he is. Never mind, I can live with that. The bigger question is, do you know what you're going to do with him? There's no point leaving it to chance. Better think it through, and if he's amenable tell him early on in the evening. Then, by the end there won't be any surprises. To really fulfil your fantasies you must know what you want, and to do that you must know yourself, and that will take time.

She was fed up with him asking all the questions.

Forget me for a second, what are your fantasies?

I should have thought that was pretty obvious. To watch a pretty girl like you, Ms X, touching herself in the middle of an upmarket gallery when she thinks no one is looking.

She smarted, but felt a tingle start between her legs and a flood of arousal run up and down her thighs. There was no way he could have known that. But I've never done that, she typed back, angrily. He must be guessing. He couldn't know such a thing unless there was a camera secretly filming her. Her eyes scanned the opposite wall but she couldn't see anything suspicious. And yet she was feeling the same way she had yesterday when Mr X had first approached her. That he was watching her. And now the feeling had turned from being a little sinister to a much more pleasant one; it was more than a little exhilarating.

Before she could give the matter more thought, a

group of people came through the door and began to ask questions about Eric's work. She tried to push the content of Mr X's puzzling e-mail aside, and, smoothing down her dress walked around the other side of the counter and led them over to a picture that was still for sale.

It was almost six o'clock when the last client left the gallery and Clara wearily switched off her computer. Again, no reply to her last e-mail from Mr X, but she had no time to think of that now. She went into the bathroom to freshen-up her face and the niggling thought occurred to her: she ought to have considered what she might like Mark to do to her. She decided there and then that, despite her misgivings about Mr X, she would follow his instructions until she felt more confident about making her own decisions.

She slicked on some lipgloss and tousled her hair, making her look as wanton as she felt. And then, as if from nowhere, a vivid fantasy popped into her head. She smiled to herself. She wondered if he could be persuaded? She heard footsteps in the gallery. Mark. Swiftly she stuffed her make-up into her bag and sprayed some perfume onto her neck and wrists. She was bubbling with a mixture of confidence and anticipation.

He was leaning against the counter, perfectly self-contained, wearing a stylish light suit. Her eyes caught his and held them for several seconds. Revelling in her new-found confidence, she held his gaze for as long as she could. In the end, he was the first to look away. In one fluid movement she stepped forwards to embrace him, her skin warm with arousal. From that glance she sensed that the enactment of her fantasy would go to plan.

They left the gallery and started to walk up Piccadilly, past the Ritz Hotel and along Hyde Park where people were lying about in deckchairs. The weather was still hot but a cool breeze was now blowing. The conversation came easily, the content light, and they talked about something and nothing. She had a feeling that he too knew that the conversation was not that important. He was looking at her meaningfully and she had an instinctive feeling that he was happy to allow her to progress at her own pace. When she was ready to take things further she would give him the sign.

They turned into Dover Street and went down a perfectly ordinary-looking staircase, which led to the entrance of the club. There were a scattering of people at the tables and a few of the men turned to look at Clara. Enjoying the glances that followed her she crossed the dining room, which was dimly lit. Clara noticed that the sumptuous velvet-lined booths that ran along the walls offered complete privacy to the diners. She walked a little way behind Mark, who was joking with the waiter, until eventually they came to a halt at a booth in the far corner. To Clara's surprise there was a man sitting at the table, pulling somewhat nervously on a cigarette, who greeted Mark and seemed rather surprised to see her.

'Well, this is a surprise. I didn't expect to see you here,' said Mark. Clara looked from one to the other, confused. Was this a dinner date or wasn't it?

'Clara, this is Claus, an old friend of mine. He supported my membership to join the club.'

Claus ground out his cigarette and stood up. She shook his hand and took a good look at him. Not bad, she thought, not bad at all. He was impressively tall, more than six foot at a guess, with tousled blond hair, blue eyes and a strongly defined chin. She guessed that he must be about ten years younger than Mark.

'I'm sorry,' he began. Despite his foreign name his voice betrayed no accent. 'Mark, I'm sure we agreed to meet today.' He began to colour. 'I'm afraid I've made a mistake. I'll leave you two to it.'

Mark smiled. 'Claus is a very old friend of mine. A lovely guy, but a bit forgetful. Why not join us for a drink.' He looked at Clara. 'That is, if you don't mind?'

'Sure, why not.'

Clara squeezed in next to Claus and felt the hard length of his thigh press against hers. It was a circular table and Mark sat next to her, and positioned one arm behind her along the back of the alcove. She turned towards him and took in the scent of his musky masculinity. Once the waiter had brought them their drinks Mark moved in a little closer to her.

She thought that she had probably been set up. Mark evidently wanted to show her off to his friend. Well, that was fine with her. Claus explained to her that he was a cultural correspondent for a German paper and was covering an art exhibition at the Royal Academy. She was finding what he had to say rather interesting when she felt the featherlight brush of his fingers slip under the hem of her dress and squeeze her knee.

She turned to look at Mark, who was smiling at his friend.

'Such a stressful job you have, Claus. Always trying to catch deadlines,' said Mark. 'Don't think about your work any more this evening. Time to let your hair down a little, I think.'

Claus' hand was rapidly making its way up her naked thigh. She leaned back in the booth and opened her legs as much as she was able to with the two men on either side of her. The waiter passed her a menu and she began to peruse it, not taking anything in, as Claus worked his way along her thigh. Mark said nothing and just watched his friend. Claus continued to chat about how he was enjoying his stay at the Ritz and that this was his last night here, although he was often in London and also wrote for some English papers.

Clara closed her eyes. It was so easy, she thought, to just enjoy the sensations, as Claus' fingertips lightly brushed over her panties, setting her clit aflame. She let out a sigh and looked at Mark. She assumed that he knew what was going on under the table. Instinctively she reached out to the bulge in the front of his trousers and ran her fingers over it. She was impressed both by its length and girth and pressed her palm along it, the heat from his cock pulsing through the thin cotton material. She would have him inside her later, she knew that, his big hard cock prising her apart.

Claus continued to tease her swollen clit. She felt herself lubricating against his fingers, which were rubbing over it in a figure-of-eight motion. She wanted more, much more. She felt his fingers urgently push the front of her panties aside and thrust their way into her vagina while with her other hand she still fondled Mark's cock. She was aroused, but she was damned if she was going to be their plaything. No, she had other plans.

'How about we stop this pussyfooting around, hmm, Claus?' she said and closed her legs, clamping his hand between them. Removing her hand from Mark's cock she reached coolly for the menu. A look of surprise crossed Mark's face but then he relaxed and started to look at the wine list. She felt Claus' hand reluctantly slide out from between her thighs.

They spent the next two hours enjoying an exquisite meal and polishing off a couple of bottles of wine. She did not explain why she had suddenly changed her mind about letting Claus pleasure her in the restaurant. In any case, neither of them seemed particularly bothered about it. Clara basked in the pleasant intimacy that was building between them. The restaurant was filling up and was becoming rather hot and stuffy.

Even in the flimsy dress Clara felt very warm. With the two men on either side, her pussy was again pulsing with desire, abruptly making its demands felt. The urgent ache which was now spreading out from the hub of her desire, and building minute by minute, made her decide to take action.

'Well, that was a lovely meal,' she said as Mark paid the bill. 'But how about we go back to my place,' she added, with a smirk, 'for coffee.' She looked from Claus to Mark. It was impossible to choose between the two. No, she had made her decision, she would have them both. Mr X would have approved of her quick adaptation to the situation.

They both agreed enthusiastically, and as they made their way out of the club she thought again of the fantasy she had formulated before she left the gallery. She had thought that she would like to make love to Mark on the Underground, an image that had come out of the blue.

Mark began to hail a taxi but she told him that it wasn't necessary as she wanted to take the tube. As she passed through the entrance to Green Park tube and they followed behind she was suddenly a little self-conscious. She hesitated at the top of the escalator, wondering whether she was really ready for this.

The men had caught up with her and Claus stepped onto the escalator first. Mark put his arm around her and drew her onto the escalator.

'Is something wrong?' he asked, kindly.

She looked at him, in his immaculately cut linen suit. Wasn't it ridiculous to want to indulge in this form of exhibitionism with such respectable men? And yet, she had to confront her fear. She whispered into Mark's ear.

'I wanted to make love to you on the Underground. With everyone watching. I've been imagining it all evening. But now I'm not so sure.' It all came out in a rush.

As they stepped off the escalator and went through the tunnel towards the platform, Mark relaxed and smiled at her. She walked on a little ahead and over her shoulder saw Mark say something to Claus. She guessed they must both be intrigued by the idea. Incredible. They stood on the platform waiting for the tube. Only a few other people were about as it was Wednesday and not yet ten o'clock.

Claus ran his hand slowly and sensuously along the nape of her neck. She turned towards him, feeling a knot of fear form in her stomach. It had all been settled so unexpectedly, so easily. It seemed silly now to have thought that they would not both be happy with the idea. Now she was afraid, not of anything in particular, just of the unknown. She couldn't remember ever having taken a risk like this. She knew only that Mr X had offered her the challenge, and that she had to summon up the boldness to go through with it.

The train thundered into the station and a sensation of dizziness passed over her. She felt Claus lead her towards the open door, and, as if in a dream, she stepped onto the train. She peered down the carriage and saw that there were three people sitting further up so she turned towards the empty end of the carriage.

She sat down in one of the seats and Claus moved towards her. His face was serious now, as he stared down at her. A thrill ran through her as she reached upwards and pulled him down on top of her. She wanted him with an urgency she could no longer hide, kissing him deeply, ripping open his shirt and running her hands over his chest.

A wild surge of excitement passed through her as the train started to move. Claus returned her kiss forcefully and began to pull the straps of the dress down over her shoulders. He licked her neck and, unfastening her bra took her breast in his mouth and began to suck and bite it. Delirious with pleasure, she half opened her eyes and looked to her right. All the other passengers had turned to watch the spectacle being enacted for them. She realised that she didn't care. In any case, their faces registered curiosity but no disapproval.

Looking down, she saw Mark on his knees in front of her, the beige suit scraping along the filthy floor. He had pushed up her dress and was nuzzling at the inside of her thighs. Claus was flicking his tongue over her nipples, now hard in his mouth, while Mark reached up inside her dress and unfastened her panties. As soon as they fell away he began to run his tongue along the inside of her furrow. She opened her legs as much as possible and lay back in the seat. Dimly she heard the train stop at a station, and then start up again as Mark began to circle her clitoris with his tongue, faster and faster, until she started to cry out and come in shuddering waves.

As the pleasure ebbed away she motioned for Mark to get off the floor, and once he had sat down, she unzipped his trousers, eager to see his impressive cock and to feel it inside her. Claus sat opposite now, staring at her, his eyes wide with arousal, but his body emanating an air of self-control.

She reached over and encircled Mark's cock with her closed hand, sheathing the foreskin back and forth. It really was rather impressive, she thought with delight, as she lifted her skirt and positioned it at her opening. Leaning forward she balanced herself on the shelf behind the seats and lowered herself onto his cock. His hands were busy under her skirt rubbing her clitoris and causing her to quiver as she felt the full length and girth of his cock in her, right up to the hilt.

Now the sense of urgency that was building inside her made her plunge herself down onto his bone-hard cock. She opened her eyes and watched her reflection in the window of the carriage. She revelled in how wanton she looked. Her dress was ruched around her waist and her breasts were free of her bra, bouncing just above Mark as she ground herself down along his thick length.

Mark teased her bud with featherlight strokes and she felt her climax building up inside her, at the front wall of her pussy. She turned to her right and saw many pairs of eyes, eyes glazed with desire as they watched. She caught Claus' eyes in the glass too. The train ran on, its steady rhythm somehow increasing her pleasure as it tore across the tracks. More people must have got on, for now she felt more eyes on her, male or female, she didn't care, they were just voyeurs to her. She was getting hotter and hotter, knowing they were watching, but knew too, that they were having an experience that they would never forget.

As the train shuddered to a halt Clara rammed herself down onto Mark's cock and shuddered to a climax. Rivers of heat burned through her, causing her to almost pass out as she panted against him, still riding his cock. Then he too started to lose control and to come beneath her. Still she continued to pound him until her climax had left her utterly satiated and gasping for breath.

'Come on Mark, don't be greedy,' said Claus who had moved over so he was sitting next to her. He reached out to fondle her breasts and placed a kiss on her mouth. Despite her exhaustion she kissed him back, his sexual energy making her respond, and her arousal began to rise within her again, with Mark's cock still buried deep inside her.

She eased herself off Mark's cock and tried to stand up, but the train was moving and she almost fell over. Claus grabbed her and pulled her towards him, his face buried in the soft orbs of her breasts. His hands were running up the backs of her thighs and cupping her bottom cheeks. Mark was tidying himself up when the train again came to a stop.

'Hey,' cried Mark, 'isn't this your stop?'

Clara opened her eyes. 'Oh God, yes!' She turned towards the rest of the carriage, her breasts swinging freely as she tried to pull up the straps of her dress. Claus was laughing behind her. They just managed to all get off the tube and she too began to laugh.

'Sorry Claus, you'll have to wait until we get to my place.'

'Still, I had a nice view, as did everyone else.' He helped her to tidy herself up and placed a playful kiss on the side of her neck.

'But no one said anything.'

'They were enjoying the view too much. I think the English aren't as repressed as they seem.'

'Mmm, you may have a point there.' Right now she felt very high. And the evening wasn't over yet.

Chapter Three

The next morning she played back the messages on her answerphone at the gallery. She was tired but satisfied after an eventful night. She was in no way prepared for the voice that seeped out. A voice that was both seductive and familiar. Paul had left not one, but two messages.

She pulled the lid off her cup of coffee. He must have left them early this morning. His voice was measured, easy, asking her if she would meet up with him to hear what he had to say. He put the request so charmingly, and her mood was so buoyant, that she was tempted to call him, to at least hear him out. She sipped her coffee thoughtfully. No, she decided, she was stronger than that. She wiped the messages and switched on her computer. Paul was history, baggage that she had unloaded a long time ago. She was tired of his demands. If he had changed as he claimed then so had she. Now was the time, she figured, to really find out what she needed and was capable of.

Right now she needed to tell someone about what she had experienced last night. She began to type out an e-mail to Mr X. Was he anticipating her, she wondered?

We had quite a ride last night. She took another sip of coffee, feeling the pleasurable buzz as the caffeine began to kick in. She was feeling a little the worse for wear. In my date with Mark I ended up with more than I bargained for. Almost more than I could handle! I thought that it would just be an ordinary evening. I mean, I guessed – or rather hoped – that we would end up in bed. And we did, but not after some rather unusual foreplay.

As she waited for Mr X to reply, Paul swam into her thoughts again. She realised that she would have to deal with him. Right now his renewed presence in her life, cloying and familiar, was not allowing her to move forward.

Mr X's reply caused a tremor of excitement to run through her.

Sounds interesting. It looks like this Mark is exactly the type of guy who can handle a bit of experimental sex. It makes me jealous, I might add, to think of you with him, although I have no claim on you whatsoever. Our communication will only stay like this – on the screen. But confide in me, whatever you want to get off your chest, tell me, I'm all ears.

Mr X was acting very cool, while she was still a little wired, with images flitting through her brain. She needed to put it all down in black and white. Only then would she be able to get things into some sort of perspective.

Everything had happened so fast. After Mr X had made contact with her that first time she had made the decision to experiment. She had reckoned on pushing against her boundaries little by little, testing the water. But the past few days had turned her head. There was so much out there, so many opportunities and possibilities. Reflecting on yesterday, it was a little frightening how much she still had to find out. But she didn't want to let Mr X see that she was afraid, not yet.

She took a deep breath and began to type. It was important to her how she presented herself to him, but she wasn't altogether sure why this should be the case.

Well, as you know, I was keen to share my fantasy of being watched with Mark, but it turned out that he had ideas of his own as to how to get the party going. First he took me for dinner at his club. As the waiter showed us to our seats I was surprised to see another man waiting for us at the table. A very attractive man, thank goodness, called Claus. Mark made out that there had been a mix-up in the dates but I can't say I believed him. I was wedged between them both, one blond, the other dark, and immediately I felt an erotic frisson running between us. Claus became bold, and without missing a beat of his conversation, he slipped his hands under my skirt. I played along too. I didn't want to act naive and make a fuss. Besides, I'd made my decision to follow this adventure in whatever direction it went. And he did turn me on, quite violently, as his hand ran up my leg and then slipped beneath my panties. But then an impulse took over, that I did not want him to gain the upper-hand. At first I ignored it, but he was toying with my clit and making me want to scream out right there in the restaurant and come. I didn't want that, I was certain of that, so even though I was really turned on, and fondling Mark's cock through his trousers, I suddenly became all prim and pulled away. I wondered how they would react, but the interesting thing was that it didn't ruffle either of them. I think I realised then that they would be up for any game I chose to play.

Because I hadn't found any release, the current between us built up to a high point. While we talked my mind was working away, wondering whether I should still continue enacting my original fantasy, or whether I should go along with any plans they had made between them. If they had planned to meet 'accidentally' maybe they had made further plans for my fate between them. Of course, I knew better than to ask at that point. I didn't want to know exactly what would happen. I wanted the adventure to take its course and develop naturally between us. The thought of taking on both men was a powerful aphrodisiac though, I must admit. Then, as we left the restaurant I got an idea as to how I could use the situation to my advantage.

Mark was hailing a taxi when I said, no, why didn't they both accompany me to my flat. I suggested that we travel by the Underground, and although Mark was initially puzzled by this request he happily acquiesced. As we went down the escalator, towards the tunnel, I decided that I would confide in him about what I wanted to happen, and leave him to tell Claus, who I felt less intimate with. But as soon as we stepped onto the tube, my fears left me and I embarked on the ride of my life. You can imagine the rest!

She sent the e-mail and leaned back, enjoying a smug sense of satisfaction. She was beginning to realise that she could withhold certain details from Mr X, for as long as she chose. She too could torment him. And the thought filled her with glee.

She stretched her legs out in front of her and surveyed her body appreciatively. Her shapely legs were lightly tanned and the tops of her thighs still ached from when she had kneeled over Mark as they had made love while the train pounded over the tracks. In her hurry to get off the tube at her station she had lost her red lace panties. Someone, one of the men or women watching her being fondled by two handsome men, might have picked them up.

She smiled to herself. But then a thought came to her about the panties. She remembered how Mark had deftly reached for the fastening at the side and pulled them away. He had done so with one easy movement, although not many panties fastened that way. Then she remembered that she had mentioned the side-fastening to Mr X when she was elaborating on his fantasy of making love to her over the counter. She baulked at the thought that suddenly accosted her. Was Mr X Mark? She sighed with frustration. She was tired and it was all too confusing. It was pointless to try and rationalise the situation. She couldn't ask Mr X, after all, and spoil the game that they had embarked on.

Mr X's reply flashed on her screen.

I must say that you have turned me on very much indeed. I am tempted to stop e-mailing you and just to come round right now and see you. I imagine that you're getting hot just thinking about all this.

Indeed, he was absolutely right. Beneath her dress, which was slashed low at the back, her skin was beginning to smart as she remembered graphically how she had ridden Mark's cock with several pairs of eyes tracking her every move. A feeling of hot shame coursed through her, inflaming her, and making the juices rapidly build up at her opening.

She was distracted by a man who had stopped outside the gallery. He wore a grey suit and was looking intently at one of Eric's pictures in the window. His eyes moved beyond the picture, meeting hers, brushing over her face before returning to the picture. As the anonymous man looked at her she knew without a shadow of a doubt that she was beginning to blush. She felt as if her lewd thoughts were written on her face, pouring out of her skin. Pull yourself together, Clara, she said to herself, and she continued to read the words on the screen in front of her.

You took a bit of a risk taking on two men on a train. Quite a thrill, I guess – getting them to do your bidding. Part of it was down to luck, that you met two such broad-minded individuals. Don't tell me what happened if you don't want to – you are a tease, Ms X – but I will tell you that I imagine that these two guys had made you so hot in the restaurant that you could barely wait for the doors of the carriage to close before you started to lewdly reveal your body, with scant regard for who might be watching. I bet you gave them quite a show. You have no doubt imagined, too, what the passengers saw, scarcely believing their eyes when you began to disrobe and fondle Claus and Mark. Think of the thrill they got out of it and the friends they've told. Your secret Underground session has been conveyed by Chinese whispers all over town.

Was he getting her back for withholding the details? Were they speaking about her all over town? He was making her paranoid. But she wasn't going to let on. And he was right, she was getting more and more turned on as she recalled the events.

I did make love to Mark, with him pinned beneath me on the seat, but, it was funny really – I almost missed my stop. My mind was, as you can imagine, on other things. But when we got back to my place I really saw some action.

She didn't want to tell him any more, although there was much more to tell. She wasn't sure that she should tell him anything more about herself until she knew something more about him.

I'm too tired to write more now, but I hope I've given you enough to fuel your fantasies until we meet, Mr X. When might that be?

She really wanted to see him. Who was he? But she wasn't going to make herself vulnerable like that. The ball was in her court for the moment, and she had left him wanting more of her story. But she wasn't ready to tell any more, not yet.

She was dragged back to reality by Xavier's return. He had been on a short trip to Rome and his features were lightly tanned. He often made trips abroad to visit new artists – some of them recommended to him by Clara – who the gallery might want to take on. He wore a light cotton suit that emphasised his broad shoulders.

'I had a brilliant trip.'

'Did you discover any bright young things?'

He grinned. 'Several possibles. Nothing definite yet.'

'We've sold almost all of Eric's pieces.'

She sat looking up at him as he gave her a broad smile. She noted that he was more cheerful and relaxed than he had been for a long time, and she realised too that she wanted him more than ever. The ache between her legs was making itself felt and she needed urgent relief. She remembered that she had her vibrator in her handbag, but it made a noise. There was no way that she could use it in the toilet without arousing his suspicions.

She really wanted Xavier right then, more than any vibrator. But he always acted as if he wasn't interested. And every time she had invited him for a drink after work he had said he was busy. Yet his reluctance to get involved was intriguing. Why was he not responding? She didn't care if he was her boss, she needed a man's body against hers, skin against skin. In any case, due to the amount of income she had introduced into the business she felt that she was his equal in the gallery. Yet it niggled at her that he considered her a subordinate who had still to prove her worth.

'Do you want to go out after work and celebrate?' she said boldly.

Picking up the hold-all beside him he said, 'No, I can't. I've got lots of work to catch up on. Sorry. Maybe we can all get together in a couple of weeks. Eric called me and said he would be in London then.'

The mention of Eric's name made her stomach lurch with desire.

'Yes, that's a good idea.'

She watched his back disappear through the door as he made his way downstairs and she almost stamped her foot with frustration. She had made love to three men in the past two days. All of them had shown her different aspects of sexual pleasure. It was all so new and exciting and now a jumble of images filled her mind.

She guessed that she really needed to chill-out. Maybe she would go home, have a bath and spend a leisurely hour with the vibrator. Then she had another idea. Maybe she'd give Astrid a ring. Mr X had ignited some compulsion to tell someone about her exploits. Astrid was exactly that someone for tonight – relaxed, non-judgemental and, she guessed, very broad-minded.

When Clara called Astrid she sounded delighted to hear from her and said that she would call round at the gallery later. For the rest of the day Clara tried to concentrate on her work. Once she would have been overjoyed at the amount of commission that the sale of Eric's paintings had made for the gallery. But her mind was on other things. And still the question kept return-ing, although she kept pushing it aside. Who was Mr

X and why did she have a compulsive urge, even now, as she proof-read a catalogue, to e-mail him and tell him every thought in her head?

When Astrid arrived a few hours later, she found Clara in a restless state.

'You look stressed-out.'

Clara walked around the counter and embraced her friend.

'Have you been outside at all today?'

'No.' She realised that she hadn't eaten a thing either. 'You look great.' Astrid wore a dress made of soft kid-leather that moulded itself around her curvaceous figure. It was slashed above the knee and ended in tassels. Clara fought down an impulse to stroke the tactile surface of the dress.

Astrid ran her hand around Clara's neck, gently kneading the muscles. 'You're a little tense, I think,' she said, rubbing her fingers along the nape of Clara's neck. God that felt so good. 'But don't worry, I've got some stuff in this bag that will help you relax.' She gestured to the bag beside her.

Clara leaned over the counter to dial Xavier's extension. While she told him that she was leaving the gallery, she felt Astrid's fingers running up and down her spine. She was wearing a backless dress and hardly wanted to turn around, the sensation felt so good.

Eventually she turned to face Astrid who looked at her intently from beneath her blonde mane of hair. Her grey-green eyes were serious for a second. Instinctively, Clara felt that she could trust Astrid. Clara picked up the bag containing the vibrator, and, after she slipped her bare arm through Astrid's, they walked out into the street.

'It's such a nice evening,' said Astrid, looking up at the cloudless blue sky, 'I don't think I could bear to sit in a stuffy pub. How about a walk in the park?'

Astrid's suggestion suited her just fine. They walked

at a leisurely pace down Piccadilly and Clara remembered how only twenty-four hours ago she had walked the same route with Mark. Curiously, she was now feeling a similar sense of anticipation and began, for the first time, to wonder about Astrid's intentions.

Instead of turning right into Dover Street as she had done with Mark, she let Astrid lead her into Hyde Park. After they had talked of this and that and Clara felt more relaxed, she quite naturally found herself bringing up the subject of Paul. Astrid listened as Clara spilled it all out, then told her matter-of-factly that she should confront him or she would never be rid of him. Clara found Astrid's straight-talking advice refreshing, and was relieved to have told someone about her problem with Paul. Astrid added that it might help her to get away for a bit. When Astrid suggested that Clara might want to come along to a party in Norfolk, Clara readily agreed.

They walked along a path lined with chestnut trees, which provided some well-needed shade. The park was full of couples, sitting on the grass, soaking up the evening sun, but as they walked further they saw fewer people. Clara became aware of the softness of Astrid's arm linked with hers, and the downy layer of hair on its surface. A cool breeze blew under Clara's red linen dress. How she wished she wasn't wearing panties. She wore only a black G-string, but even that felt restrictive in the open air, among the wide-open grass verges.

Astrid suddenly stopped and looked about her. To their right was a patch of bushes and to their left a large tree whose leaves were stirring in the breeze. They had veered off the footpath and were in a secluded patch of the park. Astrid spread out a large tablecloth and flopped down on it. Clara lay down beside her and for a while they lay there staring up at the patterns of the leaves against the sky. Lying so close to Astrid was suddenly making Clara nervous, and her throat was dry. For the first time she could not think of a single thing to say.

Eventually Astrid broke the ice by delving into her bag and bringing out a chilled bottle of white wine and a punnet of strawberries. Clara began to eat the strawberries ravenously. As they passed the bottle between them, Clara began to relax again.

'I'll never forget your face the other day when I caught you at it with Eric,' said Astrid, throwing her head back with laughter.

Clara, supporting her head on one arm, shifted position and one strap of her dress slipped off her shoulder, making her nipples just visible above the cloth.

Clara took a swig of wine, not sure how to answer. She decided to be bold. Astrid's clear gaze seemed to expect an honest reply.

'I was embarrassed, at first, that you had seen everything.' She turned her face away. Why was it so hard to talk about it, when it was so easy to type it to Mr X? 'But then, afterwards, I couldn't stop thinking about it. How you must have watched me, being used very much as Eric's plaything.'

Astrid reached over and, cupping Clara's chin in her hand turned her face towards her. 'Don't be embarrassed. It really turned me on, too.'

'You mean, seeing Eric, like that. I thought that you two might be involved. I hope I haven't done something improper.' She stumbled over the words. Talking about it wasn't making it clearer, just more and more confusing.

'Eric and I have been lovers, of course. We go back a long way. But this isn't about us. It's about you. You've never done something like that before, have you?'

'I've had my share of lovers. But I've never done anything –' she searched for the word, '– this daring before. Maybe Eric brought out the impulse, I don't know.'

She was not being honest at all. She knew that Mr X had activated the desire to push the boundaries. But she didn't feel that she could tell Astrid, not yet.

Clara lay back and rested her head on Astrid's shoulder. Suddenly she felt completely at ease.

'Don't you know that some of us like to watch,' whispered Astrid in her ear, making her tremble with excitement.

'I keep thinking about it. I think about you.'

'Just keep talking,' said Astrid. 'Lie down on your front and rest your head on your arms. Wait.' She reached over and pulled the other strap down so Clara's full breasts sprung free, bra-less, and Astrid looked at the coffee-coloured nipples appreciatively. Clara felt a tingle as she rolled over on her front and lay her cheek on her hands.

She observed that Astrid was unscrewing a bottle of oil. Soon she felt the oil being rubbed into her shoulders and the scent of neroli floating upwards in the evening air. Then Astrid straddled her back and Clara became distinctly aware of Astrid's quim rubbing rhythmically against her bottom cheeks through the thin panties, as Astrid massaged her neck.

Clara felt her sex become inflamed with desire as Astrid whispered, 'Let it all out, you'll feel so much better.'

'Well, after that session with Eric I realised I wanted to be watched. I knew that I had been lucky that it had all happened so spontaneously.' She felt so relaxed, breathing in the smell of mown grass and the scented oil. 'I knew that I would have to orchestrate the event, you know, take control of the situation. Well, Mark, that guy Eric introduced me to, he wanted to take me to dinner. I had a sense that he would be interested in the idea.'

She heard a buzzing, a very familiar buzzing. She turned around to look and saw that Astrid had flicked the switch of a vibrator. For a second Clara thought that she had got it from Clara's bag but then, as she looked more closely, she realised that it was different from her own. It was very realistically shaped like a cock, as large as Mark's cock had been and well-moulded into shape. She felt her pussy contract in anticipation.

'I'll just use this on your neck,' said Astrid, a picture of innocence. 'There's still a lot of tension there.' She felt Astrid press the vibrator against her neck and continued to talk.

'It all happened easily. He brought along a friend on the date and I told Mark that I wanted to have sex with him on the tube. And I did.' She told Astrid every detail that she had told Mr X as Astrid ran the vibrator over her back. Then Astrid asked her to turn around and, still straddling her, massaged the oil into Clara's breasts and ran the cock-shaped vibrator over her nipples, making them contract to hard points.

'Keep talking,' said Astrid as if she was blissfully unaware of how aroused Clara was feeling. Through half closed eyes Clara looked up at Astrid. The leather dress had ridden up and Clara could clearly see that Astrid wasn't wearing any panties and that her pubis was completely shaven.

'Well, it was only a short ride on the tube and I still hadn't made love to Claus, Mark's friend. So back at my house, I figured that because they had been so obliging in letting me enact my fantasy I would go along with whatever fancy took them.'

She watched as Astrid pulled the dress over her head. Astrid's breasts were full, but pert, and Clara felt a desire to feel their fullness in her mouth. The vibrator was making her tingle all over. Clara felt Astrid pull off her dress and pull her panties down along the length of her thighs. Now they were both completely naked in the middle of the park.

'We stripped off and soon I was engulfed by one of them on each side of me, caressing me at the same time, making me feel painfully aroused. Mark was sucking my breasts when Claus, who was lying behind me began to make love to me, very gently at first, moving his cock in and out only an inch or so. It was really tormenting at first but then I relaxed into it and . . .'

She had a memory of the feeling, a very strong memory. It was almost as if she had Claus' bone-hard cock inside her right now, moving stealthily in and out of her. She knew that it wasn't just a memory, that right now Astrid had the vibrator deep inside her and was working it in and out, expertly rubbing it against the tiny area at the front of her vaginal wall which always drove her wild. Astrid was kneeling in front of Clara now, whose legs were splayed apart, as she pushed the vibrator into her tight tunnel. Clara observed what was happening, then leaned over and unzipped her own bag. She brought out her vibrator and handed it to Astrid.

'But I was aware that I wanted Mark's cock too. It was really something – thick and long – and I needed to taste his arousal in my mouth. I told him this, but instead of moving upwards so I could take him in my mouth he positioned himself so that his mouth was level with my quim, leaving his erect cock at the right position to be taken in my mouth. While Claus increased the depth of his strokes, Mark began to lick my clit, very gently so that it felt like a peak of flame.'

As she spoke, her voice beginning to become hoarse with desire, Astrid whispered, 'Show me,' and handed her the cock-shaped vibrator. Clara drove it into her mouth, tasting herself on it, the strong vibrations against her tongue driving her arousal up a notch as she almost believed herself to feel Mark's skin beneath her tongue, so realistic was the imitation cock.

Soon she felt the other vibrator being driven into her and Astrid's tongue working over her bud in feather-light strokes. Clara squirmed against Astrid's soft mouth, which was almost duplicating the sensations of the previous night. And yet it was a completely different experience because through her half-open eyes she saw Astrid's glistening quim before her. Taking the vibrator out of her mouth Clara began to glide the head of it between the folds of flesh into Astrid's pussy.

She worked the vibrator in a corkscrew motion a little way further into Astrid's tunnel. She guessed that Astrid was as turned on by the experience as she was as she began to buck and spasm against the hard surface of the vibrator that Clara was now pushing in up to the hilt. And even though she could feel the electric build-up of energy now being released beneath her fingers as Astrid came, still she felt the point of Astrid's tongue flicking against her, making her lose consciousness.

She felt her orgasm creep up on her as if from nowhere, the nub of pleasure flickering outwards from the tip of the vibrator. Her pussy contracting violently against the cock, she gripped Astrid, feeling the soft orbs of her breasts against her thighs.

Clara had a sensation as if the current of pleasure was racing through them both as they squirmed against each other, ekeing out every last drop of ecstasy until finally Clara lay, her mouth against Astrid's thigh, breathing rapidly and revelling in the newness of the situation. For a long while they lay there, the breeze cooling the fresh sweat that had formed over their bodies. Neither had any energy left to talk.

Chapter Four

*T*he day after making love with Astrid Clara looked at herself in the mirror and noticed a distinct glow. Her whole body felt alive, as if every nerve-ending had been activated. It had been a hectic few days and Clara could hardly believe her luck. Just days ago she had craved a man, to take the edge off the frustration that had been building up inside her for the past few months. And yet, the events that had occurred, one more bizarre and unreal than the last, were also completely inexplicable. In the last few days she had tasted several different aspects of sexuality. Experiencing the variety of deeply pleasurable situations, while temporarily quenching her physical desires, had now made her start to think about which turn she would like events to take next.

Now, almost a week had passed. To her relief, she had not heard from Paul since he'd left the messages. Maybe there would be no need to confront him. The days were still languid and humid, but she needed the time to fit together the confusing tangle of images and experiences that flitted through her mind. She could not focus on anything for more than five minutes as her concentration was shot to pieces. Uncharacteristically, she felt no guilt about neglecting her work. In any case, Eric's pictures were all sold, and Xavier was off on a business trip again, so she figured she could afford to take some time out. And yet, something, a minor irritation was disrupting her state of satiated bliss. She had wanted to tell Mr X about her adventures in the open air, how Astrid had shown her what it was to be satisfied by a woman's touch.

Yet he had not contacted her and she did not feel comfortable about trying to attract his attention. After all, he had done all the running, pursuing her in the first place, then being grateful for any crumbs she could throw at him. She had enjoyed giving him snatches of images, enjoyed the subtle sense of power she had over him. She had imagined a wry smile crossing his lips as he read about her exploits. Maybe he wanted to meet her in person, he had hinted at this intention once or twice.

Her thoughts were in conflict. Part of her wanted to prolong the peculiar frisson of the relationship for as long as possible and to keep the reins of power in her hands. She was aware that the only real power she had over him was to offer or withhold information. He had seemed to want to know everything about her, and she had struggled these past days against the impulse to tell him all. Rationally, she knew that she should be focusing on more accessible sexual pleasures, for example with Mark, who had offered an open invitation to call him whenever she pleased. But instead she thought only of Mr X. He had broken through to the very core of her, dominating her thoughts, which were now tinged with uncertainty.

The night before, she had not been able to sleep. Eventually, in the early hours, she had managed to drop off, but had ended up having a vivid dream filled with sexual imagery.

She had been alone in the grounds of an old manor house, when she entered a maze made out of a hedgerow. She had not wanted to enter it, but a magnetic force had dragged her forward. She turned several corners, trying to memorise her path. Eventually she came to the centre of the maze, and by this time dusk was falling, so she sat and rested at the centre of the maze on a flat stone monument. She lay down for a second and closed her eyes, stretching her limbs along the warm stone. She felt the stone grow hotter and penetrate through the thin dress she was wearing, somehow inflaming her, making her feel aroused, more aroused than she had ever thought possible. But then, as she tried to get up she realised that her body was welded to the stone and her attempts to free herself remained fruitless. It was growing darker and darker around her, as she struggled to free herself, when she heard the sound of horse hooves approaching. She looked up and saw a masked man looking down on her, a look of amusement playing about his lips. She felt herself begin to sob with relief as he jumped down from his horse.

She noticed that his forearms were tanned and in their powerful muscularity they reminded her of Eric's. The mask was cut away at the eyes so that his gaze fixed her with a penetrating stare that was clear in its intent. She asked him if he knew how she could release herself from the stone but he replied, 'I will set you free as and when I choose to.'

Then, with slow firm movements he had ripped her dress from her body. She felt the cool night air on her skin and his hand explore her, stripping away her underwear too and exposing her nakedness beneath. She did not dare to say any more, so keen was she to free herself from the stone. A burning sense of shame was building up within her as he caressed her breasts, rolling the nipples between his fingers so that a sharp pain radiated out from them. She was completely helpless to his roaming hand, pinned beneath him, melted into the hot stone. He dragged his palm across the length of her body as if marking it out as his, taking in every dip and curve and coming, finally, to rest over her pussy.

Her body was taut with arousal, every nerve-ending sensitive to the caress of his hand. She wanted to reach out and touch him, despite herself, to fondle his cock, to rub herself against him. And yet still her voice belied her true feelings, as she cried out to him to let her go, to use his magic powers to release her from the stone.

But he paid her no heed. Removing all his clothes, apart from the mask, he lay on top of her, making her feel small and helpless beneath his bulk. Rivers of heat ran all over her body, from the warmth of the stone which now felt almost like a furnace and from the friction between her soft curved body and his, hard and powerful. As he began to butt the head of his cock into her she cried out, with the extreme pleasure of it. But this time all conscious thought had left her. She was dimly aware of the sensation she had felt with Eric that time when he had held her firmly in his arms so that she could not move.

Now, as she lay beneath this strange man in the middle of the maze, totally reliant on him for her escape, she inhaled his scent deeply. He smelled of the earth, mingled with a harsher, more animal smell. Maybe he was the gamekeeper of the manor. He pounded into her, with scant regard for anything but taking his own pleasure. And although she could not splay her legs as wide as she would have liked he continued to thrust in deeply.

She tightened the walls of her pussy around his cock, moulding herself around him. Little cries came from the back of her mouth, and she looked up at the night sky, which was studded with pinpricks of light.

Closing her eyes, she saw only blackness, her body reduced now to this burning nub of pleasure deep within her, as she dragged him further and further into her with her tight internal muscles.

Still he rode her, pushing her back against the stone, making her skin chafe against it. Her whole back and the lengths of her thighs and arms were sore against the hard grain of the stone. Yet somehow the mildly painful sensations had turned to an intense hot pleasure that began to build within her as he rhythmically neared his climax.

The intermingling of pain and pleasure suddenly broke over her, like a crack of lightning in the night sky. It was a sensation as if she had been hit with a whip and spliced in two. She cried out as a violent tremor ran through the centre of her body, making her blank out for a moment; its sheer force made her body buck up against him as he began to come, holding her shoulders firmly as he climaxed.

She caught her breath and they lay there, his head resting in the curve of her shoulder. She lifted her arm to touch him and with a start realised that she was no longer part of the stone, that somehow he had unlocked her from it. Rapidly she realised that she no longer liked this feeling of freedom and whispered, 'You have freed me.'

He grabbed hold of her wrist and pushed it back over her head. Again, she felt her flesh melt into the stone.

'You must stay here a little while longer,' he commanded.

Then the details of the dream became vague, but she recalled that she had been his prisoner, and he had taken his pleasure with her again and that she had enjoyed it all despite herself. She had woken drenched in sweat.

Now, back in the gallery, she wondered at the significance of the dream. She couldn't help thinking that somehow the man was like Mr X. The masked man had generated the same conflict of feelings, an almost nauseating wrench of desire, coupled with a tingling anticipation. It was the feeling she was experiencing now, as she sat behind the counter, her fingers poised over the keys of the keyboard. There was so much she still wanted to find out about Mr X, but was, as yet, too scared to ask. It was as if the questions could not be articulated verbally.

She wiped away the film of fresh sweat that was forming along her hairline. It was ridiculous, she knew, to be this involved with a stranger. And yet, it hit her suddenly that she had never felt so free with anyone before. Her pussy began to tingle as the blood rushed towards it.

She was determined to wipe away the heavy atmosphere of the dream. Flashes of it still played vividly in her mind, the anonymous man in the mask and the strange sexual ritual where she had blacked out at the mixture of intense pleasure and pain. She felt as if she were in a hazy trance as she began to type out her thoughts to Mr X. She noticed that she was still censoring herself, holding back. She wasn't ready, not yet, to reveal how much she desired him.

She told him all about how Astrid had known what she had needed. Clara began to revel in every little detail, making it as salacious as possible. She could imagine him reading it, aching for her, wanting to touch her; touching himself.

A fever took hold of her as she continued to type, the stream of words floating from her fingertips. When she had finished she leaned back and took several deep breaths before, emboldened, she asked, And what have you been doing? I hope you've been thinking only of me.

Setting her experiences out in black and white had activated a dagger of lust within her quim and she rubbed one breast impatiently, making the nipple harden against the palm of her hand. It had made her feel terribly lewd, writing about how she had penetrated her friend with the vibrator, while at the same moment Astrid had rammed the other vibrator into her.

She parted her legs and ran her fingers under her miniskirt along the silky length of her thigh. Rubbing her clit from side to side through the silky material of her black lace panties, she waited in anticipation, her heart thudding in her chest. As she saw his e-mail flash in her mailbox she began to ache and rapidly pushed the panties aside and sent two fingers into her lubricated opening.

Where have I been? I've been waiting here for you, all this time waiting for you to tell me what you've been up to. You have been a busy girl, exposing your lovely pussy to the open air like that. What would I like to have done? Well, I would have liked to have got an eyeful of you two, your friend straddling your back while you waited, the lips of your pussy waiting to be prised apart by that cock-shaped vibrator. I bet it isn't as good as the real thing though.

But why haven't I been in contact, well I was waiting for you to come to me. When I didn't hear from you I thought that maybe your luck had run out. Until now, you've been fortunate. The adventures have happened to you. But what if they suddenly stop?

She felt a sense of fear course through her, her fingers buried up to the hilt in her warm musky juices.

Then what will you do? Your education is still incomplete. I would say, decide what you want, then make it happen.

The words blurred in front of her and she writhed against her fingers, her orgasms coming one after the other in rapid succession. First it was just a tremor, as she opened her legs wide to accommodate the three fingers that she was pushing in. Then, as a gasp escaped from the back of her throat, another orgasm followed, more intense this time. Then more, every few seconds, sending sensations through her she had never experienced. It was as if a series of explosions were occurring, making her unaware of her surroundings and causing stars to shimmer in front of her eyes. As she shuddered to her final climax the image of the masked man appeared, a piercing light glinting in his eyes. Lying dishevelled in the chair, her skirt ruched up around her hips, her blouse hanging open, she waited until her breathing had regulated.

Then she looked at the screen, deciding whether she had anything more to say. On impulse she closed down the computer. No, she decided, she could not bear any more contact with him today.

His words burned into her brain as she tidied herself up. Make it happen.

The multiple orgasms she had experienced had energised her, and already her mind was creating a succession of new scenarios in Technicolor.

She could not have Mr X, not for now, anyway. But there were more choices than that. She reached for the phone and dialled Mark's number.

'Hello, Clara, great to hear from you. How are you?' His voice, rich and resonant, made her realise that she had made the right decision.

She ran her fingers nervously through her hair, uncertain as to how to get to the point. 'Well, I'm feeling a little restless. What are you up to?'

'Nothing very much, the weather's so hot I can't find the motivation to do anything.'

'Anything?' she asked and then laughed.

There was a pause and he said, more seriously, 'Claus hasn't stopped talking about you. He had a wonderful time and so did I. I would have called you before but I've been abroad.'

'That's OK, I've been pretty busy myself. But anyway, how do you feel about meeting up today?'

'What, this evening?'

'No. I was thinking about right now. I'll lock up the gallery.'

'Well, that's certainly a tempting offer. What did you have in mind?'

His tone was level, and this gave her an added thrill. It was as if he indulged the fantasies of women every day of the week. Maybe he did, but frankly all she cared about right now was him fulfilling her, as soon as possible. An image swam into her head, of herself, walking along the side of a road watching the passing cars.

She took a deep breath. 'I was thinking that you could pick me up in your car.'

'Where?'

'At the intersection of Old Compton Street and Wardour Street.' She had always been fascinated by the fact that her gallery was situated almost cheek by jowl with the sleazy world of Soho, with its strip clubs and sex shops.

'I'll meet you in about half an hour.'

'There is another thing,' she said nervously, 'would you pretend not to know me? You know, pretend that I'm a –' she found it difficult to say the word.

'What? A prostitute?'

'Yes.'

'Alright. And would you do me a favour?'

'Of course.'

'Don't wear panties.'

'See you soon.' She had a broad smile on her face as she replaced the phone.

She slipped off her black lace panties and shoved them into her handbag, her heart pounding in her chest. She would have to work fast. She grabbed her make-up bag and made up her face, using more make-up than usual. She shadowed her eyes darkly, liberally applied blusher to her cheeks and smeared her lips with a dark-red lipstick.

The face that stared back at her in the mirror was unrecognisable. As soon as she glimpsed her new image she ceased to be Clara. She ran some lipgloss over her lips, making them fuller and more provocative.

Picking up her handbag, she left the gallery, locking the door behind her. Mr X was right, she was going to have to make things happen. It was early afternoon, and she felt the air rushing up her skirt and cooling her aroused pussy. She walked a little way, passing other galleries, not even caring if the other gallery workers she knew saw her wearing the heavy make-up.

She turned into the hustle and bustle of Brewer Street, and walked past the cluster of fashionable cafes where people were relaxing at outside tables. She held her head up proudly and watched a couple of men follow her with their eyes. Looking around her she watched a woman standing outside a striptease joint. She had bleached blonde hair and wore a black leather miniskirt. She eyed Clara with suspicion.

She avoided the woman's glance and continued to walk on, right to the end of the street. She turned into Wardour Street and then entered a sex shop that she had often passed but had never had the courage to go into. She needed an outfit to complement her new persona.

It was cool and shady inside the shop. One wall was filled with a glass cabinet full of sex toys of all shapes and colours. She glanced into it with curiosity. She had not known that such a variety of sex toys existed. Her own vibrator had been given to her by a friend for a laugh one birthday. It had certainly got a lot of use since her split with Paul.

The female shop assistant stepped forward and asked her if she needed any help.

What was she looking for? She craned her neck to the right and her eyes fell on a selection of PVC dresses, in black, red and white. She ran her palm over the surface of one of them.

The assistant stepped forward and picked up a white dress. 'What about this?'

Clara appraised the dress, a slip of a thing, which would barely cover her modesty. She nodded and took the dress into the changing room. Quickly she stripped off her clothes and stuffed them into her handbag. She wondered what Mark would say when he saw her attire. She was certain she would give him the surprise of his life.

She squeezed into the dress with difficulty. It hugged her figure so tightly she could barely breathe, and it was cut low over her cleavage. But it was a wonderful tightness, which made her skin tingle and her stiffening nipples became clearly visible through the shiny material. The hem was super short, ending a few inches below her pussy and skimming over her tanned thighs.

She turned from side to side, marvelling at how well the dress suited her, but also at how complete her transformation was. There would be no mistaking what she was now. She had made a complete transformation into a whore.

The assistant pulled open the curtain. 'I thought you might like to try these.'

Clara gazed at the shiny red shoes and sat down on a chair to pull them on. They had a very thin heel and were narrowly cut so that she just managed to prise her feet into them. When she stood up she was six inches taller. She fully intended to drive Mark to realms of pleasure he hadn't experienced before.

When she came out of the dressing room the assistant eyed her appreciatively. 'You look fabulous. Shall I put them in a bag for you?'

'No, I'll keep them on.'

She paid for her purchases and left the shop. Buying the dress had put her on a complete high and she stepped authoritatively onto the pavement. This time, everyone turned to stare at her. The men's stares were raw and she could see their intentions starkly in their eyes. But instead of making her uncomfortable she experienced a hot flush as a well-built man purposefully brushed against her. A searing heat was building in her pussy as she leaned back. She bent one leg against the wall and surveyed the street with studied nonchalance.

Catching sight of Mark in his green open-topped Karmann Ghia, she was tempted to step forward and wave to him, but checked the impulse. He glanced at her and kept driving, up towards Leicester Square. Damn, what on earth was he doing? Her eyes followed his car as it got caught in the traffic. Where was he heading off to?

'How much?'

'What?' she said angrily and turned towards the besuited businessman who had asked the question.

'How much for full sex?'

Oh God, how was she going to get out of this one? And he was so handsome too. It was tempting, very tempting. Then she remembered that she wasn't actually a prostitute.

'Sorry, I'm waiting for a friend. Maybe some other time.'

'Are you sure?' he said, looking puzzled. Over his shoulder she could see Mark's car moving towards her.

This time he looked directly at her and drew the car up to the kerb.

The other man was still waiting to see if she would change her mind. She glanced in his direction, not acknowledging Mark at all.

'Look, I'm sorry, but I'm not doing business.'

She needed to be rid of him to start her game with Mark.

'Alright, alright.' The man held up his hand and began to move away. He glanced back at her.

She walked around the car to the passenger side and watched as Mark looked at her, the shock registering in his eyes. It was obvious that he had not recognised her before, which was why he had driven straight past. His expression quickly changed to desire, and he gave her a nod and reached over to open the door and she slipped into the seat.

As she turned towards Mark she felt a man's glance bore into her from across the street. As she swivelled her head round to get a better look at him he turned away. She just caught the back of his dark head, his hands pushed into his pockets as he turned down into a darkened alley. The height and the dark hair had reminded her momentarily of Paul. She had the sneaking suspicion that the man had been watching her. But then she was dressed very provocatively – why shouldn't he look at her?

For a second the fantasy that they were enacting had slipped her mind. She leaned back in her seat to further accentuate the curve of her bust inside the low-cut dress and gave Mark a look that she hoped was both sexy and dirty.

'Where can we go?' His voice was husky and low.

'How about we drive to your place?'

'Alright.'

'What are you after?' she said, staring at him directly.

'Just to spend the afternoon with you. Nothing in particular, just for us to do what takes our fancy. Does that suit you?'

She paused, as if processing the information and working out its financial equivalent.

'It'll cost you,' she said nonchalantly, as if, at that very moment her stomach wasn't fluttering with excitement. She gazed at his profile as he continued to look straight ahead.

'How much?'

'A thousand pounds.'

He turned to look at her briefly, his dark eyes drinking in her curves in the tight white dress. With one hand still on the wheel he reached into his jacket and pulled out a wad of notes. She counted out the money and slipped it into her bag.

The rest of the journey passed in silence. She was still marvelling at how completely and effortlessly she had slipped into her new persona when he pulled up at a tall white house. She noticed that the windows had their curtains drawn. She looked about her at the row of immaculate identical house fronts that faced onto Russell Square. She was impressed.

She walked in front of Mark. Just as she reached the door it opened and she was looking upwards into steely blue eyes. She noted no twinge of emotion as the stranger silently surveyed her body and nodded at Mark.

'Could you park the car please, Jason. I'm entertaining a friend. Sorry, I didn't catch your name?'

'Annabelle.' It gave her a thrill to realise that Mark was entering into the game as readily as she was.

Jason took her hand and gripped it firmly in his leather glove. Something about him was making her feel weak and dizzy. He was thick-set and wore a peaked chauffeur's cap over his light brown hair. Her eyes roamed along his chest, clad in a dark serge jacket studded with brass buttons and belted at the waist. His trousers were tucked into well-shined leather boots.

'Nice to meet you, Jason,' she said. He removed his hand from hers brusquely and pushed past her, brushing against her so that she felt the heat of his body through his jacket and felt a hot flush of desire within her quim.

Following Mark down the hall she looked about her at the impressive interior, which was furnished in a Regency style. The walls were dark red and covered in nineteenth century prints. He showed her into a room that had a thick pile carpet, low sofas, a chandelier and an ornate fireplace. Above the fireplace hung what, if her art history training served her correctly, was a rather fine Bonnard of a blonde woman in a cornfield.

'Jason has been my chauffeur for a while. But he's also become a friend. So you won't mind if he joins us this evening?'

'No, of course not.' She sat down opposite Mark and crossed her legs so that he could get a good view of her pussy.

He handed her a glass of wine. 'It's just that his tastes are . . . let's just say that he has peculiar sexual tastes.'

'What do you mean?'

'It's difficult to explain. But he enjoys making women his sexual plaything.' She sipped the red wine and felt herself unwind. What he was saying was intriguing, very intriguing.

'You've paid your money sir and for that you can have whatever you want, within reason. And your friend.' A smile curled across her lips as she stared at him provocatively, willing him to start what she anticipated would be a very promising evening.

The door opened. 'Ah, Jason, there you are. Annabelle was just saying how she would like to get to know you more intimately.'

He eyed her suspiciously. 'Where did you pick her up from then?'

'Soho. She was walking the streets, looking for trade.'

He threw back his head and started to laugh. Walking over to her he leaned over and, grabbing her hair, yanked it back and pressed his mouth against hers. She kissed him back and his tongue roamed her mouth. Sitting down, he pressed himself against her, so that the force of the hard buttons of his jacket went through the PVC and into her soft flesh.

He began to pull her dress up so that now her pussy was fully exposed to Mark's gaze. Responding to the hardness and bulk of his body she kissed him back passionately. His hand, encased in the leather glove, ran along the sensitive insides of her thighs and over her labia. The arousal was building up in a prickly heat over the opening of her vagina and when he began to probe into her she cried out.

He drew back. 'You like me, don't you?'

She didn't answer, not knowing what he expected her to say. Instead she spread her legs so that she could feel the rhythmic probing of his gloved finger. She began to rub her clit against the rough surface of the glove, feeling her orgasm approaching rapidly.

He started to bite her neck gently, but it was enough to make her skin inflamed with desire. He ran his tongue along the neck of the dress and licked her between her breasts, making her shiver as she reached out to pull him towards her. He continued to bite her through the material, all over her breasts and nipples, causing a sensation as if many tiny needles were being pushed into her.

Her nipples were hard and rubbing against the inside of the dress, driving her excitement up another notch as she began to spasm against him. His hand was still driving her wild, rubbing all over the sensitised surface of her vagina and, with precise, deft movements pounding into her, pushing her over into her orgasm, which gushed over her with a force that left her dazed.

Clinging onto the hot serge of his suit she revelled in the aftermath of her orgasm and looked about her. Her eyes focused on the shimmering crystals of the chandelier and then fell on Mark, who was leaning back on the sofa opposite. He had a look that she had never seen on his face before. His eyes were black – pools of darkness – and all traces of humour had left them. She felt a little afraid. After all, she didn't know exactly what she was getting herself into.

Jason turned towards Mark. 'I think I've warmed her up nicely.'

Now Mark was advancing towards her. 'Take off your dress,' he demanded.

She obeyed and felt her arousal return. The two men were watching her measuredly and showed no obvious signs of excitement. Now, though, she looked more closely and could see that the bulge at the front of Jason's trousers belied his deadpan demeanour. She could just make out the shape of his erect penis.

'That's enough looking for you, my dear,' said Jason. Leaning forward, she saw that he held a scarf in his hands and looked up at him quizzically. Thereafter she was disorientated, as he tied the scarf around her eyes so that all around her was blackness. It was disconcerting, as the soft pile of the carpet muffled sound, preventing her from judging where the other two were in the room. She sat there for a while, not daring to move.

'Get down on your hands and knees.' It was Jason's voice, and although it was a command rather than a request she began to feel an irrational excitement in the pit of her stomach. She felt her knees sink into the luxuriant silk carpet. Now, the only item of clothing she wore were the red high-heels. The gloved hand was being run all along her spine now, very slowly, until it came to rest gently on the nape of her neck.

'What are we going to do with her?'

'I don't know. What do you suggest?'

Her throat tightened with anticipation and fear. And yet she knew that she could not hide her excitement. She could already feel herself becoming wet and could imagine both men eyeing her moist pussy appreciatively.

'You're no whore. She's told you a fib.'

'No, that's impossible. I picked her up on the corner of Old Compton Street.'

'No, I've seen her before. In one of those fancy galleries. Dressed in a nice little suit. I know how she must be feeling, all those long hours can cause people to get mightily sexually frustrated. Isn't that right?'

She didn't know what to say. She would wait until he prompted her.

'When I talk to you I want you to answer, sir. Now answer the question. You're not a street whore, are you?'

'No.' She felt a smarting sensation as the leather glove landed on the cheeks of her bottom.

'No, sir.' His voice was barely above a whisper.

'No, sir,' she repeated, the tears welling up in her eyes. Her bottom ached.

'Nevertheless, I think a little punishment is in order, for lying to Mark.'

'But why?' she began to protest.

But before she could say any more the gloved hand had made contact with her bottom cheeks again. The pain was distracting and disconcerting. But once she began to relax into it the blows took on a calming quality. Now, she felt a heat, almost a numbness, penetrating her body and she began to enjoy the sting of the leather glove on her bare cheeks. But as abruptly as the punishment had begun, so it stopped.

She was aware that someone was standing in front of her. Jason? The serge of his trousers was brushing against her face, as she continued to balance on her hands and knees. Involuntarily she nuzzled against the warm cloth and then, moving her head lower down over his trousers, her lips came into contact with the hard, shiny leather.

'Do you know, Annabelle, I think you enjoyed that spanking. You are a very bad girl. Did you enjoy it?'

'No, sir.' A blur of coloured shapes swam before her eyes. She was no longer sure of anything.

'Clean my boots.'

'What?'

'My boots. They need a good licking. I want you to get them really clean.'

Puzzled by the request at first she began to run her tongue along the leather, licking in circular motions, like a cat. When she had finished licking all the way down one boot, she gained Jason's grudging approval.

'You're not doing too badly.'

She felt the familiar texture of the leather glove, this time running along the fold where her sex lips met. Mark must be wearing the gloves now, she guessed, as she ran her tongue along Jason's other boot. She felt two fingers slide into her and prise her open in a scissor-like motion, making her groan and bite against the hard leather.

She was licking the sides of the boot now so that her bottom was sticking up in the air, no longer sure how much time had passed. Time had stopped the moment

Jason had put the blindfold on her. The gloved hand was drawing forth quivers of sensation from her swollen pussy.

Suddenly, as she continued to make light work of the boot she felt the familiar feel of Mark's cock pushing into her. She wanted to lift her head up to make it easier for her to push herself back onto the head of his cock. A tremendous ache was making itself felt within her. What she needed was to feel his rock-hard cock, the whole delicious length of it, prising her apart. She felt his gloved hands brush her hips and hold onto them as he rammed the full length of himself into her and she bit into the boot leather to stifle her cry.

'Hey!' said Jason, 'I didn't say that you could stop.'

There was so much coiled-up energy inside her now; she felt as if, at any moment, she might explode. Mark's rhythmic thrusting was making her lose consciousness. Jason was saying something but she couldn't make out the words. Only the delectable sensations that were being brought forth from deep within her pussy were important now, as the head of Mark's cock butted against the wall of her cunt. She began licking the boot again, tightly contracting her muscles to drag him deeper within her.

'Move up a little bit further.' She felt Jason's hands pull her up by the shoulder. Dimly she was aware of a zip being opened. She parted her lips and licked tentatively at the head of his penis, which was erect before her. Maybe he was kneeling in front of her. Making her tongue into a point she flicked the underside of the head, then ran her tongue under the ridge where the head met the shaft.

She reached up to hold Jason's cock, balancing herself tentatively on one arm and immediately felt the ripples of her climax cut through her and make her shiver with ecstasy, then ebb away.

Taking a deep breath she took Jason's cock in her mouth and again circled the head rapidly with her tongue until she heard him crying out. Still Mark pounded within her and she felt him make one last thrust as he came against her.

Putting the balance of weight onto her other arm she pulled Jason's cock out of her mouth and rubbed the foreskin back and forth with her hand until she felt his balls buckling and then she again took him into the back of her throat, relishing the spurts of semen that she drained from his cock.

For a moment she felt as if she had no energy left at all. Jason took his cock from her mouth and again she heard him zip himself up. She thought for a moment about how she had adapted to the experience, how she had enjoyed Jason's commands and the way he had held her in submission. She wondered what Mr X would think if he could see her now. And then there was no more time for thoughts because Jason was speaking to her again.

'You have been a good girl, haven't you? What about trying something else, hmm?'

Before she could ponder on what he was going to do she felt a gloved hand on her bottom and then a cool sliver of cream being rubbed into her secret portal. Although that area of her had never been explored before she knew that now was the right time.

She felt all her muscles relax as the gloved finger explored her passage, centimetre by centimetre, until she felt it all the way inside her. She did not know whose finger it was, nor did she care. Her body was just acclimatising to the strange sensations when she felt a cock entering her vagina, slowly and stealthily.

The finger withdrew a little and then plunged along the lubricated tunnel, in a sensuous rhythm. The cock too was prising her apart at a similar leisurely pace so that the feeling of fullness within her two passages was for an instance overwhelming.

For a moment she felt as if she were in the middle of a lull, hearing only the breathing of someone behind her and the creak of the leather boots. Then someone placed a kiss on her lips.

Then the strange pleasure began to build, as if it had been coiled deep within her and was now creeping upwards towards release. She reached out her right hand and felt a warm body sitting beside her, and she steadied herself against him, steeling herself for the tumultuous crescendo that brewed like a distant thunderstorm within her arse and deep inside her vagina.

Then, like the crack of a whip on a horse's flank, she felt her muscles contract and a shower of intense sensations course through her, causing her to see blackness in front of her eyes. She trembled against the anonymous person beside her, Mark or Jason, she no longer knew, as a deeper sensation erupted like red-hot lava from her core and radiated around her body until she started to cry out and tears flowed freely from her eyes.

Much later, when she woke up, she glanced around. She was still naked, apart from the red stilettos, and was sprawled across Jason's lap. He remained in his trousers and boots but his chest was bare.

It was getting light outside and she watched him sleeping soundly. Gently she eased herself off the sofa and picked up the dress that now seemed inappropriate in the early dawn. Slipping into it nevertheless, she saw that Mark was wrapped in a dressing gown and asleep, exhausted from their session.

She walked out into the hall and picked up her handbag. A long navy coat hung on the coatstand and she slipped into it. Tentatively she opened the front door and peered out at the deserted street steeped in a pink light. She hesitated, then turned and walked back into the front room. It didn't seem right, somehow, to be carrying the thousand pounds now that the game was over, so she placed the notes on the table. She turned and smiled at them both, then walked out of the house, pulling the door gently closed behind her.

Chapter Five

*I*t was a Saturday afternoon at the end of August, and almost two weeks since Clara's adventure with Jason and Mark. She had locked the gallery and was taking down Eric's paintings and wrapping them up in bubblewrap and brown paper. She hummed to herself. She could not remember a time when she had been so content. The show had been an unqualified success, but that was only part of the reason why she felt herself glowing.

The heat inside the gallery was beginning to get to her and she was starting to sweat with the exertion of handling the heavy pictures. They were to be delivered to their purchasers, and the next show would have to go up on Sunday for Monday's preview. She hoped that Xavier would help her to hang the show this time, but she wasn't worked up about it.

Mark had been as excited as she was by the game of prostitution. Since then they'd met a few times and she'd been surprised at his prodigious capacity for imaginative sex. Regular contact with him had left her charged up and buzzing with sexual energy. She'd been so sated with him that she hadn't even contacted

Mr X. Maybe that was all behind her, she thought, wiping her brow which was now covered in a light film of sweat. Recently she'd begun to get a disconcerting feeling about Mr X, one that she couldn't shake off, that he wasn't necessarily someone whom she could trust with her innermost secrets.

She wondered how much her attitude towards Mr X had been coloured by Paul's unwanted reappearance on the scene. She could have sworn it had been him who had been watching her as she stepped into Mark's car. And if he was capable of following her around, maybe he was capable of putting on a persona, one that was totally opposite to his own, and contacting her via e-mail, in a cheap bid to trick her into falling for him again.

Only today she'd received another letter from him. He'd sent one nearly every day for the past fortnight as well as having left numerous messages on her answerphone. This letter was typical of all the rest. 'I want you, I need you back. I can't live without you. I will never love again.' With distaste she had torn it into small pieces and put them in the bin.

Paul was the only shadow hanging over her happy state and even he could not dent her ebullient mood as she fastened the last picture into its wrapping and stood up to survey her handiwork. She wore a pair of shorts and a tightly fitting T-shirt. Because she hadn't had to deal with customers she'd dispensed with a bra.

There was a flurry of movement behind her and she turned to see Xavier and Eric gesticulating at her from behind the glass. She took a sharp intake of breath. Xavier hadn't told her that Eric was back in town.

She took in his muscular form, which was clad in a white T-shirt and faded jeans. He looked more devastating than ever. All the same sensations came back from the last time, when they had made love in Xavier's office. Now, a sense of a barely containable excitement was making her flustered. She couldn't help herself from wanting him. His eyes roamed over her nipples, stiffening beneath the thin material of the T-shirt, as she stepped forward and fumbled to turn the key in the lock.

Xavier stepped into the gallery and glanced at the bits of paper and string strewn around the room.

'Look, I really appreciate you packaging up the pictures but could you just tidy up a bit. The place looks like a tip from outside.'

Clara was determined that no one was going to interfere with her mood and decided to ignore the comment. Eric had locked his eyes onto her shorts, which fitted snugly over her bottom and tanned legs.

'Actually, I'm absolutely famished. I'm going to get a sandwich.'

'That's just as well, because I wanted to have a quick word with Eric.'

Why did Xavier have to be so unpleasant? She would have thought that they could all have chatted about business together. Well, whatever was bothering Xavier, she wouldn't let herself get ruffled by him.

'See you later,' she said, turning around to pick up her handbag. But Eric and Xavier had already walked the length of the gallery and disappeared down the stairs to Xavier's office.

As she stepped out into the street and locked the gallery behind her she was aware of the familiar tingle between her legs. Eric had something, it was animalistic, a presence that made her feel completely helpless. She wondered if she'd be able to get rid of Xavier later and have some fun with Eric.

As she walked down a side street she started to wonder about Xavier. Why couldn't he just relax and enjoy the fact that the gallery was doing well? It was such a waste, too, a gorgeous man like him, spending his time worrying about profit margins when there was so much more to life.

It was early evening and a breeze was blowing against her naked thighs as she hurried along the street. She was aware of her body's restlessness, which had been activated by Eric's stare. Her breasts, bra-less under the T-shirt, jiggled as she walked, the soft cotton rubbing tantalisingly against her nipples.

When she had reached the shop she went in to order a sandwich and as she waited for it to be prepared she noticed that a sleek car had drawn up outside. It was slate grey with tinted windows, and as she watched, drumming her fingers on the counter, she saw a window being slowly wound down a couple of inches.

She stared at the car, her mind still idly wondering about how she might dampen down the burst of excitement that was rippling up within her. Then the window was rolled down a fraction more and abruptly, out of the darkness in the car Clara felt some eyes dart in her direction. Turning her head a fraction more to the left she saw a pair of eyes dart a penetrating ice-blue stare in her direction.

'Here you are, dear.' The woman handed her the sandwich.

Clara began to fumble in her handbag. Anxiety rushed through her like pins being driven into her skin. In her haste to find the money and leave the shop, a hail of coins clattered to the floor and she bent down to pick them up. Still on her knees, she lifted her head and saw that the car window had been closed and that the car was now inching forward. The man inside the car was driving away because he had seen her looking at him, she thought, as she stuffed the coins into her purse and straightened up.

The woman behind the counter was looking at her with a puzzled expression. Clara grabbed the sandwich and slammed down the money on the counter.

Was someone following her, and if so, why? It was an inexplicable fear, and one that now rose up within her, mingling uncomfortably with her heightened state of arousal. In fact, she was surprised to find that the anxiety had made her feel more turned on than ever.

As she walked along the streets back to the gallery she felt faint with nausea and could feel her heart beating loudly in her chest. There was no sign of the car now as she walked purposefully towards her destination. Her breathing had almost regulated when she saw the grey car, not a hundred yards away, passing at right angles at the end of the street. She stopped dead in her tracks, wondering whether she should keep walking or turn back.

She decided to take a right turn off the street and take another route to the gallery. She was convinced now that this was something to do with Paul. Tears prickled in her eyes as she walked as fast as she could, her chest now drenched with sweat. The flowers, phonecalls, the frequency of his letter-writing; it all added up to one thing, that Paul was obsessed with her and could not bear to have her out of his sight.

Bursting into the gallery she quickly locked the door behind her. She was about to run downstairs to Xavier's office to tell him what had happened. Swivelling round she stared out into the street – filled with the soft orange glow of early evening – her eyes searching the street for the car. But she checked the impulse to tell them and collapsed behind the counter and buried her head in her hands. They would probably just dismiss what had just happened as a coincidence; they might even laugh at her.

She switched on her computer, knowing that there was only one person she needed, needed right now, to assuage her fears. She knew it in a split second. Mr X was the only one she could really confide in. How had she doubted him for an instant?

She began to rapidly type her e-mail.

I've just had the most awful experience – by the way, let me say I'm sorry that I haven't contacted you recently but a lot has happened. I'm convinced that someone is following me, and I'm sure that it's someone, maybe a private detective, who my ex-boyfriend Paul has hired. Don't ask me how I know, I just do, deep down. I should have dealt with him when all this started, told him face-to-face that I didn't want him bothering me. Maybe I'm being hysterical about all this, but the other day, when I was playing at being a whore in the street, I'm pretty sure that I saw him watching me from the other side of the road. I just don't know what to do or which way to turn.

She waited for a few minutes, suddenly hungry, and began to devour the sandwich. When Mr X's e-mail came back she felt a palpable sense of relief.

This Paul seems still to have a very powerful hold over you. You say that this is in the past, but it seems that it isn't really, and that you've only got over it on a surface level. Also, it seems to me that somehow you want it to be Paul. Maybe you like the knowledge that you have a hold over him. Think about it some more. I'm not convinced that Paul is following you. One's imagination can play all sorts of little tricks, especially now that you have opened your imagination to all the many possibilities of lust. You might also find that your fear can be turned around to become a powerful source of pleasure.

Clara put down the half-eaten sandwich with an air of annoyance. That wasn't the answer she had been looking for. Now she felt more confused than ever and angry at Mr X for making light of the matter. If it wasn't Paul, then who was it? She switched off her computer. Her good mood had completely evaporated.

She heard the sound of Xavier and Eric coming up the steps. Her heart leaped. Maybe they could all go for a drink. A bit of relaxation and civilised company was exactly what she needed to calm down. And who knew what might happen after closing time?

'I was thinking, why don't we all go over to the pub?' she said, giving Xavier her broadest smile.

He looked at her distractedly. 'I'm sorry, but we've got other plans. I'll see you tomorrow, though, to help you hang the pictures.'

She gasped. She was pleased that she hadn't had to beg him to come in to help her but felt deflated, knowing that she was now destined to spend the evening alone, apprehensive and turned on. She was tempted to ask Eric to walk her to the tube, as her stomach was still tightly coiled with fear.

Xavier slipped out the door and Eric turned to her and gave her a wink.

'Might see you soon?'

'Yes, sure.' She wondered what he meant by that.

After they had left she sat in the gallery until dusk darkened the street outside. She chastised herself for being so stupid. But the irrational fear still pulled at her, that Paul might be waiting for her. Finally, she threw on a light coat and left the gallery. She walked purposefully down towards Piccadilly, her head held erect and her eyes staring straight ahead.

Then, out of the corner of her eye she saw to her left that the car was following her again, moving very slowly now. Her heart beat hard in her chest. She chastised herself for getting so worked up. She was telling herself that whoever was in the car could not actually harm her, when the car drove a little way ahead and ground to a halt.

A lump came to her throat as she slowed her pace and stopped walking. Slowly the window was wound down. The light was dim and she couldn't quite make out the features of the man inside the car. She was frozen to the spot, her gaze drawn to the window like a magnet. The face moved forward.

'Hello Clara.' The steely blue eyes were turned towards her. 'Or should I say Annabelle?'

'Jason!' Relief spread through her, heating up every inch of her body. 'Thank God it's you! You gave me such a shock following me like that.'

'Sorry.' But he didn't look the slightest bit apologetic. In fact there was a sly smile playing at the corner of his mouth. She remembered what Mark had said, that Jason liked to have women as his playthings. The memory of the night the three of them had shared came rushing back, making her blush.

'Get in,' he commanded.

'But where are we going?'

'Stop asking stupid questions. What are you worried about? I'm not going to hurt you.'

Suddenly the back window was wound down. Mark leaned over and looked out. He held up a bottle of Champagne.

'Get in,' he said softly. 'You look like you could use a drink.'

She was relieved to see Mark and got into the car. After the humidity outside it was a relief to step into the air-conditioned interior. She slipped out of her coat and leaned back into the leather seat, feeling the tension of the day begin to flow out of her. She was about to tell Mark all about her suspicion that Paul had hired a car and had her followed but suddenly it no longer seemed important. His proximity was making her feel sensual, wanton. She longed to touch him.

He was dressed informally, in a sea-green shirt, unbuttoned at the neck, and a pair of chinos. She had never seen him so laid-back. Leaning into the padded seat she took a delicious pleasure in wondering what the evening held in store. A current of arousal was already rippling over the entrance of her pussy.

The car moved forward smoothly. It's interior was a soft cocoon where nothing could touch them. It had been stupid to be afraid. It was just the two of them now, in this private den. And Jason of course, whose piercing eyes she could see reflected in the mirror. She felt her palms tingling with expectation as Mark leaned forward to pop open the Champagne.

He poured the pale liquid into a tall fluted glass and handed it to her. She sipped at it, wondering how much longer she could hold out. But then, when he turned towards her, she saw a devilish look in his eyes, a look full of naked promise, that changed the mood in the car completely. He turned to her and in a soft, sexy voice whispered close to her ear, 'I've always thought that it's such a waste of good Champagne to drink it out of glasses.' He prised her glass out of her hand and set it down. His eyes locked into hers as he continued.

'Take off your shorts.'

For a second she was taken aback, but the throbbing between her legs was already making its demands felt. Her body was heating up rapidly, even in the coolness of the car. She wanted to feel his hands and mouth all over her body. In that split second she knew that she was ready to do anything his desire demanded of her. Eagerly, she wriggled the shorts down over her firm bottom and pulled off the T-shirt. As her breasts swung freely he shifted towards her. She kicked off her shoes.

'You might feel more comfortable wearing this,' he said, slipping a blindfold over her eyes. It was disconcerting to find herself plunged into darkness. But then the thrill took over. She was getting a kick out of it, even though she had done it before. Maybe it was something to do with knowing that Jason was drinking it all in but couldn't touch her.

'Now, just relax,' Mark commanded.

For what seemed like an eternity she heard nothing, just the hum of the motor as they glided forward. She had kicked off her trainers, and her feet were imbedded in the silky softness of the carpet. A drop of icy liquid fell onto her breasts – first one, then the other. She winced at the startling sensation which teetered between pleasure and pain. Then she felt the warm roughness of his tongue as he licked the Champagne off her nipples, which were blossoming hard. Rapidly he alternated the cold liquid, which fizzed on the quivering aureole, with his ravening tongue.

'Mmm,' he murmured, pushing her gently down so that she was lying at a slight tilt. She heard the pouring of more Champagne and the bubbles fizzing against the glass. As he tongued her breasts he pushed open her legs and moved his mouth lingeringly down to her stomach.

He trickled the Champagne down the plane of her stomach, licking in small, swirling motions until he came to the tops of her thighs. She spread her legs. Now she was wide open, her urgent need displayed to him. Her desire went up another notch as she waited for what seemed like an eternity, hearing the hum of the air-conditioning and the rustling of his clothes as they brushed against the leather seat.

Then at last she felt his fingers brushing against her bush. Maybe because she had been so frightened before, her sense of touch had become magnified, and now, this small movement started off a sensation that was akin to burning, a hot flush that spread all over her skin.

As he continued to toy with her, skimming her clit and holding open the entrance of her aching tunnel with his fingertips, the nerve-endings under her skin amplified each touch into a peak of pleasure. It was a powerful sensation that flowed over her like the sound that rushes out from inside a seashell when held against an ear.

He tilted her up at an angle as she trembled in anticipation. Now tiny volts of pleasure were running all over the surface of her skin. She cried out as again the liquid was splashed onto her, this time onto her labia, the Champagne flowing into her hot molten wetness.

Soon his mouth was on her pussy, lapping at the Champagne, making her writhe and jerk on the seat. He pushed his tongue deep into her, licking a point on the front wall of her cunt from which began to flow a buzz of pleasure, as if he had activated a powerful motor. Her senses were thrown into disarray as he pinched her nipples hard while moving his tongue in and out of her with an ever-increasing momentum as she trembled against him, the sensations radiating from the hot area of contact between his tongue and her pussy.

She reached up to tear off the blindfold. She was seized by an urgent desire, the need to see his face, the naked lust in his eyes. But he grabbed her hand. 'No, no, Clara. You'll take it off when I say.'

But something in her rebelled. Damn it, she couldn't hold out any longer.

'I'd like to get on top of you, if I may,' she said. She needed to feel him inside her, needed to take control and have him beneath her, so that she could ride him to her satisfaction.

'Well, well, I was thinking the very same thing.' She felt to the right for him and encountered exposed skin. She ran her fingers lasciviously over his naked flesh and along the hard length of his thighs. At last her hands came to what she was looking for. She felt the smoothness of his rock-hard erection along its substantial length.

Greedily she started sucking the tip while caressing his balls with her hands. He began to moan. She teased him a little more, pulling back the foreskin and flicking her tongue across the head in rapid skilful strokes. It was too much for her to bear. Swiftly she hoisted herself up onto the seat, and with her knees imbedded in the soft leather guided him into her.

She felt his cock slip inside the tight tube of flesh, prising her apart. She began a silky smooth ride along the length of his cock, moving up and down, revelling in the delicious friction. The springs inside the seat were providing ample leverage for her knees so that she could keep thrusting herself gloriously down onto him.

To her delight, he started to run his fingertips over her clit, teasing it with small circular motions that amplified the sensations that were streaming through her. She rammed down on him harder and faster.

Faster and faster his finger worked her clit until she felt the waves of pleasure fluttering deep within her. He began to spasm and she felt him begin to come inside her, as she shuddered to a halt, leaning against him as he pounded her from beneath until, with a drawn-out moan, he had completely satiated himself. She fell on top of him, breathing in deeply the smell of fresh perspiration until she felt him pull away from her.

'Sorry to break up the party.' She heard Jason's voice float up through the darkness. 'But we've arrived.'

Pulling off the blindfold she glanced at Mark, who was putting his clothes on. She moved to do the same but he gripped her by the arm.

'Oh, I don't think that'll be necessary.'

Jason opened the door and gestured for her to get out. She looked left and right. She realised that they had drawn up outside Mark's house. She noticed that there were quite a few people taking an evening stroll.

She hesitated. 'I can't just get out like this!'

'Oh, come on,' said Jason. 'You don't want me to have to drag you out do you?'

She felt Mark's hand in the small of her back, pushing her forward. It didn't look like she had a choice. After everything that she had done these past few weeks it still seemed like a big deal to walk down a street in Central London completely naked. She trusted Mark implicitly, although she wasn't so sure about Jason.

Resolutely, she stepped out into the night air and walked the short distance to the front door, savouring the cool air blowing against her pubic hair and folding her arms across her breasts in a hopeless gesture to veil her nudity.

Still a little dazed from her experience in the car she stood outside Mark's door. But when she turned around she realised that the car was moving away and several passers-by were turning in her direction. She felt a prickle of humiliation run over her body. Were they just going to leave her there?

But before she could think about it any more the door swung open and Astrid stuck her head out.

'Astrid! What are you doing here?'

'Come in and I'll tell you all about it.'

'I didn't even know you knew Mark.' She kissed Astrid, who returned the kiss warmly.

'Well, I do, in a way, through Eric.'

'Eric! Don't tell me he's here too?'

'Well, he was, I don't know where he's got to.'

Astrid pulled her along the hall and into the sitting room. Clara sat down on one of the sofas. As Astrid seemed to be unconcerned by her nudity Clara decided that there was no point in mentioning it.

She noticed that Astrid looked different. Her face

was heavily made-up and her lips covered liberally in shocking pink lipgloss. She wore white platform boots, tiny black PVC shorts and a shiny red bustier. The effect, combined with the tumble of blonde curls, was electrifying.

She leaned against Astrid, breathing in the exotic perfume, and closed her eyes.

Astrid put her arm around her. 'Hey, what's wrong?'

'Well, you know that ex-boyfriend I was telling you about, Paul?'

'You did tell him in no uncertain terms where to get off, didn't you?' Astrid leaned over to a table at the edge of the sofa and mixed them two drinks.

'No. God, I only wish I had.' She sipped at the drink. It was very potent but delicious. 'Things have got out of control. He won't leave me alone. Letters, practically every day, phone calls. I tell him not to call me, but he just carries on regardless.'

'You shouldn't let him get to you. That's what he wants.'

'I know, I've become so paranoid. Today I thought that Mark's car belonged to a private detective that Paul had hired to have me followed. It frightened the life out of me!'

Astrid moved closer to her. 'Put it out of your mind.'

'But what should I do?'

'Let me think about it. I've dealt with this kind of pest before. I'll work out a plan.' The door opened and Eric and Mark burst in. 'We'll talk about it later.'

Eric bent down to kiss Clara. 'See, I told you I'd see you later!'

They all settled down and began to chat. It was light-hearted banter but filled with references that Clara knew nothing of. And the way in which Astrid was ribbing Mark in that intimate way made her think that Astrid had known him for longer than she was letting on. After drinking two more cocktails she felt completely relaxed, leaning against Astrid in the intimately lit room.

She had noticed that the name Daniel kept cropping up.

'Who is this Daniel?' she asked.

'Oh sorry, Clara,' said Mark. 'Here we are rambling on and you don't know a thing about him.'

'Oh, come on Mark, don't spill the beans, you know how Daniel likes to think of himself as a bit of an enigma. Why doesn't she find out for herself what kind of person he is?'

'Is he coming tonight?' said Clara.

'No, he hardly ever comes down to London these days. But, he is having a party soon to which you must come,' said Mark.

'I've already invited her,' said Astrid.

'Yes, it's sure to be a lively weekend,' said Mark. 'He lives in this ancient country mansion.'

'Plus, he's also a very talented artist,' said Eric.

'Well, he was,' Astrid said. 'He's been working on a new project that he's keeping under wraps.'

'What kind of medium does he use?' said Clara.

'He was a brilliant painter. But his new stuff, I don't have a clue what that'll be like. But maybe if you're nice to him he might show it to you.'

'Fat chance of that!' Eric exclaimed and began to laugh.

'So are you coming?'

'Well, sure, why not.' This Daniel certainly seemed to be an important person in their lives.

The evening had turned out much better than she could have envisaged. She now felt enveloped in an intimate ambience. Clara noted Astrid's hand rubbing rhythmically along Mark's thigh. An involuntary flash of jealousy passed through her. It was not so much the fact of Astrid and Mark sleeping together that made the situation difficult to accept, rather, it was the strangeness of it all. She had met Astrid independently of Mark and now they seemed so close.

She watched as Astrid whispered something in Mark's ear and as he ran his hand up her thigh and slid it under the tight confines of her shorts. No, she reasoned, it was more to do with the fact that although Astrid had pretended not to know Mark at Eric's opening night, Clara was beginning to get the feeling that Astrid knew Mark very intimately indeed. She wondered why Astrid hadn't mentioned it. The thought was rapidly followed by a rush of paranoia. Was Astrid somebody she could trust with her secrets, her problems with Paul?

She noticed Eric, who was sitting opposite her and watching her pointedly. It was so warm in the room that she had momentarily forgotten her nudity. She turned towards Mark, who was running his fingers along Astrid's inner thighs while they kissed, her tumble of hair obscuring his face. She watched as he unzipped the shorts and slid his palm down into them. Clara could clearly see Mark's hand stealthily moving over Astrid's shaven mound. Clara bit her lip, her excitement mounting. It was as if her own fingers were, at that moment, moving down and slipping into Astrid's warm pussy.

At that moment Astrid lifted her head and gave Clara a long meaningful stare as Mark continued to plunge his fingers into her. Clara felt herself melting, dissolving into the gaze, her body tingling with a hot flush as she began to toy with her nipples.

Leaning back into the sofa she lifted her legs up as she began to rub her nipples, one with each hand, moaning softly as her legs fell open, so that she was showing herself to Astrid and Eric.

Mark had his head buried in her neck, and Astrid continued to look at Clara through half closed eyes as he licked her neck, working his way down her cleavage, then pushed the bustier down so that the orbs of her breasts protruded. Clara felt her nipples hardening as she pinched them, trying to stem the hot waves of excitement that were now building in her pussy. She watched as Mark pressed Astrid's breasts together and started to lick, with a passion she had experienced little more than an hour ago, over the surface of Astrid's breasts.

Her hand ran down the flat plane of her stomach and she jumped as her fingertips made contact with her clit. Her gaze moved from Astrid, who had now unzipped Mark's trousers and was bending down to take his cock in her mouth, over to Eric. Eric was evidently enjoying looking at Clara's shapely legs, wide open to his gaze. She pushed her fingers a little into her opening, and dragged the fluid generated by her arousal back over the nub of her desire, creating a smooth hum of pleasure beneath her questing fingers.

Clara stared back at Eric, whose eyes were trained directly on her pussy, causing it to prickle with antici-pation. When was he going to touch her? She ached to feel him against her, the heavy weight of his body on top of her, his hands pinning her down while his cock ground into her.

She looked longingly at the clear outline of his erect cock straining against his jeans. His eyes, the colour of melted honey, briefly met hers. Should she get up and join him? She was incapable of making a decision. Any moment now she was going to come. She held herself open to him with one hand, while with the other she pistoned two fingers into herself.

She stared, transfixed, as Eric began to unzip his jeans, slowly, then lowered them over his hips. She saw the outline of his cock more clearly now, lying against the blue cotton boxer shorts.

She watched as he slipped the shorts over his hard, shapely thighs and threw them aside. Relaxing back against the sofa he gripped his cock at the base and smiled at her as he rubbed his fist all along its length. She heard Astrid moaning as if she were in the throes of an orgasm. Clara, hungry now to feel Eric's cock, hard and heavy in her mouth, felt her pussy tighten around her fingers, sucking them in deeper as she felt herself climax in sharp, hot waves.

Eric appeared unmoved by the spectacle, and continued his slow elaborate exploration of every inch of his magnificent cock. As the ripples of her climax died down and her breathing regulated she felt a familiar twinge of anger. This was Eric's favourite type of game, she knew that much. But as he continued to fondle his straining cock in his hands, with a studied nonchalance, she felt a fierce yearning build up over the surface of her overheated skin.

It was so frustrating, after all that she had learned about her sexuality, under Mr X's expert guidance. She had had some success in turning her fantasies into reality. She knew enough about the rules of this game to understand that she must hold out indefinitely until Eric gave the signal. She knew too that the longer she held out the sweeter the pleasure would be. She swivelled her head to look at Astrid who lay on her front as Mark, divested now of his clothes, plunged his cock into her as she moaned beneath him.

Her hand, which had been idly toying with the lips of her vagina, now came to a standstill. The sexual tension between them was electrifying. Suddenly, out of the blue she came to a decision. She would go over to Eric and to hell with the consequences.

She saw a look of surprise flash across his face as she walked over to him.

'I don't think I asked you to join me over here,' he said.

'I don't need your permission,' she said and climbed

onto the sofa so that she rested on her knees, her breasts inches away from Eric's half open mouth.

'Oh, you don't think so, hmm.' She gazed down at his face, flushing attractively now with the effect that her proximity was having on him. She pushed her right breast into his mouth and he began to suck hungrily on it.

'Stop teasing me,' said Clara. She bit her lip to stifle a moan. His musky male scent was making her feel as if she would pass out if he did not plunge himself deep into her immediately.

He gripped the backs of her thighs and pulled her towards him with one violent gesture. She cried out as she felt her clit make contact with the hard muscles of his stomach as she rubbed herself against him. He pulled her up unceremoniously so that she found that he was now lying flat and had positioned her pussy over his mouth. As soon as she felt the expert lapping of his tongue her insides turned to jelly and she could not control the waves of release that now flowed out of her. It was mixed up, tantalisingly, with a feeling of control. That she had him under her and had him drawing the pleasure forth from her, giving her what she needed.

Reaching behind her she ran her fingers lightly over his cock and heard him moan. She moved down over his body so that her pussy was positioned over him. She kissed him deeply, prising his mouth open with her tongue, feeling him respond with an animalistic urgency. Without saying another word she sank down on him. He started to protest. 'I didn't say you could.'

She started up a hard pounding rhythm, driving his rampant cock deep inside her, feeling her insides mould themselves around his cock.

'I think that the time has come to stop playing games,' she said, breathlessly, grinding herself against him, feeling sweat drip down between her breasts from her exertions.

She looked straight into his eyes and with a force she did not know she possessed drove him further into her, up to the hilt, until she began to cry out. Supporting herself on her arms she threw her head back, moans escaping from the back of her throat as she descended into the blackness, bent now on totally extinguishing the last embers of pleasure that burst like spurts of flame within her. She felt him come too and falling against him she began to laugh, delighting in the situation.

'You can't tell me what to do any more,' she said, playfully.

He reached up and encircling her wrists smiled back at her. 'You've won this time, but watch out, you may pay for it next time.'

Then she stretched out beside him, running her fingers over the dips of his body and closing her eyes. Eventually she heard someone speaking and opened her eyes. Mark sat opposite her with Astrid nakedly sprawled along his lap.

'I was just saying that you're welcome to stay in one of the spare rooms.'

'Oh God, I really am so tired.'

'Well, it's upstairs, first on the left.'

'What time is it?'

Astrid looked at her watch. 'Nearly one o'clock. I don't feel tired at all. But you go on to bed.'

Clara got up and stretched. Then she leaned over and kissed Eric on the lips. Tentatively she turned to Astrid and Mark and kissed them too. She was suddenly incredibly tired.

She staggered up the stairs and without turning on the light went into the big room on the left and crept under the duvet. She fell immediately into a deep sleep.

Later on she was woken by the sound of music from downstairs, mingled with uproarious laughter. She couldn't help feeling a twinge of uncertainty; she still had much to learn. Would they always be one step ahead? It appeared to Clara that they viewed each erotic adventure as a game, with many subtle variations. With Eric she had felt a smug sense of satisfaction that she had beaten him at his own game. She turned over and buried her head in the pillow. Astrid's laughter trickled up the stairs. Soon she was asleep again.

As she woke she took in the majestic sweep of the room. It was understated, like everything about Mark, done out in autumnal shades of russet and brown. Stretching in the big bed she listened for signs of life. Nothing. Wrapping herself in a man's dressing gown that she found hanging on the door she went to investigate.

She walked down the corridor, and pushed open one of the doors leading from it. She smiled as she saw Eric and Astrid, their limbs tangled up in each other, sleeping deeply in the kingsize bed.

She made her way downstairs, then along the corridor, with its red intimate glow, until she reached the kitchen. In the middle of the airy room was a breakfast bar, of about waist height, and she sat down for a moment on a stool beside it.

She gazed around the beautifully fitted kitchen, furnished in terracotta and coloured enamel tiles, remembering with a jolt that she had, as far as she knew, left her clothes in the car. She made herself a cup of tea and sat sipping it thoughtfully, wrapped in a cloud of lazy contentment. Glancing at a calendar on the wall she remembered with a jolt that tomorrow was the first of September, the day of the opening. Glimpsing a notepad on the counter she scribbled a note.

Hope to see you all at tomorrow's opening –
starts at seven. Had a great time last night!
   Clara x

She got off the stool, tore the note from the pad and
leaned over to prop it up against the fruit bowl when
abruptly she felt two hands clasp her waist.

Chapter Six

'What the...?' She swivelled round and found herself face to face with Jason. He too wore a dressing gown, loosely knotted to reveal an expanse of well-muscled torso.

'Good morning,' he said and leaned over to kiss her on the mouth. His hands were now cupping her bottom through the silky material, as he pulled her towards him. In one fluid movement he was tentatively pressing his naked thigh between hers.

She disliked Jason, disliked the way he had just come over to manhandle her, as if she was his property. And yet as he pulled open the knotted cord of her dressing gown and began to toy with her nipple she realised that the situation was also tremendously exciting.

Over his shoulder she could see the clock on the wall, signalling that it was already one o'clock. She really needed to get to the gallery. Jason had both his hands on her breasts, rubbing their whole surface against his palms, then playfully pressing his fingers into their soft pliable surfaces.

'I really need my ...'

He pressed his mouth against hers and pushed her

roughly back, so that the hard corner of the sink unit pressed into the small of her back. His hand ran the length of her body and soon he was pushing two fingers into her with a barely controlled brutality that made her catch her breath.

She turned her head away. 'No, Jason, really, I just need to get my clothes. Can you get them out of the car?'

He was skilfully manipulating her clit now, pulling it from side to side so that a red haze passed before her eyes and she felt herself drifting towards oblivion. Sharply she pulled herself back to consciousness. She twisted away and out of his grasp.

'No. Not now.' There was danger, she could sense it, seeping out of every pore of his skin. There was an unknown quantity about him and she wasn't sure that she could handle it.

Drawing away from him she ran her hand through her hair and pulled the dressing gown over her nakedness.

'Please. You'd be doing me a massive favour,' she said.

He stared at her, his penetrating gaze drilling through her with such intensity that she had to look away. 'I'm just going to grab a shower.'

'Your wish is my command,' he said, and then began to chuckle, in a way that Clara found disconcerting.

Upstairs she pulled the shower curtain aside and stepped in. Switching on the faucet she hoped that the powerful surge of water would dampen down the intense excitement that Jason had generated in the kitchen, just moments before. She ran the soap over the curves of her body, trying to think about what she had to do in the gallery. But as she ran her fingers over her bush her clit jumped to attention and she could not stop herself from rubbing herself urgently against her hand. If she could just come, maybe she could get her head straight. She closed her eyes, enjoying the hard pounding of the water on her skin, playing with herself, until she felt poised on the edge of an orgasm.

Her eyes flew open as she felt the rustle of the shower curtain.

'Have I interrupted something?' He stood in the shower cubicle, tipping his head up to the stream of water.

'Jason.' Her eyes were drawn to his body. He towered above her, his feet firmly planted in a stance that radiated supreme self-confidence. She hated him. How dare he just come in like that? But then his presence made her melt, his sheer bulk and physicality, which radiated a heat, a powerful sexuality laced with a thread of danger. He reached out and moved her hand from her clit, replacing it with his own.

'Why don't you leave me alone?' But as she said it she leaned back onto the tiled wall and parted her legs to allow him better access.

'Do you really want that?' he whispered.

She could not formulate an answer, as she felt his skin, hot and wet, pressing against hers, making her body immediately turn to jelly as she began to kiss him, hungrily. The anger she felt towards him was still mixed in with her lust, but this only served to turn her arousal up another notch. She needed him to fill her up, right to the hilt. Yet still he teased her clit, with featherlight strokes. She hated him knowing that she needed him, but her pussy was slippery with water and her own juices and needed to be satiated.

The heat of his cock was burning against her hip bone and she felt herself writhing from her pinioned position, trying to get her opening in contact with him.

'Do you want it?'

The water rained down on her upturned face. She closed her eyes and savoured the sensations. Words were beyond her now. Only a soft moan escaped her lips. He positioned himself so that the head of his cock was butting against her. Pressing her back against the tiles, she levered her pelvis forward, desperate for more contact.

He moved back a fraction. 'Not so fast.'

'I need . . .' she murmured, her eyes half closed as he bit her neck from ear to shoulder.

'You were a bad girl, weren't you?'

She opened her eyes. 'What?' What was he talking about?

'Getting me all worked up, looking at you in the back of the car. Letting Mark drink Champagne out of your pussy.'

'Please.'

'Bad girl,' he whispered. 'I shouldn't really do you any favours. You don't deserve your clothes, or my cock. Say it, "I've been a bad girl".'

She squirmed against him, but her lubrication and the water had caused his cock to slip away from her opening. It rested tantalisingly, centimetres above her pussy.

'Say it.' His voice was harsh, menacing, making her feel that she no longer had any choice in the matter.

'I've been a bad girl,' she whispered. She didn't care what he made her do, what he made her say, she just needed him, now.

With one powerful thrust he was in her. She cried out, her nails clawing at his biceps as he pistoned back and forth. She was so aroused now, his cock enclosed by a tight tunnel of flesh that sucked him into her, so that it was with difficulty that he drew out to plunge into her once more.

'You'd better behave yourself in future.' His voice filtered through the water. It had a sinister edge, but that only served to heighten her arousal. Then she became lost in the tremors that flickered in the pit of her stomach, building to a peak.

She felt her pussy spasm and a wave of heightened sensation hit her so that she was almost knocked off balance. This was followed by another wave, a piercing pleasure that caused every muscle inside her to reverberate against his hardness. They came together, thrusting against each other, as he found different spots inside her that caused her to come in little waves, a long drawn-out stream of sensation. She bucked against him with the last of her strength, as the last crest of pleasure peaked deep within her and, utterly spent, she collapsed against him.

When she had finally extricated herself from Jason she hastily made her way towards Russell Square tube station. The weather had cooled down a little, and in the cold light of day she felt self-conscious in the little shorts and T-shirt, even with her coat pulled over them. At least Jason had kept his promise and got her clothes out of the car, after much cajoling. She reasoned that she didn't have time to go home and change, it would take too long and besides, she knew that Xavier was waiting for her.

She smiled to herself as she sat on the tube, thinking of all that had happened to her in the last twenty-four hours. For the first time in a while Mr X flashed into her mind. What would he make of it all, she wondered.

When she arrived at the gallery she found that Xavier was busy filling in holes in the wall with plaster. The pictures that were to go up were stacked against a wall. He was wearing an old shirt and baggy navy trousers. She realised that she hadn't ever seen him out of a suit and he appeared more human, vulnerable somehow.

'Hi Xavier, sorry I took so long. I had a bit of a late night.'

When he turned towards her she noticed that he, too, looked as if he had not had much sleep.

'Hi,' he mumbled. If he had noticed that she was wearing the same clothes as the day before he was not going to comment on it. She noticed that he had traces of stubble on his angular face. She took a deep breath. Evidently, he had not had quite so fulfilling a night as she.

She went to the back office and put on the coffee machine. While she waited for it to drip through she thought about Jason. She still resented him, even though he had given her so much pleasure in the shower. Still, she reasoned, she was unlikely to see him again. He had humiliated her, making her say she was bad, then forcing her to beg for her clothes. She vowed that she would get her own back on him, somehow. As she poured out the coffee she smiled to herself. She would enjoy getting her revenge.

Back in the gallery Xavier had completed his plastering and was sitting on the rungs of a stepladder staring into space. She sat on the floor and watched him absent-mindedly sip his coffee. She switched on the radio, hoping that the pop music that blared forth would break the heavy silence that hung between them.

'I'm sorry,' Xavier said. 'I'm not in a very good frame of mind.'

'Anything I can help with? Or did you just drink too much last night?'

A wan smile crossed his lips. She realised that she knew hardly anything about him, who he socialised with or even whether he had a girlfriend.

'No, if only! I had a rather sad evening going through the accounts. What with all the travelling I've been doing, it's all rather piled up.'

'Everything's alright though isn't it? Eric's show was a sell out.'

'I know, and you've done a tremendous job. But, as you know, the rent on this place has shot through the roof, and we really need Hilary's show to be equally successful if we are to break into profit.'

Clara digested the news. She walked over to the stack of pictures. The artist, Hilary Fenton, had a good reputation. She looked through the paintings, vivid watercolours of seascapes, fish and beach scenes.

'I don't think we need to worry. These are some of the best pictures she's ever done. Hilary's told me that she's coming up from Devon and, considering her reputation, I don't think we'll have any trouble getting the media coverage a personal appearance will generate.'

'I hope so, I really do.' Was there something else on his mind? She hated the way he didn't confide in her. She was as passionate for the gallery to be a success as he was, so why didn't he let her in a bit more? Or maybe what was troubling him had nothing to do with the gallery. Well, there was no time to worry about it now. She picked up some sandpaper and began to file down the lumps of plaster on the wall.

They lapsed into a companionable silence while they painted over the filed-down spots of plaster, then hammered the nails into the wall and finally begun to hang the pictures.

He stood on the stepladder and as she lifted the pictures up to him and their hands brushed she felt a tremor of excitement run through her. She looked up at him and saw him blush, then quickly turn away. Obviously he had felt the spark between them too.

The work was slow-going and she felt her arms and legs begin to ache. But eventually, they stood back and surveyed their handiwork with satisfaction.

'Sorry I ruined your Sunday. We should be able to afford an assistant to do this stuff. And we will, soon.'

'That's OK.' She wiped her grimy hands on her shorts. His change of mood was a little perplexing but she was too tired to analyse it further.

'Well, I'll see you tomorrow then.' He gave her a broad smile and his green eyes twinkled. He looked a little more relaxed.

He began to walk to the far end of the gallery and she walked over to the counter and picked up her bag.

'Clara.' She swivelled round and he gave her a look that penetrated her skin. This time there was no mistaking its intent.

'What?'

But in an instant he switched off the smile and moved back inside his shell. 'Nothing, it can wait.'

'What? Look, is there anything else that's bothering you?'

'No,' he said abruptly and turned to open the door that led downstairs to his office.

A turmoil of emotions wrestled within her. 'I'm just going to check my e-mails.'

He lifted an eyebrow and looked at her over his shoulder. 'Can't that wait until tomorrow?'

'Probably. But I'll have a hundred and fifty things to deal with then.'

'Well, goodnight.' He disappeared through the door.

She positioned herself behind the counter. She felt that Xavier had been about to spill something out, but then had thought better of it. Maybe Mr X would be able to shed some light onto the matter.

To her delight she saw that there was an e-mail from him. Quickly she read it.

I've been thinking about you more and more, Ms X. I've been thinking that it might be time to take things a step further. Maybe it's time that I gave you a clue to my identity. It seems that you are very fond of games, aren't you? You're very much a split personality. Who else would have known that behind this rather serious career girl lurked this very playful, well, insatiable appetite for pushing the boundaries of pleasure?

Clara smiled as she read it. He was right. She would never have believed herself to be capable of half the things she had recently experienced. Mr X had given her permission to do something that she had not had the confidence to do before. He had allowed her to take the leap into the unknown. In fact, that first day when he had contacted her, and the subsequent session with Eric, had immediately tipped her into this strange, new, lawless universe.

At first things had just happened to her, but now she felt that the circle was slowly turning. She was beginning to make her own decisions, testing herself to see how far she could go, and she guessed that ultimately she would gain control over herself and her desires. She smiled to herself. Maybe her capacity for inventiveness would one day surpass Mark's or Jason's or any of theirs.

She typed back an e-mail, telling him everything, about the exquisite sensations in the car that she had experienced with Mark.

Later, Eric tried to play one of his power games. He was sitting opposite me, completely naked, just idly fondling himself. Meanwhile Astrid and Mark were really going for it, moaning and groaning. And there I was, completely naked, excited, sitting not two metres away from Eric, while he feigned disinterest. I knew though, that he wouldn't be able to hold out forever and in the end I managed to have my way with him and tame the beast.

Mr X replied,

He sounds like a challenge, but I'm not sure that you've completely tamed him yet. What about Paul? Have you heard anything more from him? You need to get that situation under control before it gets out of hand.

No, mercifully he seems to have disappeared. But I was almost frightened out of my wits yesterday when I saw a car following me. I got it into my head that it was something to do with Paul, that he was thinking of some other way of getting at me, because I refused to take his calls. In the end it was some stupid game that Jason, Mark's chauffeur, was playing. If Jason was trying to terrify me out of my wits then he succeeded. This morning, he didn't explain why he'd done it. Then he wouldn't give me my clothes until I made love with him. He really ended up humiliating me, although I must admit I got a buzz out of the mental games we played.

She waited for a long time until Mr X sent back the e-mail.

I think you need to get it out of your head that Paul is having you followed. He sounds like he doesn't have the nerve or the imagination. I don't want to talk about him any more. Nor do I want to scare you any further, but how do you feel about the fact that I know that right now you're wearing a tiny pair of shorts and a rather tight T-shirt? Hope you don't freeze to death. There's a chill in the air today. She felt a tremor run up and down her spine. So, think about it. I'm the only one who's watching you. But who am I?

She typed rapidly. She thought of all the people she knew.

I don't know. Who are you?

Eric, Mark, Astrid, Paul. No, Mr X was right, none of them quite fitted the bill.

She waited for a moment until his e-mail came up.

Has it ever occurred to you that you might know who I am?

The thought came to her, like a clap of thunder. It was Xavier. It had to be. A wave of nausea fell over her. Suppose that Xavier was Mr X, and was, at this very moment, typing her e-mails from his office downstairs? It was far-fetched and yet, at the same time, entirely probable. Suddenly his shifty behaviour had an explanation.

She got up, and realised that her hands were shaking. Suddenly Mr X was no longer a fantasy figure onto whom she could project her dreams and longings. But why, if he did like her, had Xavier not made his intentions clear? She had made it perfectly plain that she liked him. Well, she decided, it was definitely time to take action.

Crossing the floor she made her way down the stairs, making as little noise as possible. When she got to the door of his office she hesitated, then moved closer and placed her ear against it. There was a sound, muffled but distinct, coming from his office. There was the faint sound of buzzing, a sound that she couldn't quite place.

Tentatively, she put her hand on the doorknob and twisted it. The door would not budge. Now the metal doorknob was slippery beneath her hand, which had become clammy. But again she turned it. Nothing. He had locked the door from the inside.

There was nothing for it now, she would have to make her presence behind the door known to him. Maybe he'd seen the doorknob turn. She knocked on the door and waited for what seemed like forever. The buzzing grew a little louder. Finally, she banged impatiently on the door with her fist.

She waited, then heard the buzzing cease and the sound of a key being turned in the lock. He pulled open the door and she was inches away from his startled face.

'Clara! You gave me a shock.'

She smiled, trying to keep up the pretence of normality. 'Sorry if I scared you, I just needed a file from the office. Why did you lock the door?'

He held the door open a little wider. In his left hand he was clutching an electric razor. His casual clothes were gone and now he was back in a suit.

'I thought you'd gone.'

She walked over to the shelf of books behind his desk and grabbed a file on Hilary Fenton. Then she spun round and stared directly at the illuminated screen of his computer.

He walked over to her. 'I thought you were a burglar.'

'You don't usually lock the door.' She skimmed her eyes over the screen. Frustratingly, she saw only a spreadsheet, crammed with numbers. But that didn't prove anything. He could have closed down his e-mails in a second.

'I just locked it for a second while I was getting changed.' Now he had relaxed again and was waiting, the razor poised while he peered at himself in a mirror on the desk. Of course, she thought, the razor was the source of the mysterious buzzing.

'Well, goodnight then,' she said.

He switched the razor back on and gave her a brief smile. He had gone back into himself and now his expression was a blank mask. So much for her detective work.

Closing the door behind her she made her way back up the stairs to the gallery. His explanation was perfectly rational, or was it? She sighed. Why would he have bothered locking the door if he'd thought she'd gone? It made no sense at all.

Wearily she walked over to her computer and

switched it off. She feared that Mr X's words had induced a sense of paranoia that had allowed her imagination to run out of control. And yet, as she left the gallery she still could not shift the idea, that somewhere, somehow, Xavier was watching her.

The next day passed in a buzz of activity. In the cold light of day her intrusion into Xavier's office seemed to her to have been a foolhardy act, one which she felt inexplicably ashamed about.

Clara had dressed formally in a well-cut red suit that contrasted with her dark hair that hung down loosely. She felt the tension in her shoulders. Xavier had made his position perfectly clear. She was to make sure that the evening was a success and she was determined that it would be.

She had ordered an extravagant buffet of Thai food for the evening and the fridge was crammed with fine wine that had strained the preview budget to its limit. But it was worth it for Hilary, who was somewhat eccentric, in her mid-forties and claimed to have a vague sort of aristocratic background. Notoriously fussy, Clara was sure that she would find everything, from the food to the freshly cut flowers that adorned the gallery, to her liking.

Then at midday, disaster struck. Hilary, who lived on the Devon coast, phoned to say that she had caught a bug, was laid up in bed, and wouldn't be able to make the drive up to London. Clara had cajoled her, using every trick in the book to flatter her ego, but Hilary had remained firm in her decision. Then Clara had had to break the news to Xavier, and watch as his face took on that stony expression which she knew so well.

Now she stood by the door of the gallery waiting for the first guests to arrive. Hilary's non-appearance couldn't be helped, she tried to tell herself, yet she knew that something would be missing from the atmosphere, without her haughty, elegant presence.

She caught sight of Mr and Mrs Raleigh, an ageing couple who had always had a soft spot for Hilary's work.

'I think you'll find her new work bolder, a little different from her last exhibition but nonetheless, we're very pleased with it.'

She saw Xavier appear and shake hands with the couple. He was ushering them over to the wine table, his face friendly and open. He could certainly turn on the charm to two wealthy clients, Clara thought glumly. But his smile, to Clara, appeared fake. She smiled over at him, and he nodded briefly in her direction. She hoped that the couple would not be too disappointed that the artist could not be bothered to make an appearance.

The next hour was wearing. She had to explain to several photographers from art magazines that Hilary was not going to be able to make it. Everyone gave her positive feedback on the pictures, and were quite content to help themselves to the wine, which was dwindling rapidly, but no one was buying.

The room was filling up, and the smell of expensive perfume hung in the air, mingled with cigarette smoke. She had the beginnings of a headache and the chatter around her seemed to grow louder and more insistent with every passing minute.

Then she saw Astrid from across the room and waved at her. She looked sensational, as ever, and was wearing a shimmering emerald-green dress, which was cut low at the back and skimmed her firm bottom. She pulled Mark behind her.

'I'm so glad you turned up. I'm having one hell of an evening. Where's Eric?'

'He sends his apologies,' said Astrid. 'He had an

appointment he couldn't get out of. But he said that he hoped to see you again.'

'Did he?' Clara said and laughed.

Mark pulled her towards him and playfully kissed her neck. His suit, of dark plum-coloured velvet, was clearly expensive and fitted around his broad shoulders like a second skin.

'You look wonderful. But you seem a little glum. Where's the infamous Hilary? I'd like to see what she looks like in the flesh. I've only ever seen her in the society pages of *Tatler*.'

'That's just it. She can't make it. And it's going to cost us a heck of a lot of publicity.'

He ran his hand along her shoulders and let it rest on her neck, squeezing her in a reassuring gesture that unexpectedly caused a little shudder of pleasure to run through her. Astrid had turned away as if someone had just caught her attention.

'Don't let it get to you. I'm sure you'll do OK.'

She pulled away from him, not wanting to feel his hot fingertips press into her because it was clouding her thoughts and she needed to keep her wits about her.

'Goodness, Astrid, you never give up, do you? Surveying the field for likely prey, are you?'

Astrid giggled. 'As it happens you're spot on. Who's that handsome guy over by the door. Do you know him?'

Clara looked over to where Astrid was signalling. Suddenly, it appeared to Clara that time had frozen, and all the noise and buzz of the room fell away, leaving a tense hum of silence inside her head. His figure was unmistakable. The tall, rangy frame, his overgrown fringe hanging across one eye. At that moment he looked up and caught her glance.

'Yes, I know him,' she said. 'It's Paul, you know, the one who's pestering me.'

A look of concern crossed Astrid's face.

He was coming over, weaving his way through the crowd.

'Hello, Clara.' He towered above her, his hands pushed into the pockets of a suit that looked a little crumpled.

'Hello,' she said. 'What are you doing here?' She saw Astrid and Mark moving away, towards the back of the gallery, and felt the panic rise within her.

'I've been watching you for quite some time, wondering why I let you go and wanting to do this.' He pulled her against him, pressing his lips down on hers, so that she could barely breathe. All the memories came tumbling back. His kiss was as exciting as it had always been – urgent and filled with passion. She wrenched herself free, hating the way that he had got to her.

'You've been drinking.' She could smell the alcohol on his breath. 'This really isn't the time to discuss anything.' She noticed that people were staring at them. He had a wild look in his eyes. He had often been a little dangerous when under the influence of alcohol and she didn't want to risk causing a scene.

Out of the corner of her eye she saw Xavier looking at her disapprovingly. He came over. 'Are you alright?'

'Who the hell are you?' Paul stepped towards Xavier, swaying a little. He was clearly drunk.

This time it wasn't her imagination. The conversation around her had ebbed away and more heads swivelled round to see what was going on. It was imperative that she keep the situation under control.

'Look sir, I think you'd better come into the back room.' Xavier reached out and touched Paul's arm but he shrugged him off.

'I'm sorry.' Paul hung his head. Clara wondered for one terrible moment whether he was going to start crying. 'I love you. I've always loved you. I can't live another day without you.'

His voice echoed around the room, much to Clara's embarrassment. He had evidently just begun to say what he had come to say.

'OK, look Paul. This isn't the place. Why don't you just come through to the back and we can discuss this.'

'What am I meant to do? You won't speak to me on the phone, you don't reply to my letters. I'm going to pieces. I can't write, I can't eat, I can't think straight any more, without you.'

To her horror she watched Mr and Mrs Raleigh look at him with a barely disguised distaste.

Mark came over and spoke to Paul softly. 'Look. I can see you're upset. Clara wants to talk to you. You look like a civilised man.'

Paul took a step towards Mark and Clara watched as his eyes slowly focused on him.

'You. I know who you are. You've had her. You've screwed her, haven't you!' His face turned red and as he staggered backwards Clara thought he would fall off balance. Instead, the unthinkable happened. He steadied himself and swung a punch at Mark, whose head swivelled to the side with the force of the blow.

'Oh God,' said Mark. He was evidently shocked and drew his hand up to his eye where Paul's fist had made contact.

The next few minutes were chaotic. People began to leave. She watched as Mr and Mrs Raleigh, two of the gallery's most prized clients, moved rapidly towards the exit.

Xavier had grabbed Paul and pulled him away as Clara looked on in horror. She noticed that Astrid had put her arm around her and was saying soothing things in her ear.

Later they sat in Xavier's office. Astrid was resting

117

an ice pack on Mark's eye. Clara could not stop apologising.

'Who was that madman?'

Xavier came in. 'I've got rid of him, I think. Do you know him?'

Clara gulped. 'I'm sorry.' She glanced from Xavier to Mark. She began to cry then, not knowing how to stop herself. Why had he turned up like that and ruined everything? 'I knew him once. I've tried to put him out of my life. But he won't leave me alone.'

She watched as Xavier's face softened. 'You never mentioned anything about him before.'

Astrid stood up and smoothed down her dress. 'I'm going to take Mark home and sort his eye out.'

'I'm really sorry, Mark,' Clara said weakly.

He held up his hand. 'No hard feelings. But you do need to get that guy under control.'

When they had left Clara sat in the big executive chair and Xavier poured her a brandy.

'What about Mr and Mrs Raleigh? Were they going to buy something?'

'Yes, they were. But forget them. Are you sure you're OK?'

She had never seen this side of Xavier before. He sat on the desk and rested his arm on her shoulder. Sipping at the brandy she felt herself slowly gaining control of herself again.

'It makes me so angry. How dare he just burst in here like that!'

'Do you love him?'

'If I ever did, this incident has killed all that.' She shook her head. 'I don't want to talk about him any more.'

'OK.' She looked up at Xavier's face, illuminated by the soft glow of the table lamp. His eyes were filled with concern, and then, she was sure of it, she sensed the gleam of desire mixed in.

'He doesn't deserve you,' he whispered. She almost laughed at the situation. It took her ex-boyfriend to make a gigantic scene in the gallery to make Xavier take notice of her. Not as his business partner, but finally, as a woman.

He leaned forward and brushed his lips against hers. She responded, prising his lips apart, drawing him further towards her. A heat was building in her with such ferocity it was frightening. It felt like she was breaking a taboo as she kissed Xavier. He was her boss after all. A stream of conflicting feelings raced through her and suddenly she drew back.

'You don't know how long I've waited to do that. And now isn't the time to stop.'

'But you're my boss. You've always made it perfectly clear that you . . .'

But before she could finish her sentence his mouth was on hers again and all doubt flew from her mind. She reached out to unbutton his shirt and rubbed her hands through his luxuriant chest hair. He moaned and pulled her up onto the desk with him so that she was lying across him, pulling off her jacket and top, and kissing him, with difficulty, at the same time. He rapidly stripped down to his boxer shorts, then reached up behind her back to unclasp her bra.

She pulled away and as he began to nuzzle her breasts the unwanted thought sprung into her consciousness. What if Xavier was Mr X? She sighed as he pulled one nipple into his mouth and encircled it slowly, tantalisingly. It was so frustrating, not knowing. And yet, Xavier was just as she had imagined Mr X: dark, moody and passionate.

He lay back, his fingers toying with the tips of her hard nipples, causing them to tingle. He sighed, as if he was offering himself up to her as a gift and was now waiting for her to satiate her desire. She was puzzled for a moment, then she leaned over him and

119

ran the tip of her tongue along the side of his neck, savouring the smoky aroma of male sweat.

She bent down and whispered, 'What do you want? Is this what you want?'

He looked up at her, his green eyes becoming murky with desire. As he closed his eyes she noticed how beautifully long and dark his lashes were.

'Do anything, anything you want.' His voice was soft, pleading, and caused an unexpected surge of desire to rush up the tops of her thighs and build up at her entrance.

She pulled off his boxer shorts and straddled him. Pushing two fingers up inside herself she revelled in her wetness. She ran her fingers, coated in her juices, along his cock, which was already hard and throbbing beneath her questing fingers. She ran herself over it, back and forth along its length, creating a delicious friction. She longed to place his cock inside her, but there would be time for that later. She wanted to string out her pleasure for as long as possible.

Slowly she moved her pussy up over his body, smearing him with her wetness. She felt his hands reach up and brush the outside of her thighs, gently, like butterfly wings. She lifted herself up on her knees and lowered herself down onto his mouth. She could feel how much he wanted to explore her by the way his grip tightened on her thighs, pulling her pussy down onto his mouth. He parted his lips and began to run the tip of his tongue between the lips of her pussy.

It was all she could do to stop herself from rubbing herself hard against him, but she sensed that for the pleasure to be exquisite she would have to follow the rhythm of his tongue, as it circled her clit, causing flutters of pleasure to radiate out from the hard swollen bud. Working the flat of his tongue against the whole area of wetness, he increased the pressure and rapidity of his strokes until her pussy felt like molten liquid, dissolving between her legs.

She began to moan softly as he now held her open and probed his tongue down her tight tunnel. Supporting herself on her hands she took a deep breath to prevent herself from shuddering to a climax there and then. She was ready to hurl herself over the top but was determined to do it her way.

She moved down his body again, the whole surface of her pussy burning with sensation. Taking his cock in her hand she slid its length into her. The penetration caused a sharp, intense pleasure to run up inside her. She reached down and, finding his hand, placed it on her clit.

'Gently now,' she whispered as he touched her, causing her clit to quiver from the searing pleasure that he had caused.

Moving her pussy in a sensuous rhythm up and down his shaft she sat upright and took both her breasts in her hands, pressing them together with a restless urgency. Her orgasm was deep within her and beginning its slow climb to release.

She revelled in the multiple sensations, the pressing of her fingertips into her sensitised nipples, his fingers, featherlight, brushing over her clit, and the steady strokes of his cock, deep inside her. She closed her eyes.

At first she saw only blackness and then Paul's face appeared, wearing the expression it had worn in the gallery, an expression that seemed to say that he had hunted her for a long time and now that he had found her he wasn't about to let her go.

To her surprise, she felt a tremendous swell of excitement in the pit of her stomach. The image activated a violent reaction in her body. The separate areas of pleasure were melting and tumbling into each other. Gradually the string of sensations broke down, leaving only the slow release of pleasure, pouring out of her body in long drawn-out spasms, so intense that the image of Paul was blurring in front of her eyes, as she gave her whole self over to the orgasm's powerful hold.

Her pussy continued to throb as she thrust herself against Xavier one last time and he came, crying out as he did so.

As she lay against him she smiled. Their spent bodies entwined, she lay back against the arm that was around her shoulders and looked down. Piles of papers were strewn, higgledy-piggledy, all over the floor.

'These papers must have fallen off the desk, what with all our activity.'

'Oh, I'll sort them out later.' He sat up and twisted round so that his legs were hanging over the edge of the desk. She reached out to stroke his back, wanting to elongate the intimacy that had passed between them only moments before. But to her annoyance, he shifted away from her hand, got down from the desk and started to retrieve his clothes, which lay mixed in with hers in a pile on the floor.

There was nothing for it, thought Clara, she would have to get dressed too. She couldn't just lie on the desk on her own. She pulled on her clothes and smoothed down her skirt and blouse. An uncomfortable silence hung between them.

She wanted to go to him, to pull him into an embrace, but already the worried expression had crept back into his face, warning her that he was once again out of bounds.

'Thanks,' she said, as she did up the buttons on her red suit-jacket.

'What for?' His voice registered cold and distant.

'Well, for being so understanding about Paul. I don't know how I'm going to explain it to Hilary, that he cleared out the gallery before we made any sales.'

'Oh, don't worry about it,' he said, dismissively, sitting down to tie his shoelaces. 'I'll explain it to her.'

Clara sighed to herself. Was this Xavier's way of telling her that yes, their heated session on the desk had been fun but that was the end of it? Her body still hummed with the satiation it had experienced. And their lovemaking had also had the benefit of pushing her out of the wretched state she had been in after Paul had caused a scene.

Clara paused at the door of the office, remembering how she used to be. It hit her how different she was becoming, even in these short weeks since Mr X had encouraged her to become a risk-taker. Once she might have been hurt by Xavier's coldness, feeling that it was a rejection of her. Then the thought came to her that maybe she was feeling the way men did. It was as if Xavier had been a conquest and now she had conquered him.

She had longed for him, but as the months had gone by the possibility of them ever getting together had become more and more unlikely. Then suddenly, in a moment of weakness, he had let his real feelings slip, shown her another side, that he was a flesh and blood man who desired her with an equal intensity. Now, he was the bashful one, not sure how to deal with her. Well, she figured, maybe he would have got his head around the situation by tomorrow.

'Well, goodnight,' she said as she pulled the door behind her.

What a strange evening it had been, she thought as she left the gallery. But as she began to walk down the street in the direction of the Underground, she began to think of Paul, and what else he had in store for her. Whatever it was, she thought, she would be prepared for him.

Chapter Seven

A week had passed since the tumultuous events of the opening. Now, Clara sat in the gallery idly perusing her mail. She wore knee-length leather boots and a short russet-coloured dress. She felt a little agitated, and crossed and uncrossed her legs so that her sheer stockings rubbed together, causing a tantalising friction to run up the insides of her thighs.

Since making love with Xavier she had needed a rest. The whirlwind of events, her experiences with Eric, Jason, Mark and Astrid had made her blood flow faster, had added a spring to her step. But Paul's appearance had put a dampener on things. Since then she had shifted the problem to the back of her head.

She answered the phone. It was Mark. His voice lifted her spirits. She had meant to call him, but was too embarrassed to mention the incident.

'I'm sorry I haven't called you,' she said.

'That's alright. Listen, I wondered if you fancied meeting up later?'

'How's your face?'

'A bit of bruising around the eye but nothing too

serious. That boyfriend of yours certainly has some strength in him.'

'Oh, that idiot. He's got a lot of explaining to do, if only I could face speaking to him.'

She glanced down and looked at the envelope in her hand. She recognised the familiar spiky handwriting as Paul's. 'I've just received a letter from him this morning.'

'What does it say?'

'I don't know. I don't want to read it. I should really toss it in the bin.'

'Look, don't let him get to you. He's really not worthy of you my dear. Shall we meet up after work?'

'Yes,' she said, her mood shifting up a gear as she placed the letter to one side. 'That's a wonderful idea.'

'Oh, listen, I'm a bit tied up this afternoon. Is it alright if Jason picks you up?'

His name caused her heart to give a tumultuous jolt. The memory of the way in which he had humiliated her, making her beg for her clothes, now made her smart. At the same time she felt, with a barely controlled feeling of anger, that the lips of her pussy were engorging and tingling with the prospect of seeing him again.

'There's really no need.' She was worried about whether she would be able to handle Jason and his vexing little games of humiliation. Mentally she made a note to quiz Mr X more about how she should handle the situation.

'I'm sorry, got to go, I've got another call. I'll get him to pick you up at about six. See you.'

'Bye,' she said, although Mark had already put down the phone.

She looked up and saw Xavier hurrying out. He gave her a curt wave and pushed open the door. Since their session on his desk things had reverted very much to the way they had been before. She would just have to accept that it had been a one-off.

She picked up the letter and started to open it with the paper knife. She'd been running away from confrontation for too long. She took a deep breath and unfurled the sheets of paper which were torn from a cheap notepad.

Dear Clara,

I have been too embarrassed to contact you since that debacle at the gallery. What can I say? I behaved very badly. I had been drinking all day, trying to get up the nerve to come and see you. I had hoped that we could have a quiet chat, finally clear things up between us once and for all.

For what it's worth, I feel lost without you. I haven't so much as looked at another woman since you. I know I should move on, you've told me enough times on the phone. But the fact is that I'm concerned about you. I barely recognise the woman you've become.

I happened to be in Soho a few weeks ago when I saw a woman who looked familiar. I presumed that she was a hooker plying her trade. She was dressed in a very tight white dress and was wearing red heels. With a shock I realised that it was you, my beloved Clara. I didn't know what to think. Then a man pulled up and you got in. The very same man I saw you with at the gallery. What am I expected to think? I don't know what's happened to you in these months since I haven't been around to take care of you.

The closely written text swam before her eyes, and she began to sweat as the familiar fear crept over her. There was no coincidence about his being in Soho. He'd been following her, she knew it, instinctively.

Again the thought occurred, was he Mr X? She hoped against hope that he wasn't. But how else could it be explained that Mr X had known what she was wearing? She read on.

I didn't know what to think. I still don't. Are you short of money? Is that it? If so, I can help you out. My novel is doing well. Yes, I know, you can probably hardly believe it!

When they had been together he had managed to get a publishing deal for one of his novels. She was happy for him, but felt utterly detached. He was no longer anything to do with her life. She read on.

And instead of being happy about it, I can't be. I'd rather have nothing if it meant having you. So I have money, should you need some.

Where did I go wrong? You used to be so different. I really wonder if I know you at all or ever really knew you. But to sink to such depths of depravity. I think you need help, I really do. I'm telling you as a friend. What I saw was a cry for help. I think you are lonely, that you need someone. I want you to know that I'll always be there for you, if you want to discuss why you did this terrible thing. I will always love you and if you are willing we can put this whole thing behind us, start again. I know I'm not blameless. When we lived together you said that you felt trapped with me. But it was a difficult time. I was trying to finish my novel and therefore stuck in the house while you were busy at work or out with friends and I felt left out. I was under stress, what can I say? Only that I'm sorry. But I sincerely hope that we can work something out. If only you'll agree to meet me.

She despaired of ever getting rid of Paul. She felt like crying. She had met new people, was having the time of her life and he was determined to spoil everything. At least she knew the boundaries between business and privacy. The scene he had created at the gallery would not be forgotten in a hurry and, while Xavier had been very understanding about it, they had lost two key clients. That kind of behaviour really was unforgivable. She felt invaded, as if he had climbed into her head. Was there no escape from him? She had tried to be nice, to be patient and had hoped that he would have got the message by now. But from this letter it was obvious that he would continue this campaign for as long as was necessary to get her back.

She was determined to pull herself together. It was completely impossible that Paul could be Mr X. Paul had always had a pretty matter-of-fact approach to sex and although she had not really had any complaints in that department, in the end she had begun to itch for something else, something a little more dangerous, some variety. When she had suggested experimenting to Paul he had baulked at anything differing from the norm, claiming that if she really loved him she would be satisfied with things as they were.

She started typing to Mr X.

This ex-boyfriend that I was telling you about, he's determined to pursue me. He confronted me at an important opening and punched a friend of mine, Mark. I've never been so humiliated in all my life. Why doesn't he just leave me alone?

Mr X's reply followed.

It sounds to me as if you need to take the matter firmly in hand. He needs putting in his place. Maybe he needs a spot of domination, you seem to be getting rather adept at that.

Clara wondered what he meant by that. Did he mean her session with Xavier? No, it was impossible, he had no way of knowing about that.
She typed back.

I'll give it some thought. But my more immediate problem is Jason. He's coming to collect me later and he's bound to try one of his little humiliation games. I'd like to confuse him, not give in to his demands. It's so difficult, because although I hate him he does something to me and then I hate myself for getting turned on.

She was getting excited just thinking about Jason.

Do what he's least expecting. Turn the tables. Get in control of the situation. That's something I'd like to see. I'd like to be a fly on the wall inside that car. My patience is running out, having not seen you for so long. And as we reveal ourselves, bit by bit, I feel that I know you and you know me. It's silly, I suppose, but I feel close to you, as if our thoughts and desires are in perfect synchronicity. I can't help wishing that we could meet.

Clara was puzzled. Was there some impediment that meant that they could not meet? Maybe he was in another country, she reasoned. She could not stop herself from starting to type.

Whenever, wherever, I want to meet you too. If only you'd give me some clue to your identity. You say that I know who you are, but what do you look like, what colour are your hair and eyes, how tall are you?

The time is approaching when we shall meet. But you still haven't stretched yourself far enough. There's a lot more to learn, but now you need to learn to take control. Until we meet, I'll dream of you. Of all the beautiful things in the world, I think that seeing you come would be one of the best. Be patient.

She felt a little agitated. A longing rose in her throat. How much easier it would be if they met up, she thought. And yet, the thought of meeting Mr X made her feel sick with nerves; fantasy would finally become flesh. She did not doubt that he would be everything that she had dreamed of, but after their e-mail communication, which required little risk-taking, it was somehow terrifying.

Looking down at her desk she began to start some work that she had been putting off. It was only two o'clock. She wondered if she had the strength or energy to deal with Jason. She looked at the phone. She need only call Mark and call the whole thing off. She knew that she should. But Mr X had made her feel extremely horny. She was happy to play a game with Jason, up to a point, as long as she was fully satisfied by the end.

She became so immersed in what she was doing that the time passed quickly. Suddenly she became aware that she was beginning to feel a prickly heat running along her neck, as if she was being watched. She looked up and saw hands, encased in leather driving gloves, resting on the counter. Letting her gaze run up his navy uniform her eyes rested on his harsh, impassive face, which was thrown into shadow under a peaked cap.

'Are you ready to go?'

'How long have you been watching me?'

'Only a few minutes.' He took a few steps towards the window and stood with his feet firmly planted on the floor, his body turned fully in her direction.

She jumped up from her chair. He was making her nervous, but she was determined not to show it. She walked around the other side of the counter, then leaned over it to pick up her bag, which was hanging from her chair. She felt his eyes running up her high-heeled brown leather boots, the expanse of sheer stocking and the hem of the dress that ended inches below her pubic hair. As she picked up the bag she remembered, with a start, that she wasn't wearing panties. Spinning round she found that Jason had taken a step nearer, a smile playing at the corner of his mouth.

She neatly stepped to the side and moved towards the door and pulled it open. She was determined not to let him get the upper hand.

Once she had got into the car and sunk back into its soft leather seat she waited for Jason to start the engine, but he gave no intention of doing so. She clicked open her handbag, noticing with delight that her vibrator was at the bottom of it.

'Are you still upset with me?' he said.

'No, why?'

'You left in quite a huff last time. I suppose that you found it unreasonable that I made you beg and plead for your clothes.'

'I needed to get to the gallery, that was all, and you seemed determined to keep me there, well, indefinitely.' She noticed that her voice sounded a touch patronising, which she hoped would terminate the conversation. The sooner she got to Mark's, the less chance there was of her getting into a scrape.

'Well, I must say I'm sorry if I offended you. But it is rather fatal for a woman with a body like yours to wander around in a silk dressing gown, then to sit around in the kitchen with it clinging to your skin.'

'Shouldn't we be getting going?' she said, reaching over to her handbag and removing her powder compact.

He started up the motor, and as she dabbed the powder onto her face she caught his glance in the rearview mirror. She smiled to herself. He was clearly a little taken aback by her good humour. She positioned herself until she could see the tops of her thighs and the dark shadow of her pussy in the mirror. She leaned back luxuriantly and pulled her dress up a little. She couldn't see his eyes clearly, as they were still in shadow, but she knew he was watching.

The motor hummed beneath her as they drove slowly along the streets of Central London. Clara casually uncrossed her legs to give him an eyeful. She quickly crossed them again and stared out of the window, as if she were unaware of what she had done.

He was separated by the glass partition between them, which was only partly open. Because he could look and not touch, she reasoned, she could do what she pleased in the back. She smiled to herself as she remembered how much he had hated having to be a voyeur the last time.

Slowly, tantalisingly, she pulled her dress up, inch by inch over her body. Then she pulled it off over her head and threw it aside. Her full breasts were cupped in a bra that was underwired, deepening her cleavage and making her even more voluptuous. She looked into the driver's mirror and took in the scalloped lace material that skimmed her breasts and her dark nipples, just visible beneath the filmy material.

She ran her hands over her body, from the shoulder down to the flat plane of her stomach, feeling its heat beneath her fingers. Then she unclipped her bra and toyed lightly with her breasts, cupping the fullness with one hand, and pinching the nipple so that sharp pulses of pleasure ran through it. With the flatness of her palm she ran down the smooth expanse of her stomach, sliding over her pubic hair and coming to rest over her pussy.

She cupped her mound in the flat of her hand and rubbed it slowly in a vertical motion, dragging the hood of the clit back and forth over the little bud of nerves. She was so aroused now and knew that she would climax immediately if she wasn't careful.

She took a sharp intake of breath and began to brush her fingers softly over her clit. Her arousal was mounting in layers, each stroke of her fingers winding her body one notch higher.

'I'm glad that you're showing me exactly what you like.' It was Jason's voice, filtering through her consciousness. The nerve of him – did he really think that she was putting on a show specifically for his pleasure? Pretending to ignore him, she reached over to pull out her vibrator and then switched it on. Her body jerked as she placed the cool plastic device against her inner thigh. At once, tiny currents of pleasure radiated from her, causing her pussy to feel the current further up. She continued to play with her swollen bud, this time with firmer strokes.

Tentatively, inch by inch, she moved the vibrator up her leg until it rested and purred against her pubic bone.

'I don't think you can take much more,' he said. She closed her eyes, twisting her body towards the vibrator, desperate now for it to penetrate her, but also keen to prolong her pleasure.

Now the tip of the vibrator was running back and forth over her labia, brushing across her fingers. As it touched her clit, her body responded with a sharp dagger of pleasure. Before she could recover from the strong sensations she rammed the vibrator deep inside, causing her to emit a cry. At any moment she feared she might spasm against it. As she moved it slowly in and out of her tight tunnel she felt as if every nerve within her had been awakened and that she was floating on a stream, letting the current wash over her again and again.

His voice burst through into her dreamlike state. 'I wish that I was doing that,' he said. But he was louder than before as the car had stopped moving and the motor was off. She glanced up to see him beside her, still wearing the chauffeur's cap, his hard bulk inches from her.

He removed the cap and placed it on her head, then began to pull down his trousers. She waited, frozen with anticipation as to what would happen next, and hating herself for letting him get the better of her.

'Close your eyes,' he said, softly. Soon she felt something brushing against her lips. Instinctively she opened her mouth. To her delight it was his cock, engorged to its full length. She licked off the liquid that had collected at its head and opened her mouth so that he could slip it inside.

He made soft gasps as he slid his cock, which she held firm at its base with her right hand, in and out of her lasciviously parted mouth. She caressed it with her tongue and lips, holding it for a moment and flicking her tongue across the head and then allowing him to move rhythmically in and out.

Lower down she pushed the vibrator into herself, in the same rhythm. Over and over again she pulled it almost all the way out and then plunged it in again, embracing the exquisite sensations, and savouring the taste of his cock.

His cock was now rasping the roof of her mouth as he began to step up the pace. As he did so, her hips, overloaded with pleasure, rammed the vibrator deep within herself. At that moment he climaxed, the salty liquid hitting the back of her throat as she greedily sucked the last vestiges of pleasure from him. Her orgasm rushed over her a split second later, her body bucking wildly against the vibrator, still deep within her, as stabs of pleasure ran through her and exploded in her clit.

In a state of semi-consciousness she felt him withdraw from her mouth and the vibrator being slipped out of her pussy and switched off. An indeterminate amount of time passed, while her body continued to buzz with the deep pleasurable currents that had recently passed through it.

She raised her head to look up at him. He had pulled his trousers up, and was still wearing his jacket. He smirked, his eyes crinkling up at the corners. Despite everything, he was still in control.

She turned away from him and began to dress.

'You really had no right, getting in the back like that.'

'You didn't seem to mind,' he said, his hand resting on her thigh. She brushed it off.

'Where are we?' She looked out the window. They were in an anonymous side street. Despite the pleasure that she had experienced she still disliked Jason, and the sneaky way that he had called her bluff.

'Let's get to Mark's,' she said, pulling on her dress. 'He must be wondering where we've got to.'

A phone began to ring in the front of the car. She heard Jason talking, but he spoke quietly so that she could not hear what he was saying.

He passed her the phone. 'Mark,' he said.

'Hi! We're just on our way to your house.'

'That's what I was ringing about. I'm really sorry to let you down like this, but I don't think that I'm going to make it. I met some friends this afternoon in Henley and now I'm stuck in a traffic jam.'

'Do you think you'll be here soon?'

'I really don't know. And I'd hate to think of you waiting for me all evening. Let's do it some other time?'

'OK,' she said despondently.

'Jason looking after you alright?'

'Yes,' she said curtly.

'I'll make it up to you soon, I promise.'

As she passed the phone back to Jason she wondered what she should do now. Despite herself, she was tempted to spend the evening with him. He was watching her in the mirror, awaiting her instructions. Yet she felt sulky, like a child, that Mark had let her down like this.

'Do you want to come back for a while?' No, she decided, there was no way that she was giving him the satisfaction. Without Mark there she would be completely at his mercy. She didn't trust him enough to take the risk.

'I'm tired. Could you drive me home?' she said dismissively.

Chapter Eight

Clara was awoken on Sunday morning by the trill of the phone. Wearily, she leaned over to the side of the bed and picked up the receiver.

'Yes?'

'It's Paul. I'm sorry to wake you. Have you had time to digest my letter?'

'Do you know what time it is?' Her alarm clock showed half-past eight.

'I'm sorry, I really am. But I thought that we could talk. Maybe today?'

'Do you really think that there's anything to talk about?'

'Well, what about the things I mentioned? I am concerned about you.'

Clara stretched luxuriantly. It was time to take the bull by the horns. 'OK, I'll meet you, but not today. I'll call you to arrange it. Then we can thrash things out.'

She put the phone down and rolled over, nestling deeper into the softness of the pillow. She managed to doze off, but at the back of her mind, an uneasiness lurked, which she associated with Paul.

In the end she decided to get up, and her eye was

caught by the eclectic mixture of colours in the picture that hung above her bed, which had been a present from Eric. Even though she was still groggy it triggered something within her subconscious. It would be fun to meet up with him again soon. She thought with regret about how she had failed to get the better of Jason in the car. She was determined that she would be stronger this time. But she didn't have Eric's number. Maybe it would be fun to call Astrid, and then the three of them could meet up.

But to her disappointment, when she called Astrid's number the answerphone sprang into place. She left a message. Then she went to the kitchen, made herself a coffee and took it to her computer.

It was warm enough indoors to sit there by the window without any clothes on. Recently, she had spent as much time as possible at home in the nude. She had developed a taste for it.

After switching on her computer she rapidly brought up the list of e-mails. There were a few enquiries about Hilary Fenton. Hilary's exhibition was doing quite well. Around half her pictures were sold, but it wasn't really good enough. Clara decided that something needed to be done, to take the gallery in a new direction. An exhibition that would make the public sit up and take notice, that would really put the gallery on the map.

She decided to go into the gallery and go through some of the files that featured new artists that she had been too busy to look through recently. A buzz of energy ran through her as she thought of this new project.

Xavier was out of town sourcing new artists in Paris. Hopefully the fortunes of the gallery were about to take a turn for the better.

She was upset to find that there was nothing from Mr X. She toyed with the idea of writing to him, but, in the end, decided not to. She could wait a little longer, she figured. She pulled on some Capri pants and a T-shirt and left the flat.

In the gallery she checked her computer; still nothing from Mr X. There was nothing for it but to settle down to do some work, even though her body was taut with a strange and inexplicable excitement. She looked for the relevant files, and when she couldn't find them, decided that they must be downstairs in Xavier's office.

Making her way down the stairs she caught her breath. She paused on the stairs, her hand clenched on the banister. She had heard a sound. But where was it coming from?

She continued her descent and waited outside Xavier's door. She was being silly, she told herself, no one else had the keys for the gallery apart from Xavier and there was no evidence of a break-in.

She pushed open the door apprehensively. But in the end nothing prepared her for the sight that accosted her.

Xavier's desk had been cleared of clutter and Astrid lay across it, her wrists and ankles secured tightly with rope. She lifted her head and gave Clara a wide grin. Eric stood before her, also stripped bare, looking at her spreadeagled body as if wondering what to do with her.

'How did you get in?' said Clara, stepping into the room.

Eric turned towards her, startled. His face was angry and she was genuinely frightened by his expression. Her eyes travelled down his tanned chest to his cock, which was stiffening beneath her gaze.

His voice, when he answered, was laced with menace. 'Didn't anyone ever teach you to knock?'

'I'm sorry.' She was about to go on when she realised that Eric was immersed in a game of role-play and that if she wanted to stay she had better play along.

139

He grabbed her by the wrist, so hard that the skin beneath his fist began to smart. He pulled her close to him, so that she looked up at his eyes, which were cloudy with rage. 'You need to learn some discipline. Evidently another lesson is in order.'

'What do you want me to do?' She could feel the heat from his body, even through her clothes.

'Take your clothes off.' She glanced over at Astrid, who now had her eyes closed. Clara stripped off her trousers and top and unclipped her red see through bra. She stepped forward.

'Get these off, too,' he said, gesturing towards her red panties. She slipped them off and stood naked before him.

'Look at poor Astrid. She's been lying here for such a long time that she really needs warming up. Or rather, you'll warm her up. Now.' He moved to step behind her and placed his hand around the back of her neck and pressed hard. She twisted from side to side, trying to escape his grasp. Abruptly, she felt a hard slap on her bottom.

'Ouch!'

'Stop it! Stop it right now! Are you willing to do as I say?'

He was pinching the back of her neck, making it ache, but at the same time her pussy was filling with pulses of sensation that were impossible to ignore.

'Right.' He pushed her forward so that she stood directly over Astrid, looking down on her biscuit-coloured skin, her eyes drawn to the slit of her shaven pussy.

'Now, I want you to put her out of her misery. Make her come. You've made her wait long enough.'

She climbed up onto the table and knelt in the gap between Astrid's wide-open legs. She feared that if she made a wrong move Eric would punish her, so she knew that she would have to do her best under his watchful gaze.

Her bottom still smarting from where Eric had smacked her she crouched over Astrid and kissed her. She revelled in Astrid's soft, lush mouth and felt her return the kiss. Clara's breasts were hanging over Astrid's and she could feel Astrid's nipples hardening against the soft skin of her breasts.

Clara reached down and ran her fingers over one of Astrid's firm breasts. Kissing along Astrid's neck she bent down and pinched her nipple till she heard her moan. She sank her mouth onto the breast and started sucking it hard, the bud growing more erect in her mouth, knowing all the time that Eric was watching every move she made.

She felt a mouth moving up the back of her neck. She recognised it as Eric's touch. She pressed her back towards him, feeling the ripples of his muscular chest hot against her spine. As she continued to fondle Astrid's breasts she felt something hard prising open the cheeks of her bottom. She heard the familiar buzz of the vibrator and waited, wanting him to push it into her but knowing that he would make her wait.

He had lifted up her hair and was covering her neck with soft feathery kisses. She felt lost between the warm softness of Astrid's body and the hard probing vibrator behind her, which was almost boring into her. It was a perfect complement of sensations. At the same time Clara wondered what would happen next.

Clara moved over Astrid's breasts, swirling her tongue in the furrow between them, tasting the sharp tangy sweat. The scent of her was bringing forth the desire in Clara to press her fingers deep into Astrid's pussy. Stroking Astrid's shaven mound with her fingertips, she tentatively pushed a finger in.

'Now,' whispered Eric, 'make her come.' He put his hands around Clara's waist and pulled her backwards, so that she was bending over the desk, her mouth hovering over Astrid's pussy. As Clara ground two fingers into her, Astrid gave a little gasp of pleasure. The hot sensation of knowing that she was pleasuring Astrid made Clara bold and suddenly impatient. She supported herself on her elbows, her bottom poking towards Eric, and buried her mouth in the silky wetness of Astrid's pussy.

She buried her mouth in her juices, a sweet musky scent rising up between them. She felt something enter her from behind, slowly, sensuously prising her open. Eric was sliding the vibrator in, inch by inch, causing her to gasp and pause for a second. With one hand holding her hips steady he slid it out of her again.

Clara began to circle her tongue around Astrid's hot pink bud.

'Come on, now,' Eric said, 'you can do better than that.' Again she felt the sting of his hand on her bottom. 'Maybe you need an incentive,' he said, pushing the vibrator in, up to the hilt. Clara felt desperately that she was about to come and she knew that if she did she would not be able to concentrate on the task in hand.

'Don't be greedy. Let Astrid come first. She's waited so long.'

She took a deep breath and Eric rammed it into her again. She tried desperately to control herself as she felt him dragging the vibrator out all the way and then ramming it back in. 'No, don't come yet, let Astrid come first.' She pressed her tongue directly onto her clit, pushing back the hood and flicking over it with greater intensity.

Looking up she could see Astrid's breasts shaking as she twisted her head from left to right. Feeling the energy that was building up inside Astrid's pussy she pressed her tongue hard against her so that Astrid began to cry out, and then abruptly jerk her wet pussy up against Clara's mouth.

She couldn't hold out any longer and began to buck against the vibrator. Eric noticed what was happening.

'Bad girl,' Eric said sharply. 'Oh, you'll pay for this. No self-control at all. Now, finish what you started.'

Clara gasped, still feeling the vibrator lodged in her entrance and pushed her tongue against Astrid's clit. Immediately she felt the electric current of Astrid's climax, which flowed along Clara's body and built up inside her pussy so that she once again started to come.

Then Eric untied Astrid. Clara guessed that she had not behaved altogether as Eric had wished, but it had been so hard to keep herself from coming.

'Now, Astrid, let's see if you can do any better. This time let's see if you can let Clara come first.'

Clara took Astrid's place on the table and Eric tied her limbs securely to the legs of the desk so that her whole body was stretched out. She looked up at the two pairs of eyes roaming over her vulnerable naked flesh. Closing her eyes she trembled with anticipation, waiting to see what would happen next.

Then she felt Astrid's mouth on her, her tongue teasing her clit at first, then transporting her into seventh heaven by increasing the pressure.

Through half-open eyes, Clara could see Eric behind Astrid. From her restricted position Clara lifted up her head so that she was looking directly into Astrid's eyes. It seemed to Clara that a current passed between them, an understanding. Then Astrid moaned as Eric began to penetrate her while at the same time reaching around to touch her bud.

'Hold on, Astrid. Let's see if you've got a bit more self-control.'

Astrid continued to move her tongue in rapid circles around Clara's clit, building up the heat there to fever pitch. Nevertheless, despite Eric's warnings, Astrid gave a yelp and started to come, her body shaking as Eric rammed himself into her. Clara was racing towards her climax, lifting her hips up to get into contact with more of Astrid's tongue. Soon the excitement was too much for her over-stimulated body to bear and she shuddered into a climax. At the back of her mind the fear started, of whether Astrid would be punished.

'Well,' said Eric, walking around the side of the table and beginning to untie the rope around her wrists. 'Looks like you both have a lot to learn.'

Clara sat up and began to rub her wrists. She watched as he pulled Astrid towards him and pulled her over his knee. Then he ran his hand over Astrid's small, pert bottom, and brought his hand down. Astrid let out a cry of pain.

'I told you to let Clara come first, didn't I?'

'Yes,' Astrid mumbled.

'I despair of you both. Why should I even waste my energies punishing you? No, I've a better idea. Why don't you punish Astrid. Maybe that'll teach her to do as I say.'

He pushed Astrid away and untied Clara's feet. Clara wasn't at all sure about Eric's plan. She had never inflicted pain on another person. But as she sat on the edge of the table and felt Astrid settle her petite body over her knees she felt a thrill, as if she were once again crossing over into unknown territory.

'Come on, come on,' said Eric. 'We haven't got all day.'

Steeling herself, she brought her palm down on Astrid's arse.

Eric's face became red, and looking down she noticed that he was fondling his burgeoning erection.

'Put some effort into it!'

Fearful of what else Eric might do if she did not

comply with his demands, she brought her hand down harder, again and again, until Astrid's behind became warm. Her hand was aching now and despite herself she was getting a kick out of what she was doing. Astrid was quiet now. Clara hoped that she hadn't hurt her too much.

'Isn't that enough?' He drew Astrid up and turned her around. Her face was dazed, but she was still smiling. She stood unsteadily on her feet.

Clara's eyes were drawn to Eric's magnificent erection, which she wanted in her mouth. Surely she had appeased his anger now? She walked over to Eric and kneeled down. She removed his hand, replacing it with her own. Taking the head in her mouth she sheathed his foreskin back and forth. Circling the shaft tightly with her hand to prevent the whole of its impressive length from entering, she took more of it into her mouth, moving deliciously along its length and tasting the stirrings of his arousal, which was leaking from the tip. She was lost in her sensual activity but noticed that Astrid had gone behind Eric and was rubbing herself against his back.

Clara pulled back, rubbing her saliva along its hard length, and looked up at Astrid, who was pushing her fingers in and out of Eric's secret passage. He was emitting soft moans, and Clara put his cock into her mouth again, watching while Astrid now held both his wrists in her hands, drawing him against her.

'Why don't you sit down and make yourself more comfortable?' Astrid whispered.

He sat down without taking his cock out of Clara's mouth. It grew in her mouth and she was sure that he would come at any moment. Then, hearing a click, she looked up momentarily. She wondered whether there was someone else in the gallery. She looked up at Eric, whose eyes were half closed and then at Astrid who smiled at her mischievously. She noticed that Astrid held a piece of the rope that Eric had just discarded in her hands and guessed what she was up to.

As Eric started to come, Astrid swiftly tied the rope around his chest. Without being told, Clara knew what was expected of her. She climbed onto his lap and held him down as best she could.

'How about you do what we want for a change?' said Astrid, in a low, gravelly voice. He struggled but he was still a little weak from having come moments before.

'He should be safe for a while. I've cuffed him,' said Astrid.

To Clara's surprise, Eric began to laugh. 'Why, you mischievous little vixen! I'll get you for this, you'll see if I don't.'

Astrid was looking down at his cock, which was growing hard again.

'It's a bit stuffy in here and Clara and I fancy a little walk outside. Now, we won't be gone long. Amuse yourself as best you can, won't you.'

Grabbing a bundle of clothes, Astrid put her arm around Clara and led her out of the door. They laughed uproariously as they walked upstairs.

'Do you fancy a drink?' said Clara. 'I think there's some Champagne in the fridge.'

They took turns drinking from the Champagne bottle. Clara was feeling very high, but was unsure of what their next move would be.

'A brilliant piece of work, Astrid.'

'I thought so!'

'How long are we going to leave him like that?'

'Oh, as long as it takes our fancy. He'll really be randy for us when we go and see him again.'

'You can't really go out like that,' she said, glancing at Clara's nakedness, while pulling on a leather mini-skirt and a halter-neck top, 'but I really do need to get some cigarettes. I won't be long.'

'But nothing's open around here on a Sunday,' Clara protested. A distinct sense of unease crept over her.

'Oh, there's bound to be a pub somewhere.'

When Astrid had left, Clara drained the last of the Champagne and chewed over the problem of what to do next. Should she untie Eric? She realised that even if she did, Astrid still had the key to the handcuffs. Also, they were in this together and she wasn't sure that Astrid would want her to untie him without her.

She walked back into the gallery, still naked. It was no big deal, she figured, as there was hardly anyone in the street.

Sitting down behind the counter she began to face facts. What if Astrid didn't come back for some time? There was something a little scary about the situation. No sound came from downstairs. She couldn't imagine Eric accepting his entrapment without a fight. What on earth should she do? She switched on the computer. Mr X would know, she was sure of it. Rapidly she began to type.

I've got myself in a bit of a fix. It all started as a bit of fun. I walked in on Eric and Astrid at the gallery who were making themselves very comfortable on Xavier's desk. Well, I didn't know if they wanted to be interrupted, as they looked pretty self-absorbed. So here's my problem – do I wait for Astrid to come back, or do I untie Eric and take the full force of his wrath? Although it's a game I know he's furious that the tables have been turned and he'll find some other way of punishing me, I know it.

She sent the e-mail and sat looking through the window for signs of Astrid returning. Staring agitatedly at the blank screen, she willed Mr X to get a move on.

She thought of Eric, his muscular body held in place

by the ropes, unable to escape. She let her fantasy run away with her, wondering what it might be like to keep him permanently as her prisoner in the basement. She could treat him with contempt, then use him as her sexual slave. She would do whatever she wished with him and he would be forced to comply because he had no choice in the matter. She clicked her mouse, out of nerves and impatience, and stared at the blank computer screen. Damn him! Mr X was not responding.

And then it hit her. She didn't need Mr X to tell her what to do. He had taught her well, and she guessed that she was now more than capable of finding her own solution. How much she had learned in so short a space of time!

Stealthily she made her way downstairs. Pushing open the door, she saw Eric's bulk, strapped into the big leather chair. He was indignant.

'Hey, this joke's not funny any more. Get me out of here. You've had your fun.' She said nothing, merely stepped forward so that her full breasts hung a few tantalising inches from his mouth.

He wriggled a little, the rope chafing against his arms. She pressed her mouth against his, feeling his resistance as he twisted away to avoid it, desperately trying to regain the upper hand. She reached down and ran her nails lightly along the base of his cock. She heard him moan and relax as she grasped his cock more firmly and shifted the foreskin back and forth. She swirled her tongue against his until she began to feel a tingling all over the surface of her breasts and the throb of desire started between her legs.

'Do what I say and you'll be free soon.'

She held his gaze and, keeping a tight grip just under the head of his penis she whispered, 'Remember, I could do something painful to you, if I wanted to. Now are you going to be quiet for me?'

He said nothing.

She rubbed the base of her thumb against his frenulum. 'Are you?'

'Yes,' he whispered.

'Can't take any chances.' She picked up the T-shirt she had discarded earlier and tied it around his mouth. Straddling him she positioned herself over his erection and rammed herself down hard on it. Using her knees for leverage she pushed his cock deep into herself, feeling the power she had over him whip her up into a higher level of arousal as she began to claw at his shoulders. She smiled as she made love to him, and looked into his eyes, which were now hazy with desire. That would teach him to punish her for scratching him.

'You're enjoying it now, aren't you? Seeing what it's like when I'm boss.' Putting her weight on her arms she gripped his shoulders and manoeuvred herself so that his bone-hard cock penetrated deeper into her.

Driving her pussy up and down along his cock she began to fondle her breasts with one hand, twisting the nipples hard and feeling the pleasure radiate in streams of heat over her breasts. Her orgasm was coiled inside her, rising up towards release. She revelled in the sense of power that ran through her, making her feel light-headed and giddy, from the knowledge that he was tied up and helpless beneath her, and from the fact that she was using his cock for her own pleasure. She felt him thrust upwards as she moved her hand down to rub her clit as she felt her orgasm spill out, pushing her over the brink.

She began to cry out at the same time as Eric writhed beneath her. She came in waves, jerking against him as he too came. The spasms went on and on as still she thrust against him. Her pleasure had reached a sharp peak but she still continued to ride him with an added urgency, soaking up the last tremors of pleasure before they began to ebb away.

To her horror she heard the sound of laughter behind her. It was a man's laugh. She turned her head to look at the door. Her eyes opened wide with recognition. It was Xavier.

Behind him she could see Astrid who was giving her an expression which seemed to say, 'What could I do?' Abruptly he stopped laughing. He didn't look shocked at all.

'I see that you have managed to tame Eric,' said Xavier, smiling at her.

Clara climbed off him, not knowing what to say. 'I didn't expect you. I just came down to get a file,' she began to mumble, pulling on her panties and the Capri pants.

Xavier was in a remarkably good humour. 'No need to explain.' He waved his arm in Eric's direction. 'It's all crystal clear.'

'I thought you were in France,' said Clara.

Astrid had gone over to Eric and started to untie him. She was trying to keep a straight face but Clara could see that it was only through remarkable self-control that she was managing not to burst into laughter.

'I saw a few artists, but nothing particularly promising. Anyway, this isn't the time to talk shop.' He turned towards Eric. 'Have you still got those keys I lent you?'

'Yes. We were just driving past,' said Eric, 'and we felt a bit frisky. Astrid thought that it might be a laugh to come in here. Hope you don't mind.'

Eric stood up so that Astrid could unlock the handcuffs. He was remarkably unperturbed. 'Well, we'll get out of your face.'

It was odd, thought Clara, that Xavier should be so nonchalant about the whole affair. But maybe he had seen enough to fuel a hot masturbatory session for himself later. She had given up trying to work him out.

'Do you want to get something to eat?' said Astrid.

'Yes,' said Clara. 'I'm absolutely ravenous.'

'Are you two coming?'

'No, I've got something I need to chat about with Xavier.'

'Suit yourself.'

They went up the stairs together and were about to leave when Clara said, 'Hang on a minute.'

She went to her computer and was about to switch it off. Mr X had not replied. Oh, well, she reasoned, maybe he had lost interest in her. The thought saddened her for a moment. Then she switched off the terminal and exited with Astrid. Out in the street Astrid began to laugh.

'Oh, if only you could have seen your face when you caught sight of Xavier. It was hilarious!'

They walked a while until they had reached Soho and went into an Italian bistro. They shared a bottle of red wine as they ravenously devoured their pasta, laughing over everything that had happened.

'Listen,' said Astrid. 'Remember that party I was telling you about, in Norfolk?'

'Yes.'

'Well, it's next weekend. You're still coming aren't you?'

'Yes, of course.' She sipped her wine, feeling a warm glow spread through her. It was so intimate, sitting in the snug restaurant, a candle flickering in front of her. The time was right to confide in someone.

'Look, there's something I need to tell you. If I don't, I'll go mad.'

'What is it?'

'You remember Paul? Of course you do! That scene he made at the gallery won't be forgotten in a hurry.'

'Did you tell him where to get off?'

'No, I'm too much of a coward. He wrote me a really

awful letter. Calling me a whore. He took the moral high ground, says I need saving.'

'God, what a jerk!'

'I'm at my wit's end about what to do about it.'

'I'd love to teach him a lesson.'

'Actually, there's something else.' Suddenly Clara felt drunk and in need of opening up to Astrid. 'It's complicated. Well, I know that Paul's been following me, at least I think so. But I've also started corresponding with a guy who calls himself Mr X, on the internet.'

'Sounds interesting.'

'The really weird thing about this Mr X is that he seems to know so much about me, well, things that no one could know unless they were somehow . . .'

'What?'

'. . . watching me the whole time. Now that I say it out loud it just sounds so far-fetched, I wonder whether I'm going mad.'

'What's he like, this Mr X?'

'He's the complete opposite of Paul, imaginative and unpossessive. I just know he'd be sexy, although I've never met him.'

'What's the problem?'

'It's all become tangled together, Paul and Mr X, and I no longer know what's reality and what's a figment of my overwrought imagination.'

Astrid leaned forward, so that her face was illuminated in the candlelight.

'Haven't you ever considered the possibility that Paul might be Mr X?'

'No, that's ridiculous,' Clara said defensively. 'Paul's my worst nightmare.'

'Well, it's a possibility. Look, I can't help you find out who this Mr X is, but I can help you with Paul.'

'How? I'm at the end of my tether.'

'You need to call his bluff. Surprise him by inviting him to come along for the weekend.'

'I hardly think it's his cup of tea. He'd probably explode with rage!'

'Oh no, don't tell him what will really be going on. Why not tell him it's a civilised get-together at a country house. Tell him anything you like, as long as you get him there. He'll see some sights he won't forget in a hurry. And he'll see his precious ex-girlfriend indulging in things that'll change his opinion of you irrevocably!'

'I don't know.'

'The way I look at it, it can't fail. And don't worry, once you get there, I'll take things in hand.'

Later on, after she had taken a taxi home, Clara lay on her bed, giggling to herself at the oddness of Astrid's suggestion. She glanced at the phone. Knowing she was more than a little tipsy had filled her with Dutch courage. It was almost midnight, but she feared that she might not have the courage to call Paul when she was sober.

Propping herself up on some pillows and kicking off her shoes she reached over and dialled his number, amazed that it was still lodged somewhere in her memory.

As she waited for him to answer the phone she felt tense with anticipation. She had never acted in quite such an underhand fashion before, but, she realised, it was all part of a general change in her over the last few months. She would show him that she was in control, that he could no longer manipulate her.

'Hello?' His voice was groggy as if she had woken him.

'Paul? I'm sorry to ring so late.'

'Well, this is a shock. I didn't expect to hear from you.'

'I've been thinking about things. What you did at the opening was unforgivable.'

'I know, I can't tell you how sorry I am about that.'

'But you're right, we do need to clear the air between us and really have a proper talk.'

'Well, I'm amazed to hear you say that.'

'Are you free this weekend?'

'I think so, why?'

'A friend's invited me up to a weekend away in Norfolk. It'll just be a few people who I've got to know recently.'

'I don't know.'

'If you don't want to, that's fine.' She felt a sudden panic, that things were not going to plan.

'I just don't understand your sudden change of heart.'

'I'm too tired to talk now. How about you pick me up at the gallery around midday on Saturday and we drive up?'

'Are you sure?'

'Yes, it'll be a chance for us to get to know each other again. It'll be fun, trust me.'

'Alright. If you're sure that's what you want.'

'Yes, it is. But I'm not promising anything. It'll just give us the opportunity to talk. Now I'm really tired, goodnight.'

'Bye.'

She noticed that she was trembling as she replaced the receiver. It was exhilarating wondering exactly what Astrid had planned for Paul. Wearily she pulled off her clothes and slid between the cool sheets. Soon she fell into a deep sleep.

Chapter Nine

On the morning of the trip to Norfolk Clara paced the gallery impatiently. The plan that Astrid and she had drunkenly hatched at the restaurant was now about to come to fruition, and now Clara waited for Paul to arrive, with a mixture of conflicting emotions battling inside her.

She had slept badly and on waking had remembered her dream vividly. The same masked man who had previously figured now reappeared, making love to her with a fearsome brutality. But half-way through the dream she had opened her eyes and found that Astrid's face had replaced the mask, but it was not the Astrid that she knew, kittenish and playful, but an altogether more sinister presence.

How well did she really know Astrid? How did she know that Astrid wasn't planning to have some fun at her expense? But she quickly pushed the thoughts aside and focused on trying to appear calm and collected.

Slipping behind the counter she tried to focus on some work that she wanted to finish, but the figures swam before her eyes. Maybe she'd check her e-mails.

It had piqued her somewhat that Mr X had still not replied.

But now, as she saw his reply flashing on the screen and began to read it, she could not help feeling a sense of exaltation.

Clara, I trust that you sorted out your little dilemma.

Well, she thought crossly, it hadn't been quite such a small problem at the time. She read on. So, he wasn't going to explain why he hadn't replied. Why should that bother her, anyway? After all, they had no obligations to each other. That was what she loved about their exchanges, the complete freedom and anonymity.

I think I know you well enough to know that you handled the situation well. Eric certainly deserves to be taken down a peg, and no doubt, if you did dominate him, as I think you did, he thoroughly enjoyed himself.

Have you thought any more about how to deal with that bothersome ex-boyfriend of yours? I'm sure that you are more than capable of figuring out a plan that will banish him from your life forever.

Yes indeed, she typed. I realised that it was hightime to deal with him. With everything that has happened to me recently, I haven't had the energy to confront him. But a masked man keeps appearing in my dreams, a dark presence, and somehow his presence reminds me strongly of Paul. So, I've decided to go away for the weekend with him. We are going to stay at a house in the country. An artist called Daniel is holding a house party. Astrid tells me that it could be rather a wild experience. But Paul doesn't know that. He thinks that it will be an opportunity for us to build a few bridges. I just hope that he will be so shocked at what he experiences that he will realise that I am not the one he wants after all. But apart from that, I intend to thoroughly enjoy myself.

An excellent plan, Ms X. Sounds like it will be a very eventful weekend and I look forward to hearing about the outcome. Have you thought of any more fantasies you will play out? You have experienced so much now that no doubt your fantasies have become more refined, and maybe a little more way-out? Don't be afraid of your imagination. It will push you in the direction that you need to go.

She thought of her dream, of Astrid's face emerging from the face of the masked man and she felt the excitement build up. Dare she tell Mr X about that? Boldly she typed, I have a fantasy, about Astrid. We have made love a couple of times and it was intimate – an extension of our friendship. But now I think that I'd like to have her make love to me, less like a woman, but roughly, passionately, like a man. Do you think that's completely weird?

Nothing is strange as long as you are in control of your desires and what you want to experience. I think that Astrid is close enough to you to know what you want, you just need to nudge her in the right direction. You would both get a terrific buzz out of this scenario, blurring the boundaries of sexuality. At the end of the day, what we believe to be male and female characteristics are not set in stone. I wish you all the best in mapping out your own destiny. Remember, don't be afraid. Thinking of you. Mr X.

It helped, somehow, knowing that Mr X was thinking of her. She had a tough task ahead of her, but suddenly she was sure that she was more than up to it. As she tidied up her desk, she thought about how

157

she would put Paul firmly in his place and felt an unexpected surge of adrenaline.

When Paul arrived she was surprised at how different he looked. He had been in a sorry state on their last encounter, his hair mussed-up and his eyes glazed with alcohol. But as he bounded into the gallery she felt his powerful presence. She noticed uncomfortably that his brooding dark gaze was making her heart pound.

She picked up her weekend bag, walked over to him and kissed him on the cheek. As she began to pull away, he pressed her close and kissed her on the mouth. Although his lips only lightly brushed hers, they generated a pulse of desire between her legs. Confused, she took a step back.

'You look lovely,' he said, running his eyes over her tight black trousers and snugly fitting red polo neck.

'You don't look so bad yourself. Let's get going shall we?'

As they got into his car, the seats of which were badly in need of repair, she thought of how Paul and Mark were miles apart. An unexpected image flashed before her eyes of herself, luxuriantly leaning back in Mark's back seat while he supped Champagne from her pussy.

'I would have thought that you could have bought a new car with all the money you're earning from your novel,' she said as Paul started up the car.

Paul laughed. 'I love this old car, you know that. Couldn't bear to part with it. I've spent a bit of money on getting the flat redecorated though. You must come round some time. You wouldn't recognise it.'

Clara began to relax. She was pleased that Paul was making an effort and that he was in a good mood. As they drove to the outskirts of London and onto the motorway their conversation came easily, and she was reminded of why she had once liked him so much. She felt herself become lulled into a false sense of security and had to sharply remind herself of the obsessive letters, and of what the objective of their trip was.

Towards three o'clock they found the place. It was an impressive building, with a melancholy air about it, built of ancient grey stone and set up on a hillside.

'Wow,' said Paul. 'This artist bloke must certainly have a bit of cash.'

Paul got out of the car and went over to the passenger side to let her out. He then insisted on carrying her bag as well as his own, and she was happy to let him be chivalrous. That was a side of him that she had not seen much of before. He was evidently determined to win her over.

They walked up the long gravel drive and knocked at the door. When there was no answer, Paul knocked again, this time more forcefully. Eventually the door was opened by a beautiful oriental girl, with black hair that fell to her waist. She wore an exquisite dress, of a silver gossamer material that clung to her lithe figure.

'Hi, I'm Lina. We thought you'd got lost!'

Out of the corner of her eye Clara noticed that Paul was taking in Lina's body appreciatively.

'Do come through. We're just finishing lunch. But there's plenty left over.'

Paul dumped their bags in the hall and they followed Lina along a carpeted corridor. Soon they found themselves in an airy dining room. The table was strewn with wine bottles and overflowing with delicacies.

'Why don't you come and sit beside me, Paul,' said Lina, pulling at his hand.

'Clara!' said Eric. 'Come and sit next to me.' She did so, and kissed him on the cheek. She looked about her. Mark was opposite her, leaning back in his chair and sipping at a glass of red wine. Lina was piling food onto a plate for Paul. There were two other women around the table, who were introduced as Veronica, with fragile features and a tangle of red hair, and Leila, dark-skinned with her black hair cut into a bob. Clara wondered where Astrid was.

'And this is Daniel,' said Eric, introducing her to the man on her right.

She glanced at him as she shook his hand. He was in his late thirties, she guessed, with olive skin, dark wavy hair and intense brown eyes. His face was familiar somehow, although she could not place it exactly.

Clara ate ravenously for a while, then leaned over to talk to Mark.

'Jason's not here, I see.'

'Actually, he is. Astrid took him off somewhere. There's quite an impressive maze in the grounds that he feigned an interest in. But I think he may have had other plans.'

'Do you think they'll be back soon?' She really wanted to have a talk with Astrid to discover what plans she had for Paul.

'I shouldn't think so,' Mark replied, 'but she did mention something about your little problem.' His eyes rested briefly on Paul, who was deep in conversation with Lina.

'Well, fingers crossed, it should all work itself out.'

'I'm sure it will.'

An hour passed and Clara had drunk several glasses of wine. Eventually she managed to drag Eric's attention away from Veronica.

'Do you know what Astrid's up to? Did she tell you about my problem with Paul?'

'Oh yes, she mentioned it. But Astrid is very secretive, and didn't say all that much. You look fabulous. But aren't you a little hot in that pullover?'

Now that he mentioned it, she was rather warm. She guessed that if Paul hadn't been there, she would have pulled it off without a qualm and sat there in her bra, but she didn't want to shock him, not yet. She knew that she would have to bide her time.

Feeling Eric's hand travelling up the length of her thigh did not surprise her, it was what she had come to expect from him. Paul glanced her way, and she smiled as she felt Eric's fingers graze her pussy through the restrictive material. As he began to stroke her quim through her trousers she glanced at him inquisitively. She began, not for the first time, to ponder the idea of whether Eric could be Mr X.

It was frustrating to be wearing the trousers. She would have liked to dispense of them too, and now the sensations Eric was generating were becoming agonisingly pleasurable.

'Hey,' she said with mock indignation. 'Keep your hand to yourself.'

He moved his hand away. 'I never heard you complaining before.'

She leaned towards him and lowered her voice. 'Listen, I've been meaning to ask you something.'

'Oh yes?'

'Someone's been sending me anonymous e-mails. A man, calling himself Mr X.'

'So?'

'I was wondering if it was you?'

'Why would I do that?' Eric said guardedly.

'I don't know, something you said made me think. The first time he sent me an e-mail he described the way I looked, the way the gallery was set up and how he wanted to make love to me over the counter.'

'Well, what of it?'

'When I first met you, you mentioned that you had watched me before. As far as I knew you hadn't been in London while I was working there. And downstairs, in the basement, you said that you'd seen me before. How do you explain that?'

'Oh, Clara, you are paranoid. You need to relax.

Maybe we can do something about that later. But yes, I was in London once. I passed the gallery and saw you, and guessed who you were. But I was in a hurry and didn't have time to pop in and say hello.' He smiled. 'Does that solve the mystery?'

'I suppose so.' But, looking at Eric's mischievous expression, she wasn't entirely convinced. Still, she had other things to think about right now, like when Astrid would be coming back.

Then unexpectedly, Daniel, who had been silent up until that point, leaned over to her. 'I could tell by your face when we were introduced that you don't have a clue who I am,' he whispered.

'I'm sorry, you do seem familiar.'

'Well, my name's Daniel Stanford. Don't get me wrong, I love it when someone doesn't give a damn who I am!' Of course, she had heard of him, now that he mentioned his surname. He had been famous, mainly for his large-scale nudes, she remembered now, about a decade ago.

'Of course I remember your name. But didn't you used to have a beard?'

'Yes indeed. I think it's great that you didn't recognise me. It's one of the reasons why I dropped out of the whole art scene. People thinking that I was public property.' A far-off look crossed his eyes as he began to reminisce. 'It was strange that as soon as I became famous I began to loathe the attention. The papers were interested in my private life and not in my art.'

'So to get away from it all you moved to the middle of nowhere?'

'Yes, and it suits me down to the ground.'

'Have you given up nudes forever?'

'Yes, I've really exhausted the artistic possibilities of the human form. For many years it was my subject, especially beautiful women. But then, I don't know, I ran out of ideas.'

'What, just like that?'

'Yes, just like that.'

'Do you miss creating things?'

'Well, I do still create, but in a rather different – I think – rather unique way.'

'What have you been working on?'

'Well, I've been studying technology, communication fascinates me, and I've really been learning everything that I can about computers and the internet.'

'But I don't understand. What's that got to do with art?'

'Well, art can be many things. It's not just paint on a canvas, is it? To me, art is about breaking new boundaries, freeing people from social restrictions.'

'Could I see something? Have you got anything here?' He was drawing her in, making her feel special, pulling her into his secret world.

'Yes, I have as a matter of fact. I might show you, later. I've been working on it for almost a year now. No one else has seen it yet, but I think you'd find it interesting.'

Suddenly she turned round to see Paul standing behind her chair.

'Sorry to interrupt, but I really fancy taking a look around the grounds,' he said.

'Well, OK, why not?' she said, irritated. 'Anyone else want to come?'

In the end, the others professed to be too full to move so she left the room with Paul. First they went up to their first-floor room and tossed their bags into it. She looked around the spacious room, which, she noticed, had only one double bed. One wall was taken up by a large window overlooking the countryside, while a curtain was draped over the opposite wall.

'Come on,' he said, 'let's have a look round before it gets dark.'

Once outside they walked around the house and along a winding path that led down the hill. The air was cool but a warm breeze fluttered through the leaves in the trees, which were just beginning to turn brown.

They walked along in silence for a while until Paul said, 'I feel terrible for hitting Mark the other day. Do you think I should apologise?'

'Well, if you like, but I don't think he holds a grudge.'

'I can't tell you how much it shook me up when I saw you in Soho. I couldn't believe it. When we were together you were so elegant, so refined. To see you like that, it really turned my stomach.'

'I'm still refined. Besides, it was just a bit of fun.'

'Oh really!' he said, stopping suddenly and grabbing hold of her arm. 'And how many of the other men in there have you had fun with?'

His hand was digging into her arm but she shook it off. It really wasn't any of his business, she thought angrily.

She began to walk on again, not looking behind to see if he was following her. In the distance she could see the well-trimmed hedges that she guessed were part of the maze that Eric had referred to.

Earlier on, when Eric had teased her clit through her trousers she had been turned on. Now, she started to resent Paul's presence. If he had not been here she would definitely have been able to start looking forward to the evening's events with a growing sense of expectation. Instead she was feeling agitated and frustrated.

'Don't let's have a row, please,' she said, as Paul caught up with her.

His eyes were lit with an inner flame and his body was coiled with repressed energy. 'I want to know. What can Mark do for you that I can't?'

'Every man is different,' she said dismissively. 'And besides, I'm not your property any more.'

'Why did you invite me up here?'

'So that you could see for yourself that I'm not as depraved as you might imagine. You were getting on well with Lina weren't you?'

'Yes, they all seem nice, but I've been so worried about you. I think you need someone to take care of you.'

'Oh, come off it, Paul! I can look after myself. If you only tried to relax a bit you might end up having a good time.'

They entered the maze and she tried to concentrate on the route they were taking, trying to memorise the twists and turns. The maze felt familiar. Then it hit her: it was like the maze in her dream, when the stranger had pressed her down into the hot stone. A tremor of pleasure coursed through her.

'We had something good together. I'll never understand why you left.'

'You know why. You were too controlling. What I've learned these past few months is that I want to be free, to do what I want to do.'

'I've changed, you know. But my feelings for you haven't.'

Before she knew what was happening he had pulled her into his arms and was devouring her face in urgent kisses. She was melting, melting into his warm embrace, and excited to feel the hardness of his cock pressing against her. She kissed him back, a turmoil of emotion welling up inside. She feared that she was rapidly losing control of the situation.

Pulling free, she broke into a run, not knowing any longer in which direction she was going, knowing only that at that moment she had to get away from Paul. She had to stop herself from succumbing to the urgent need that he had generated in her, to make love with him right there and then. The pull was so strong, and partly nostalgic, a need to once more drink in the familiar scent of his skin.

It was getting dark now and she realised that she was completely lost. She tried to retrace the route that she had come. When she stopped for a moment she thought she caught Paul's voice calling her name, but it was distant and indistinct. Breathing heavily, she stumbled on and abruptly came to a clearing. Her eyes were inexorably drawn to the flat grey stone in the centre and the naked male that was kneeling in front of it. It was Jason.

Taking care not to make a sound, she took a few steps to the side. Jason was so involved in what he was doing he did not notice her. Astrid was sprawled on the stone, her legs spread wide, her eyes closed, and Clara blushed as she heard the familiar moans that Astrid emitted when she was nearing her climax. Jason's mouth was buried in her pussy, lapping at it in stealthy strokes.

Clara stood, transfixed by the scene. A strong compulsion was drawing her closer to it. She wanted to lie next to Astrid, to feel the harsh surface against her naked skin, to have Jason drink the nectar from her pussy, releasing the pressure inside her that had been building up this past hour.

Astrid cried out louder now, her hips jerking up towards Jason's mouth as she began to come. Clara took a step forward, then felt two arms grab her from behind.

She swivelled round to see Paul. She could see that he was about to say something, but she was aware too, by the way that his eyes had become round as saucers, that he found the view as delectable as she did.

Nevertheless, she couldn't be sure that Paul wouldn't make some sort of scene, so she beckoned to him and pulled him back into one of the shadowy

166

paths. Her skin was aflame with arousal. She knew that if he touched her now, she would be helpless to resist him, and yet she knew that she must if she was to carry out her plan.

'Friends of yours?' Paul said, eventually.

'Yes. I suppose you're appalled?'

'Well, yes, frankly I am. And I think you would have been, a year ago. Who is that guy?'

'Jason? He's Mark's chauffeur.'

'Have you slept with him?'

'I don't really see that that's any of your business.'

She needed to be free of him, to get her thoughts into some sort of order. His presence was overwhelming, stifling. But she knew that he could not resist a challenge.

'Listen,' she said, trying to make her voice sound as seductive as possible. 'Do you want to play a little game?'

'No, I want to get to the bottom of just what is going on here and which of these guys has slept with you.'

Ignoring his comment, she said, 'How about we split up and try and make our way out of the maze separately? See who makes it to the house first. It'll be fun. What do you say?'

'I don't know. It seems stupid,' he said petulantly.

She paused as they came to an intersection. 'Now, I'll take a left and you take a right, and I'll see you back in our room. I promise I'll tell you everything you want to know then, OK?'

'OK,' he said grudgingly, shrugging his shoulders.

As she turned away from him a palpable sense of relief flooded through her. She had to keep her head clear and try and fight her body's insistent clamour for relief. She hated to admit that she was also angry with Astrid, for going off and enjoying herself instead of briefing her on the master plan to get rid of Paul.

Time passed, and it grew darker and more chilly,

and still she kept walking, in what she hoped was the general direction of the house. She took comfort from thinking of Mr X, that he wouldn't want her to despair now. Just thinking about him strengthened her tenacity.

She stopped and looked about her, and then thought that one of the turnings seemed familiar, then another, and soon she was out of the maze, looking up the hill to where the lights from the house twinkled invitingly.

But when she eventually got to the house and knocked at the door, Daniel answered.

'Ah, Clara, we were about to send out a search party.'

'Is Paul here?'

'I think he's about somewhere. But listen, while the others are in the sitting room, how about I show you my artwork?'

She wasn't really in the mood for art. She needed to find Paul, and, more importantly, Astrid, and straighten this whole confusing situation out.

He looked at her intensely. 'You need to relax a little. Trust me, I think you'll enjoy the experience very much. Follow me.'

They climbed up a flight of stairs, into a room that was adjacent to the one where she and Paul were to sleep. The room was dark, but as her eyes acclimatised to the darkness she could see that it was much bigger than the bedroom.

She felt him standing very close behind her, could feel his breath on her, making the fine hairs on her neck stand up on end. A strange electricity passed between them and she relaxed, sensing that she could trust him.

'Remember, Clara, while you are in here you must clear your mind. Forget about all your problems, and open yourself up completely to what I think you will find a very exciting adventure.'

'But what's it all about?' He placed a finger on her lips, and then she felt his hands moving over her, pulling off her jumper and unfastening her bra. She trembled as his hands brushed against her sensitised nipples and instinctively her mouth groped for his.

'No, no,' he whispered, 'remember, you're here to experience something new. Now take off the rest of your clothes.' His voice was magnetic, it pulled her in, and she began to do as he asked, removing her trousers, shoes and panties.

Eventually he picked up her clothes and left the room. She heard the soft click of the latch falling and felt a momentary flutter of panic. She stood in the centre of the room for a long time, then looked down because she thought that she had felt fur brush the bare soles of her feet. She looked about her and noticed that two of the walls were mirrored and that she could just about make out her reflection in them.

Gradually a milky pink glow filtered into the room, emanating from the floor. Bending down she noticed that the floor was made up of individual tiles lit from below with pink light. Looking more closely she saw that some of the panels were covered in pink fur, others stretched with kid leather and latex, also in the same shade of dusky pink.

She crouched on the floor, and then stretched out on her back, feeling every inch of her body making contact with the floor. Beneath her bottom, the soft fur brushed against her pussy; her back was pressed against cold glass. The backs of her thighs rested on the soft leather beneath them which began to warm up with the heat of her body.

She closed her eyes and drifted off for a moment, but came to consciousness again. What was this strange room? She felt impatient and a little indignant. Was Daniel making a fool of her? He didn't intend just leaving her there, did he? Getting up, she walked across the tiles, which made up some sort of gigantic chessboard as far as she could ascertain. Standing at the edge of the board she wondered what would happen next. Surely he would be back soon, she thought, the panic rising in her throat.

Chapter Ten

'Welcome to the playroom, Clara,' the deep, distinctive voice intoned.

It was Daniel's voice and it was turning her insides to jelly. She spun round. Where was he? Was he hidden behind one of the mirrored walls? Or watching her from a gap between the tiles?

She walked over to the door and turned the handle but it would not budge. He had locked her in. Of all the stupid things to do! Furiously, she paced back to the centre of the room and stared down at the tiles, fighting back the tears of frustration that she felt welling up.

'This is a prototype of my new artwork.' The voice poured down on her from the walls and ceiling, enveloping her, and sinking into her skin. 'This is the computer speaking. Listen carefully. I will ask you a series of questions. If you answer them honestly you will complete the sequence and be allowed to find some release.'

'Firstly, stand on the fur square.' She did as he commanded. It was so disconcerting not knowing where he was. She realised that this was just a recording of his voice, emanating from a computer. But where was he? Could he see her? No doubt he was enjoying seeing her trapped in the room. What kind of game was this?

'Remember, if you do not answer the questions honestly, I will know. I know you too well. You will not complete the sequence, not be allowed to find release and will have to remain in the room until such time as you decide to play my game.'

'Now, let's begin. Do you enjoy exposing yourself in public places?' An image of herself being pleasured by Claus and Mark on the tube flashed into her head. A hot coil of desire began in the pit of her stomach and started to unravel, creeping down the insides of her thighs. There was no doubt in her mind that the answer was yes, but she was not sure that she wanted Daniel to know that.

'To answer yes, step on the latex square, or to answer no step on the leather square.'

She hesitated for a moment, then stepped onto the latex square.

'That is the correct answer,' said the voice. She felt a small twinge of exaltation that she had passed so far.

She waited for the voice to ask her another question. But no voice came. Instead, she became aware of a video being played on the ceiling of the room, the images dreamlike and larger than life.

Tilting her head back she looked up and gradually her eyes became accustomed to the grainy image of two naked people. By looking at it more carefully she realised with a jolt that she knew the identity of the people in the video. Daniel and Astrid.

'Look at it closely, Clara. Do you desire the man in the video?'

A hot flush of rage ran over her, swiftly followed by a pulse of arousal. How vain this man was to ask such a question. And yet, seeing him naked like that in all his glory, her eye was drawn to his bone-hard cock and hard, muscular chest, the top half covered with dark hair.

They were sprawled across a double bed with wrought-iron bedposts. Daniel was securing Astrid's hands and feet to the four corners. Astrid was wriggling about a bit, as if not wanting to be tied; she was completely naked but for a pair of black stockings.

He rubbed oil in his hands and ran it all over Astrid's body, hesitating at the entrance of her pussy. Clara turned away. It was too much to bear, seeing something like that and not having any way to relieve herself. It was a form of torture.

'Do you desire the man in the video?' The voice then gave her two options to step onto, signifying yes and no. She stepped onto the square for yes. She could not lie about that, not to Daniel and not to herself. The voice told her that she had answered correctly.

The video went on and on, until Clara's head clouded. She tried to focus on it more clearly.

After having rubbed Astrid's body liberally with the oil, Daniel was pushing his cock into her, but not into her pussy. Astrid was tied to the bed face down and he was pushing his cock into her, all the way up into her anus. Instinctively, Clara cupped her full breasts and started to toy with her nipples, which stiffened beneath her fingers.

'Are you shocked by what you see, Clara?'

The computer again gave her her options. Yes square or no square, thought Clara. Inexplicably the decision was a hard one to make. In a daze she stepped onto the no square as she watched Daniel's cock go in and out of Astrid as she squirmed beneath him.

She watched as Daniel moved off her and loosened the ropes a little. Once Astrid had got up onto all fours, Daniel used a vibrator and pushed it into Astrid's cunt. The camera zoomed to a close-up of Astrid's face, the features distorted with pleasure. Although the film had no sound, Clara could almost hear the howl of pleasure. Tendrils of Astrid's hair were stuck by sweat to her shoulders.

The image spoke to some as yet unrealised need within her, it was her ultimate fantasy, to be restrained, and completely at the mercy of another for her pleasure. It was with a burning sense of shame that she realised that mingled in with the hot flush of arousal was envy, at Astrid's luck at being restrained and roughly and masterfully pleasured.

'You have answered correctly. Do you fantasise about being tied up and spanked until you can't take it any more?' said the voice.

Her face burned as she remembered how Eric had initiated her. But she was afraid, afraid of revealing any more of herself to Daniel, who she barely knew. She felt as if she was losing control of the situation, something she could not bear to happen, and so stepped onto the no square.

'You have made an incorrect move. To answer yes, step onto the glass square.'

The voice made her feel ashamed for lying. She hesitated, shocked at how the computer could see right inside her head. She felt tears prickling in the corner of her eyes. She bit her lip and tentatively stepped onto the yes square.

'Don't lie to me, it won't pay. Now does what you see turn you on?'

Standing there watching the video, knowing that he could somehow see her, was humiliating. Now a red-hot river of desire started up within her, burning her up, making her skin so sensitised that she longed to rub herself against the latex. Swiftly she stepped onto the yes square.

'Correct answer,' the disembodied voice boomed forth.

She felt weak as she kneeled down, and helplessly spread herself over the board, not caring if it was allowed by the bizarre rules of the game. The video still played on the ceiling, but she was only dimly aware of it, and of its white light raining down on her.

She reached over to one of the squares and to her surprise it gave way. She pushed it down and felt something hard. She peered at the object in her hand. To her relief it was a vibrator, but unlike any one she'd seen before. It was, like the glass squares, translucent and glowing from within with a pink light. She flicked on the switch so that it began to buzz and with an urgency she could hardly contain thrust it into her, beginning to moan, her eyes half closed as she thought of Daniel watching her.

But, to her frustration, she could find no relief. Her excitement was locked inside her, even as she pushed the vibrator harder and faster into her pussy. Then she began to be aware of another sensation, a soft trail of hair against her stomach, brushing against her, tickling her hard nipples. Slowly, Clara pulled the vibrator out of herself and put it aside.

She looked up and saw Astrid's face, bathed in the soft pink light. She watched, mesmerised as Astrid reached into another square and pulled out a strange implement. Clara could dimly make out that it was a harness with a rubber cock on it. Astrid fastened it around her narrow hips, her long blonde hair streaming down over her breasts. Clara gasped. There was something very horny about the contrast between Astrid's delicate femininity and the hard black cock jutting out from her pudenda.

'Take it in your mouth,' Astrid commanded in her gravelly voice. Obediently Clara did so, sucking on the rubber cock, until she felt it graze the back of her throat.

Astrid had picked up the vibrator that Clara had

thrown aside, and then bent down, and, placing her full mouth onto Clara's, kissed her with a heated urgency that Clara had never sensed in Astrid before.

Then she pulled away and whispered, 'I know what you want.' Clara hoped, desperately, that Astrid did. She needed to be pleasured hard with the strap-on, the vibrator or ideally both.

Astrid pushed her down, so that again she felt the fur and latex beneath her. With a controlled brutality that excited Clara almost beyond endurance, Astrid held open Clara's legs and plunged the vibrator into her opening, twisting it so that every fibre was alive inside her pussy. She felt the long hair brushing her face, and her senses were alive to Astrid's distinctive scent, an exotic oil mingled with fresh sweat.

Half opening her eyes, Clara saw the swell of Astrid's breasts and reached up to fondle them. Her body felt molten, and all the rigidity of frustrated desire was gone in an instant. She moaned. The dexterity with which Astrid was pushing the vibrator into her was taking her over the edge and she shuddered to a climax, crying out in her frenzy.

Clara felt faint now, the heightened state of arousal generated by Astrid's proximity causing stars to appear before her eyes. Clinging on to Astrid's body she bit her neck and rubbed her face against her breasts.

How had the computer, the interface between Daniel and herself, known how much she needed this? She had barely recovered from her climax when Astrid leaned over her and was securing her arms above her head with a rope that was attached firmly to the underside of one of the squares, so that when Clara tried to move her wrists met a sharp resistance. Clara relaxed, feeling her body become pliable, stretched out for Astrid's pleasure. All self-consciousness had left her as she lost herself in the sensation.

She felt a finger investigate her bumslit. Astrid had put some cream on her fingers and was widening the passage. She hooked her legs over Astrid's shoulders, opening herself up, anticipating that the rubber cock would fill her up. But Astrid was intent on taking her time. Inch by inch the cock moved up her lubricated passage, widening and stretching her. Clara kept perfectly still until, finally, she breathed a sigh of relief as it was inside her. Every nerve-ending in her passage was aflame and she felt herself hover on the edge of her orgasm as she heard the buzzing begin.

'Do you like that?' said Astrid.

'Mmm,' murmured Clara, biting her lip in anticipation of what was to come. Astrid slipped the vibrator's head into her opening and Clara's pussy sucked it in, her juices spilling out. As Astrid moved the strap-on back and forth in a rocking motion within Clara's anus a haze began to envelop her, her body buckling, overloaded with sensation, and still Astrid tormented her. She longed to feel the full length of the vibrator within her pussy. Yet this way, slowly, was both torturous and new, making her savour each exquisite moment on the cusp of pleasure and frustration.

'Please,' Clara murmured.

'You must learn to wait. It won't be long now.'

Clara pushed herself against the vibrator until it was in up to the hilt, and let out a moan as her orgasm crashed over her, causing her to buck and spasm as Astrid continued to ride her.

'You little bitch. You couldn't wait could you?' But Astrid was smiling.

They lay panting in each other's arms, Astrid's breasts smeared with sweat due to her exertions. Soon Clara had regained her energy, and was putting her mouth down to Astrid's pussy, and licking her clit in a figure-of-eight until Astrid began to come. Clara picked up the strap-on that had been flung aside, and, seized with a sense of enthusiasm and an illicit thrill, secured it around her hips.

'Are you sure you're ready for this?' murmured Astrid, at the same time already opening her legs in readiness. In reply, Clara prised Astrid's labia apart with one hand and slipped in the dildo. She felt a rush of excitement, seeing the pleasure crossing Astrid's face as she thrust into her. So this was how men felt, she thought gleefully. At last she knew.

Supporting herself on her elbows she bent down to kiss Astrid and, taking the dildo almost out, plunged it back in again. Losing herself now in the fluidity of motion, she thrust into Astrid, who bucked forward to get the dildo deeper inside.

Astrid was scratching Clara's back and screaming. 'Oh, oh, oh, yes,' she cried and with one last thrust, Clara pistoned deep into Astrid's pussy and she felt her come beneath her. As they lay on top of each other, smeared with their mingled juices, Clara dimly heard the familiar male voice.

'Congratulations, you have successfully completed the game.'

Before she could fully recover herself Astrid was on her feet.

'Come on. There's something I want to show you,' said Astrid.

'What, there's more?' said Clara incredulously.

'Yes! There certainly is.' Clara stood up and barely had time to pull off the strap-on before Astrid was pulling her towards the door.

'What's going on?'

But Astrid did not answer as she opened the door, which was now mysteriously unlocked, and stepped into the corridor. Turning to her right Astrid went up to Clara's bedroom and hesitated at the door.

'You didn't think I'd forgotten about our plan did you?'

Before Clara could answer Astrid had thrown the door open. The first thing Clara saw was Paul's face, red and distorted with rage as he twisted his head round to look at her.

'Oh God! Astrid, what have you done to him?'

'I thought a little show might do him the world of good,' said Astrid playfully.

Paul was tied into a chair, firmly secured with rope, and completely naked. He was emitting muffled sounds.

'What's he saying?' said Clara.

'I don't know, and I don't care. I stuffed his boxer shorts in his mouth.'

Clara saw that the curtain that had lined one of the walls had been pulled aside to reveal a clear view of the room that Astrid and she had just been in. She walked over and touched the surface. Of course, it was a two-way mirror.

Paul was struggling in the chair and she was tempted to untie him. She had never seen him look so vulnerable and helpless.

'Shouldn't we at least let him have some air?'

'Well, maybe, once he's recovered from the shock. What he's just seen has shaken up his moral scruples. Or maybe not.'

Clara followed Astrid's gaze. It rested on Paul's cock, which was thrust up, fully erect.

They looked at each other and burst out laughing. Then they laughed uncontrollably, until tears ran down their faces. Clara eventually recovered her composure.

'I'm starving,' said Astrid. 'I bet dinner's almost ready.'

'But what about Paul?'

'As I said, we might untie him when he's calmed down a bit. Now come on, let's have a quick shower and dress for dinner.'

As Astrid led her from the room Clara was filled

with a sense of remorse. She knew that Paul would not have been able to take the scene that he had just witnessed. She dreaded having to talk to him about it. But maybe Astrid was right. It was something that could be dealt with later.

As they shut themselves in the bathroom Clara started to ask questions.

'How on earth did you get Paul into that chair?'

'Well, when he came in I offered him a cup of tea. Naturally I slipped a pill into it.'

'Oh no, Astrid!'

'Don't worry. It was very mild. Then he went up to his room. When I went up after him ten minutes later he was out of it. Well, I stripped him of his clothes and tied him to the chair. When he came to he must have been surprised to see you and me locked in an intimate embrace.'

It was a clever plan, Clara had to admit it. 'Oh Astrid, you are naughty!'

Astrid drew back the shower curtain.

'Still, it did the trick, didn't it?'

By the time they had showered and changed things were in full swing downstairs.

'Where did you two get to?' asked Eric cockily.

'We had a little business to take care of,' said Astrid, beaming from ear to ear as she sat down at the table.

Lina frowned. 'Where's Paul? I was looking forward to getting to know him a bit better.'

Daniel pulled out an empty chair next to him and Clara slipped into it, for a moment unsure as to how to answer the question.

'He's exhausted by all the country air, I think. I left him asleep upstairs. But he should be down soon.'

She would go and untie him, when she felt the time was right. She was surprised to find that she was enjoying the thrill of power gained from the fact that Paul sat above her, helpless and bound.

Jason had his arm draped around Veronica's shoulder, her pale skin a stunning contrast against her low-cut electric-blue gown and tendrils of red hair.

Clara sipped at a glass of red wine. It was full-bodied and flowed through her veins, warming her up rapidly. She picked at the food that was placed in front of her – a spicy curry. But her throat was dry and she realised that nervous tension was running through her, making the food unpalatable. She would have liked to have had some time alone with her thoughts, to ponder over what had happened in Daniel's playroom.

While the others were chatting, Daniel turned his face towards her, his eyes lingering on her nervous hands that were twisting a napkin under the table.

'Come on now, there's nothing to be afraid of,' he said, taking the napkin away from her. 'You look very beautiful tonight.' She wore a black velvet corset, that made the orbs of her breasts swell invitingly.

She looked to her right. Mark was planting a kiss on the side of Leila's neck. She threw back her head and laughed. On Clara's left, Eric was also busy, pushing his hand up Astrid's skirt as she leaned nonchalantly back against Lina. Clara could feel the playful sexual tension in the room moving up a notch and wondered what plans there were for later.

'How did you like the game?' said Daniel.

She took a large gulp of wine, feeling a flush of embarrassment rush through her.

'Well, it was certainly nothing like any game I've played before,' said Clara. 'Has anyone else seen it?'

Eric turned towards her. She had evidently spoken too loudly. 'Hey, what game?' he said.

'I gave her a preview of my new artwork.'

'Well, you are privileged,' he said. 'None of us have seen it. What did you make of it?'

Clara glanced at Astrid, whose face had grown serious.

'I couldn't possibly divulge. But I will say that it's worth waiting for.'

'When are we going to see it?' Eric asked.

'I'm not sure. But I wanted Clara's opinion, seeing as she's the art expert.'

'Oh, I don't know about that.'

'What do you think?' asked Veronica. 'Do you think it's ready to show at a gallery?'

The idea was an interesting one. 'Well, not in its present form, no. It might offend some people's sensibilities. But maybe with a few modifications.'

The others drifted back to their own conversations. Judging by the way that the girls were starting to disrobe, art was evidently the last thing on their minds.

Daniel smiled enigmatically. He was dressed casually, in black jeans and a shirt and yet she felt his presence, his brooding masculinity heavy beside her. She could not yet fully fathom how he had known all those things about her. She thought of Mr X, and the last e-mail she had sent him, of how she had wished for Astrid to make love to her, roughly.

'How did you know?' she said softly, so that the others wouldn't hear.

'Know what?'

'All those things about me.'

He dodged the question. 'It was the computer that knew. Only, you tried to lie to it, and got found out.'

'No, but seriously, I've never told anyone about my sexual fantasies. Not Paul, not Astrid, and I hardly know you. So how could you, or rather the computer know?' Was it possible that Daniel had read her mind in so short a space of time?

Then abruptly the group stopped talking, their attention caught by the sound of a car being revved-up outside the bay window. Mark stood up and looked out.

'Hey, what's going on?' said Lina.

Mark shrugged his shoulders. 'Looks like your friend left early.'

Clara leaped up and ran towards him. But it was dark outside and she couldn't make out anything but the foreboding shadows of trees. 'But how?' she said.

Astrid began to laugh, a deep throaty laugh. 'He must have wriggled out somehow. I knew I should have made those knots tighter.'

'What, you mean you tied him up?' said Lina. 'You should have said. I would have had a great deal of pleasure untying him.'

'I'm not sure that Paul would have been up for that kind of game,' Astrid replied, turning back to Eric as if Paul's departure was of no consequence.

Clara glanced at Daniel and their eyes met in a complicit understanding. Across the table, Veronica was standing up and Mark was pulling down the long zip that ran down her back. She shrugged the dress off in one fluid movement.

'Did you know about our plan?' said Clara.

'Oh yes, Astrid told me. I don't think he'll be bothering you again. Not after the things he saw.'

'Isn't there somewhere we can go? Somewhere where we can talk privately?'

'Is that what you want to do, talk? I rather think that you have something else on your mind.'

'Well, maybe, but don't you want to?'

'You may find this difficult to believe, but I haven't been with a woman for a very long time.'

'I do find that hard to take in.' Especially as I've seen that video of you giving it to Astrid, she thought.

'When I was famous, there were always women, women on tap. They worshipped me. And for a while that was great. But then I began to feel unsure as to whether they liked me for myself or just because of who I was. I don't mean to be big-headed, you know.' Now he was blushing. He stared down at the table, an oasis of stillness amongst the bawdy goings-on in the room.

'Isn't it time you took the plunge?' She put her hand over his. 'After all that abstinence your senses will be heightened. I'm quite envious of you, in fact. I'm in quite the opposite state, I've become quite a glutton recently. I think I've explored almost every sensual possibility.'

'No,' he said, slipping his hand away from hers. 'I don't think I'm quite ready, or that you are, for that matter. I'm not really in the mood for all this. I think I'll have a lie down. But why not stay here and relax.'

There was much complaining when Daniel made his decision to retire early. Clara felt utterly frustrated. One minute they had been enclosed in a bond of intimacy, the next, he was fleeing from her touch. What had gone wrong?

'Should I go after him?' she whispered to Eric who had leaned over and was placing soft kisses on her neck. She still had so many unanswered questions. What about the attraction between her and Daniel? She had felt a connection, a feeling beyond the physical. Had that all been in her head too?

'No, Daniel wants to be alone. Besides, you've got some explaining to do.'

Someone had dimmed the lights and now only the candles that had been placed over the fireplace and down the length of the table illuminated the room. Clara glanced around her and saw that in the corner the three other women were keeping Mark well occupied. Daniel began to glide out of her thoughts.

In the half-darkness Clara reached out to touch Eric, her hand coming into contact with his bare chest. While Eric still nuzzled her neck she felt two hands come at her from behind, grasping her neck firmly. She felt her neck being bent backwards, like the pliable stem of a flower. She closed her eyes and waited, not knowing who was behind her, but not having the energy to push him away either. She heard a rumble of thunder and then a storm breaking in the distance.

Eric caressed her bosom that swelled over the corset, first with his fingers and then with his tongue.

The hands were still fastened around her neck, but had loosened their grip a little.

'Are you having some trouble with her?' the voice said. She realised that she was a little drunk and could not quite place the voice.

Eric moved his chair a little closer to her.

'Well, it really is too much. We've known Daniel for years. And woe betide if anyone ever went near that room.'

'I see what you're getting at.' Of course, it was Jason. Just the thought of him made her prickle with a heady mixture of dislike and desire. She twisted round, driven by a sudden compulsion to see his face.

'Stay like that, there's a good girl, looking at Eric.' His voice was hypnotic yet firm. She realised that she wanted to comply with whatever he had in store for her, but the old Clara still fought against the impulse.

Eric tugged at the laces of the corset. 'Then, as soon as she comes along Daniel shows her his precious artwork.'

Jason's hands had moved up over her face. He held his palms over her eyes so that her mind was flooded with blackness.

'It's not really art, it's a game,' she said, as the corset was gently pulled away from her. She felt Eric's breath against her nipples.

He sucked on one for a moment, causing her to gasp. 'Tell us about the game.'

She remained silent. Her body felt weak, craving to

185

be touched, to be used for their pleasure. As she slipped off the chair she felt two hands, Eric's or Jason's, she couldn't be sure, break her fall and lay her down on the carpet.

'She'll tell us,' said Jason. 'I'll make sure of that.' She closed her eyes more tightly, wanting to blank out the unpleasant aspect of what was happening to her, the intrusive voices. She desired oblivion.

Someone had pulled off her skirt and panties and now a strange spicy scent, which she couldn't place, filled her nostrils. One of the girls on the other side of the room laughed, and she heard another girl sigh, but she had no desire to look and closed her eyes more tightly.

'Blindfold me,' she said.

They had no objection to that, evidently, and tied some material round her eyes. The fruity smell became more pungent. She remembered the smell, it was cinnamon, and it was scenting the oil that was being poured over her breasts. She trembled as the oil ran between them and down the flat of her belly.

She felt the soft lapping of a tongue, from the back of her knee, moving in slow circles up her inner thigh. She tensed as she felt the tongue approach her swollen bud, hoping that it would move directly onto it. But instead the tongue started its ascent again from the back of the other knee, building up rivers of heat at the tops of her thighs. She spread her thighs, again hoping for the anonymous tongue to lick her pussy.

As the oil was rubbed into her breasts, and she felt the wet tongue begin to lap between her legs, she felt as if she had turned to liquid. Another tongue began to make its way from inside her ear, down the back of her neck. And soon she could not tell one sensation from another. Their tongues were everywhere and their fingers too, prising her apart and running over her well-oiled flesh. The only sound in the room now was the rain driving hard against the glass.

'Tell us about the game,' said Jason, his voice making an unwelcome inroad into her dreamy state.

'No, I can't. I promised Daniel.' If only the tongue that was working her clit back and forth would do so for another few seconds, she knew she would come. But abruptly the tongue moved away.

She sensed aggression flood the air as a hand gripped her arm.

'Tell us.' Her other arm was held down and she felt someone climb on top of her, felt the pressure of hard muscular thighs slither against her oiled skin.

She guessed that this line of questioning might just be a ruse to give them an excuse to punish her, they were both very adept at that. She struggled, knowing there was no point. What harm would it do to reveal what she had seen, what had happened? Yet, somehow, invisibly, there was a connection tying her to Daniel and there was simply no way that she would reveal what he wanted to be kept a secret. She wondered anyhow whether she could explain it. It now seemed like a dream to her, a far-off memory. Had the glowing pink room been real?

'If she won't spill the beans we'll have to punish her, of course,' hissed Jason.

'But why, why is it so important?'

'Don't ask questions.'

'I'm losing my patience. Jason, gag her will you. I can't bear any more provocation.'

'But,' she began to bite against the hand as it pushed the material into her mouth. She struggled, and somehow managed to push off the man who was sitting astride her, and roll onto her side. She breathed heavily from the exertion. Then a slap fell onto her bottom.

'Stop moving about. This is getting tiresome.' She

187

gasped as her head was yanked back and the gag was tied firmly into place.

'I thought that she'd got beyond these little bouts of petulance,' said Jason. He pushed an exploratory finger into her anus and she felt a tremor of pleasure run through her. 'But evidently I was wrong.'

As she was turned over onto her front she wondered what they had in store for her. But to her surprise, as abruptly as it had started, the rough treatment ceased. The cinnamon oil was poured onto her back and rubbed into her skin. Then the hands moved lower, over her bottom cheeks and came to rest over the entrance to her forbidden passage.

Now that the adrenaline from their tussle had settled down she felt an amazing sense of peace fall over her. She relaxed. It felt good to have the gag in her mouth and the blindfold over her eyes. The urgency that she had felt moments ago flooded out of her. She was lost in a series of new sensations, the rain drumming heavily on the window, the scent of fresh male sweat mingled with the spicy oil.

Slowly, stealthily she felt one finger move in and out of her anus. Then another finger slipped in beside it. Her whole body seemed to open up, like a flower, as more oil was dripped over her opening.

'I think she's ready now,' a voice said, but so quietly that she could not make out if it was Eric or Jason.

Stretching her arms out in front of her she felt a man's body move over her and place the tip of his cock against her entrance. She leaned on her arms so that her bottom was slightly raised, pushing herself against the tip, wanting the hard length of the anonymous cock to drive into her. At the same time she felt fingers caressing her swollen bud from the other side, pushing it from side to side and driving her arousal to a more urgent level.

The cock drove into her, suddenly activating a white-hot core of pleasure that threatened to explode. She cried out, but the gag stifled her cries of pleasure. She pushed herself back on the cock, increasing the friction between the cock and her anal passage. As the finger rubbed her clit harder still she rammed herself backwards onto the cock. The climax crept up on her, increasing step by step until her whole insides swam with a warm heavy buzz of pleasure. Then abruptly her insides lurched, tipping her over the edge, the waves running all along her inner thighs like rivers of molten lava.

Chapter Eleven

The next morning she woke up in the big bed, the sun streaming through the curtains. She stretched, slowly and luxuriantly. Someone had no doubt carried her up the stairs. Her skin was still slightly sticky with oil. Rolling over on her side she saw that the curtain had been pulled across the mirror that led onto the playroom.

Someone had placed the chair, to which only hours ago Paul had been tied, against the wall. The creamy walls seemed to belie the fact that Paul had struggled his way out of the ropes. There was not a scratch on the wall.

She began to wonder whether maybe she hadn't gone just a bit too far with Paul. After all, it must have been enough of a shock for him to have seen Astrid and her having sex on the chessboard, never mind the fact that they had tied him up and laughed at him. She knew that he had deserved it, but somewhere at the back of her mind traces of guilt lingered.

After taking a shower and dressing in trousers and a sweater she decided to go downstairs. She peeked into the dining room. The beautiful walnut table had trails of hardened wax all over it, where the candles had burned down. The faint smell of cinnamon still hung in the air, reminding her of last night's pleasures. Plates of discarded food and empty bottles of wine lay in disarray over the table. She decided to tidy up a bit and took some of the plates into the kitchen.

She had loaded the dishwasher and now sat at the kitchen table, wondering whether anyone was going to surface. Drinking her coffee, she realised that she was relaxed, and was pleased that the strain of having Paul around had been lifted.

Then Astrid came in, wrapped in a big fluffy bath robe. 'God, my head is hurting!' She ran her hand through her tangled curls.

When Clara had poured her a coffee Astrid sipped at it, staring out into the distance. Although Astrid was clearly a little hungover, Clara knew that she had best seize her chance to ask some important questions about yesterday's events before the others woke up. 'I can't thank you enough for sorting out Paul.'

Astrid shrugged. 'It was nothing. You didn't think I'd let you down did you?'

'No, but I do feel a bit guilty. After all, Paul was behaving himself and not being too much of a pain.'

'Don't tell me you're having second thoughts. It's finished. He won't be bothering you again.'

'No.' She took another sip of coffee. 'But what about that business in the playroom?'

'What about it?'

Clara felt that Astrid did not want to talk for one reason or another, but nevertheless she pressed on.

'Well, for a start, how did Daniel know about all my fantasies and what I had experienced before?'

'Daniel's very perceptive, he can read people.'

'Maybe. But I've never told anyone about this stuff, except for Mr X.'

'The famous Mr X.' Astrid began to laugh. 'At least you know that he isn't Paul.'

Clara thought about it. In fact, she was no nearer to finding out Mr X's identity than she had been before. But now everything was pointing towards Daniel being her mysterious internet admirer and yet, there were too many coincidences to make it believable.

'The thing is, only yesterday I wrote to him that I wanted you to make love to me, but not in a sensual way, but hard, passionate. And then when you came in with the strap-on I . . .'

'Actually, Daniel did suggest that. But I think that the link is too tenuous. In any case, I don't see what light I can shed on the matter.'

Astrid was right, she was going to have to solve this problem herself.

'But you know Daniel better than me. Do you think that he could be Mr X?'

'I'm sorry,' Astrid said irritably, 'this is too much for me to take in so early in the morning. Why don't you just ask him?' She stood up and moved towards the door. 'Now, I really must find some aspirins.'

Just ask him. It seemed straightforward enough, and yet something was preventing her from entertaining the idea. She wondered if she had upset Daniel in some way last night. When he had gone to bed early, she had wondered whether it was anything to do with her, until her mind had been taken up with other things. Somehow Daniel had succeeded in getting under her skin and she needed to know what was bothering him.

She was so lost in her daydream that she did not for a moment notice that Daniel had come in. When they caught sight of each other she felt the heavy aura of sexual tension fall between them, making her self-conscious. It was not like her to be lost for words and yet she felt like a stupid schoolgirl, gazing dopily at him. 'Thanks again for helping me out last night,' she said.

Daniel wore a checked shirt and faded jeans with scuffed boots. There was a tiredness around his eyes as if he had not slept properly. Shyly, he sat down opposite her.

'That's OK. But that wasn't so important to me. It was really to show you my artwork. No one, apart from Astrid, has seen it, you know.'

Clara felt herself blush. 'I thought it was incredible. Everything about it. I've never seen anything like it.'

'You're just saying that.'

'No,' she blurted, 'I really think that it should be exhibited.'

'I hardly think you'd find much of an audience.'

'Well, no, not in its present form. But if the questions were changed, made less erotically charged, I think it could be a hit.'

He shrugged. 'I don't know.' He was looking down into his coffee mug. She couldn't help noticing that he was a lot less self-assured than yesterday.

'Have I done something to upset you?' she said softly. 'I'm finding it a bit disconcerting the way you won't look at me. You leaving early yesterday, I couldn't help wondering if I'd said something.'

There was a long silence. Then she began to hear laughter from upstairs. Soon everyone would be awake and she would have lost the moment.

'It's not something that I expect you to understand. I've spent so long on my own. I needed the solitude, these past few years. And then when I met you . . .' He paused.

'What?'

He lifted his head and looked deep into her eyes. His eyes were deep pools, dense with secrets and still she needed to find out more.

'I wanted to make love to you. But something held me back.'

The intensity between them was abruptly shattered as Lina and Veronica came in.

'Hi there,' said Veronica. 'Is there anything to eat? I'm starving.'

Daniel stood up. 'There's lots of stuff in the fridge. I think I'm going to go for a walk. Tell everyone I'll be back before lunch.'

'Wait, I'll come with you,' said Clara. She sensed that he wanted to be alone but she was not in the mood to make small talk with the rest of the guests.

'I'm afraid that I wouldn't be very good company.'

'Still, I'd like to get some fresh air.'

'OK then,' he said, without enthusiasm.

Outside, the air was clear after the rain that had fallen during the night. But a warm breeze was blowing and Clara had to push back her dark hair to prevent it falling over her face.

For some minutes they walked side by side, down the path to the maze. But when they got to its opening, instead of going in, he turned to the right and she followed him. It had been a mistake to follow him, she thought angrily. And yet, it would be even more foolish to turn back now. With every step she felt him moving further away from her.

As they entered a wood his mood became a little lighter. Eventually he spoke. 'What do you want from me? You've got what you came for. You've got rid of your boyfriend.'

She stopped and grabbed his arm. 'Do you want me to go?'

He pulled away from her and continued to walk into the dense forest.

'I want to help you,' she said, breathlessly. 'You can't keep running forever.'

'And what would you know about it? You've only known me five minutes.'

'Oh God!' she exclaimed. Her sweater had caught on a bramble bush and the thorns had torn her skin. 'Help me, will you?'

As he came towards her and bent down to untangle the sweater she caught a scent of his fresh male sweat on the breeze. His proximity made her stomach knot in a turmoil of unresolved feelings.

Slowly he pushed her sleeve up and gazed down at the long scratch mark in which pearls of blood were forming. Her breathing was laboured, partly from walking so fast and partly because his mouth was inches away from her skin.

She began to pull her arm away but he clasped her wrist firmly. Then to her surprise he bent down and licked the blood away with one sweep. The unexpected contact brought all the trapped emotion inside her flooding to the fore. She reached out and pulled his head against her. In the violence of her movement he tripped on the brambles and fell sideways, onto the thick carpet of leaves.

Standing above him she looked down at his luscious body sprawled beneath her. Sexual power, of an intensity which she had never experienced before, was racing through her body. As he struggled to get up she put one palm on each shoulder and pushed him firmly down.

He opened his mouth to speak but she interrupted him. Bending down to straddle him she put her mouth close to his ear. 'You say you're not ready to take the plunge. But the fact is, you'll never be ready.' The expression in his eyes was one of terror. 'But if you won't, I'll have to make you.'

'What the hell do you think you're doing?' he said, but she felt the lack of conviction in his voice and silenced him by kissing him, hard. She felt his body weakening beneath her grasp, her hands rubbing against the soft cotton material of his shirt. Then, as he started to return the kiss, she sensed the palpable rising of passion beneath his skin. His face was hot and flushed as she lifted her head and began to unbutton his shirt.

Her tongue ran along his chest, seeking out his nipples amongst the thick dark hair. Making her tongue into a sharp point she tormented one nipple, then the other until she heard him moan. Urgently, she ran her tongue down over his stomach, and pulled at his belt, until she had opened his trousers to reveal his cock, hard and rampant beneath her questing mouth.

She hesitated, then moved away and rapidly divested herself of her clothes. For although she was aching to feel his cock in her mouth, her pussy was making its demands felt. Turning her back to him and placing her pussy over his mouth she opened her legs wider until she felt her wet clit rubbing against his face. Leaning over she reached for his cock again, feeling its thickness and bulk in her hand. His tongue was swirling around her hot bud, causing tiny currents of pleasure to radiate out from it. As he increased the pressure of his tongue her clit responded with a sharp dagger of pleasure that almost split her in two.

She slipped his cock into her mouth, savouring the sensation of fullness. It was difficult to concentrate on the task in hand because she could now feel his fingers pushing their way into her tight tunnel, and as he rammed them deeper into her, opening her up, she began to cry out, spasming against his tongue as wave after wave of pleasure flowed over her.

Her orgasm went on and on as she caressed his cock with her tongue. He began to gasp softly as he moved his hips to slide his cock, which she held firm at its base with her right hand, in and out of her parted mouth. She caressed it with her tongue and lips, holding it for a moment and flicking her tongue across the head and then allowing him to move rhythmically in and out of her mouth.

Barely had her first climax ended than another began to build. He pushed his fingers into her, in the same rhythm, faster and faster now, making the peaks of pleasure harder and more urgent. She ground herself against his fingers, feeling his tongue still teasing her clit to a point beyond endurance. As she increased the pace at which her mouth moved up and down his bone-hard cock, she felt a frenzied excitement, and all the sensations began to blur into each other.

As he began to come she did too, feeling a sense of exaltation that she had finally made a connection with Daniel. As she shuddered to her climax she relished the intimacy of the moment, their bodies locked together in the depths of the wood, away from prying eyes. She felt that it was a special moment, a turning point and knew that she would remember it forever.

Later, as they lay side by side, she savoured the breeze that blew over her naked body. Neither spoke, but as he held her in his arms she knew that his relief had been overwhelming, as it had been for her. She lay across his chest, a blissful state rising up inside her and seeping through her limbs like molten honey.

'That wasn't so hard, was it?', she said, tracing her fingers down the ridge that ran down the middle of his chest.

'No,' he said, and pushed a few tendrils of hair back from her forehead. She looked up and was startled by his gaze, which was less withdrawn than before. A tremor passed through her as she returned his glance. She turned away and reached for her clothes.

'The others will be wondering where we are,' he said, sitting up and starting to button up his shirt.

They walked back to the house in a companionable silence. Again, it was on the tip of her tongue to ask him whether he was Mr X. But, somehow, she sensed that she should not push him too far, too soon. He had just had sex after a very long drought. No doubt that was enough to keep his mind occupied for one day.

But once they had returned to the house and settled down to lunch, which had miraculously appeared, Daniel began to withdraw back into his shell.

'What have you done to Daniel?' whispered Veronica. 'He looks exhausted. If I didn't know him as well as I do I would think that you'd had your wicked way with him.' She leaned back in her chair and laughed.

'Oh, I haven't done anything to him,' Clara replied. 'Maybe all this jollity is too much for him to take.'

Veronica looked at her quizzically. 'Perhaps,' she said, turning to talk to Eric on her other side.

The chatter continued, and the atmosphere was light-hearted, filled with easy and indiscriminate flirting. Yet Clara could not concentrate. Her gaze was brought back, time and time again to Daniel's brooding figure, as he sat half-listening to what Mark was whispering in his ear.

Clara was lulled into a trance. The only person that mattered to her at that moment was Daniel. Why then was he avoiding her glance? On the one occasion when she had managed to meet his eyes he had swiftly looked away. What on earth was he up to?

As it began to grow dark outside it became clear that everyone was staying for another night. Much as she would have liked to confront Daniel about his reticent behaviour she was also pleased that there was a genuine impediment in her way – that she had to be at the gallery on Monday.

Much to her relief she saw Astrid make a move to be on her way.

'It would be great if you could give me a lift. I'm pretty much stranded without Paul.'

'Yes, sure, that's fine.'

'Just give me a few minutes to get my things together.'

Up in her room she bundled her clothes into her bag. She began to feel angry. For the first time in the last few turbulent months she had stumbled upon an insoluble problem. It was unthinkable to her that Daniel no longer wanted her. How else could his behaviour be explained, after all? Was he really so arrogant to think that now that he had had her he could pretend that nothing had happened in front of his friends? His behaviour had dented her confidence.

But then, as she pulled on her coat and turned to leave, she saw him standing in the doorway. His look was beseeching, and despite herself, she dropped the bag and went to him. Running her fingers through his hair she deeply inhaled his distinctive smell, of outdoors and woodland. She pressed her mouth to his and kissed him at length.

When he drew away, he said, 'I'm sorry.'

Despite the fact that Astrid was waiting for her downstairs she felt an urgent pulse of desire. She ran her hands impatiently over the soft cotton shirt and down over his crotch where she met his burgeoning erection. She bit his neck softly and he moaned. She began to unzip his trousers.

He pushed her away, gently but firmly.

'I can't do this.'

'But why? I don't understand.'

'I don't know that I do either. I told you I wasn't ready.'

Her hands dropped to her sides as she felt anger rise up inside her. 'I suppose you're going to tell me that I forced you to have sex with me in the wood?'

'No, of course not. I enjoyed it every bit as much as you did.'

'Well, what then?' She drew close to him again and slid her hand over the tantalising bit of naked flesh at

199

the top of his shirt. But he clasped his hand over hers and pushed it away.

'I don't know what the hell is going on here.' She picked up her bag and pushed past him. 'Look, thanks for having me to stay.'

'There's no need to be so cold. I only meant . . .'

But she no longer wanted to talk. He was letting her down gently, that much was clear. Right now she just wanted to get out of the house, as quickly as possible. She hurried downstairs, not bothering to turn around to see if Daniel was following her. Mercifully, Astrid was waiting at the foot of the stairs. But there were still goodbyes to be said and Clara felt that all eyes were on her and that everyone knew what had transpired.

When they got into the car Clara decided to sit in the back. She wanted to think everything through. But it was not to be. Astrid was in such an ebullient mood that Clara could not focus on her thoughts.

'That was such good fun. So much good sex, and yet I still feel completely high, like I could go the distance.'

'I wish I felt like that.'

'Hey, I'm sorry. Maybe you're still a bit worried about that business with Paul. But judging by his reaction, I think you'll be rid of him.'

Paul, thought Clara. He had hardly figured in her thoughts at all this past day. 'He was a pain. Always touching me and pulling me towards him, like I was some sort of rag doll.'

'Mmm, I know what you mean. But what about if the boot was on the other foot?'

'You mean with Paul? I think he'd enjoy it.'

'No, get Paul out of your head. It was just a thought. I just figured that it might turn you on.'

'What do you mean?'

They glanced out the window at a couple of girls who were hitchhiking.

'I feel bad not giving them a lift, but what with all

200

my luggage in the front, we've really only got room for one.'

Later, Clara watched the trees, silhouetted against the sunset, as the car sped along the motorway.

'You must remember what it was like,' said Astrid. 'When you went hitchhiking as a student. The hassle you got from men.'

Clara began to remember her youthful travels. 'Yeah, every time they'd shift the gearstick they'd accidentally brush your thigh.'

Astrid gave a throaty laugh. 'And were any of them ever attractive?'

'No,' said Clara, warming to the subject. 'They were mostly middle-aged businessmen in shiny suits.'

'Or truckers who hadn't washed!'

'I got into a few scrapes, I can tell you, but nothing serious.'

'It's always been one of my fantasies to pick up a really cute young guy. Then hassle him a little, intimidate him, find out how he likes it.'

'I shouldn't think he'd complain.'

'Ah, fantasies, just fantasies.' The subject was dropped and they talked of other things, but something about the idea had got under Clara's skin. The idea of seducing a young, fit guy was quite irresistible.

Clara realised that she was starving. What with all the excitement of Daniel's presence she had not indulged in the copious amounts of food on offer. When the sign for a service station flashed ahead of them she leaned forward in her seat.

'Do you mind if we stop quickly. I'm really hungry.'

'No, not at all, I might grab a sandwich too.'

Once they had parked, they walked across the car park which was dark but illuminated with spotlights. Once inside they took their sandwiches to a table and began to devour them ravenously.

'What do you think of Daniel?' said Astrid.

'Daniel,' she repeated. 'I think he's a very talented artist.'

'Yeah, yeah,' said Astrid, 'but there's more to it than that isn't there?'

Clara wondered why Astrid had avoided the subject that morning and was now eager to discuss it.

'The way you were looking at him. It was like a schoolgirl with a crush. Everyone noticed it.'

'Oh, don't be silly, Astrid.'

'Don't get me wrong. I think it's really cute.' She chewed her sandwich thoughtfully. 'Just remember that Daniel isn't like Mark or Eric or Jason.'

'How do you mean?'

'Oh, forget it, it's really none of my business.'

'Go on.'

'He's highly strung. Takes things seriously. He's intense. We were all surprised when he took such a shine to you.'

'Oh, thanks a bundle.'

'No, it's just that he hasn't shown any interest, you know, sexually, in a woman for years and years. And don't think that the girls and I haven't tried to tempt him!'

Clara smiled. So they really didn't know that she had made love to him in the forest clearing? It was a good feeling, knowing that only Daniel and she knew.

'What are you saying?'

'I think that you could be the one to bring him out of his shell. But don't be heavy-handed. Maybe get involved with him on a business level first, have a show at the gallery.'

'Oh, I don't think he would show with us, do you?'

'I don't see why not. But in any case, win his trust slowly.'

'Thanks for the tip.' It wasn't like Astrid to take such a serious tone but Clara appreciated her advice. After all, Astrid had known Daniel a lot longer than she had.

Back in the car, they were just about to leave the carpark and drive onto the motorway when they saw him. They almost missed the shadowy figure holding up a piece of cardboard.

Astrid slowed the car down and looked at the piece of card on which was scrawled 'London'. Clara ran her eyes appreciatively over the young man. From his crew cut hair down to the tight, well-worn jeans and scuffed boots he was utterly delectable.

'Will he do?' said Astrid.

'What do you mean?'

'The conversation we had earlier. Do you want to play?' Astrid had driven the car level with the youth and he was looking over with interest.

'Oh God, Astrid, I don't know. He's a total stranger.' He bent over to lift up his rucksack and she took in the curve of his buttocks and the strong sinewy line of his thigh.

'He's all yours. I can't do anything while I'm driving the car.'

'But . . .' Suddenly she was scared, scared of the unknown, but also extremely excited.

Astrid rolled down the window. 'Looking for a lift?'

'Yeah, I am.'

'Put your bag next to me and hop in the back with my friend,' said Astrid with a barely contained smirk. 'She'll look after you.'

Clara waited until he had stowed his bag. Then he slipped in beside her. Clara turned to look at him. He had an open expression, and the clear untroubled eyes of youth, of a hue somewhere between amber and brown.

'Hi, I'm Mike,' he said, holding out his hand. She shook it, taking in the dewy skin and shy smile. He had a cute accent.

'Clara, and this is Astrid. You're American?' Astrid drove the car out onto the motorway.

'From Boston. I've been travelling around Europe before starting college.'

'How old are you?' said Astrid.

'Nineteen.'

He pulled off his coat and settled back into his seat. He told them about his travels and plans for college and they listened politely. Clara was much more interested in the boy's crotch. The jeans were evidently well-worn and frayed, especially around his cock. Was it her imagination, or was it growing under her inquisitive gaze?

'Have you met any nice girls since you've been in England?' said Astrid.

'No, not really. I don't think I've talked to anyone in a couple of days. So it's great to meet you two, although you're not really girls, more like women.'

Clara caught Mike's eye. There was a yearning in his expression that she responded to.

'I'm really broke and the reason I've got to get to London is because –'

Clara let her hand casually rest on Mike's thigh. He stopped speaking for a moment, and a warm flush coloured his cheeks.

'– my father has wired me some money. The bank's in London.'

'A good-looking guy like you,' said Clara, 'and no girlfriend?' She let her fingers trace the line along the inner seam of his jeans. He leaned back and parted his legs a fraction.

'I do have one, back in Boston.'

'That's nice,' Clara said, cupping his balls in her hand and giving them a gentle squeeze.

A sigh escaped from his lips, which parted to reveal a row of gleaming white teeth.

'You're very well-developed,' she said, moving her hand up along his stiffening cock, 'for a boy of your age.'

Clearly very excited, he leaned over to kiss Clara.

'Hey,' she said, pushing him away with her free hand. 'Just lie back and think of England.'

'I hope you don't feel that my friend is taking advantage of you in any way,' said Astrid, sounding so prim that Clara had to stifle a laugh.

'No, she can do whatever she wants with me.'

Clara decided to tease him for a little while longer and ran her nails, hard, along his inner thighs. But the sight of his cock, packed into the jeans, was making her work up a sweat and she longed to pull off her top. She could see that that was going to prove difficult within the confined space.

'Take off your T-shirt,' she said. She sat back and watched as he peeled it off, to reveal a lean chest, well-defined and hairless.

'Nice, very nice,' she said, running a finger over one nipple, then the other.

She leaned forward, as if they were two guys who had just picked up an eager young girl. 'He's got a really firm body. Hope you're getting a good look in your rear-view mirror.'

'Yes, I'm getting an eyeful,' said Astrid. 'And he certainly fills those trousers.'

Although it was dim in the back seat there was just enough light from the headlights of the car behind to see what she was doing. Lying across Mike she began to pull off her trousers. To her relief he helped her to divest herself of her shoes, trousers and panties and then began frantically unbuttoning his fly.

She kneeled on the floor and took off her top and bra. The friction caused by rubbing her naked breasts against his lean muscular thighs was making her nipples tingle. Gripping his cock in one hand she began licking the base of his balls. She took one into her mouth, and, hearing him sigh with pleasure, felt it swell beneath her tongue.

After toying with his balls for some minutes she ran her tongue along his length, then worked his foreskin back and forth, slowly, so as not to push him to the point of no return.

'Oh, I really need to come,' he said breathlessly.

'Patience, patience. All in good time.'

'Just a little bit more, please.'

She flicked her tongue over the head of his penis, then held it firm behind the head. His excitement was infectious, but she didn't want the party to be over too soon.

'Hold on, I've an idea.' Releasing his cock she got up from the floor and crouched over him, so that she was facing Astrid. He began to kiss her neck, and she felt his raw passion and urgency transmitted through his frenzied kisses.

She slid onto him, wriggling around to make herself comfortable. Holding on to the back of Astrid's seat she sighed as she felt his cock widening and stretching her. She felt his fingers cup her breasts from behind and pinch the nipples hard as he began to thrust beneath her.

Holding on tight to the top of the seat she stayed perfectly still. She was savouring the way that he was thrusting powerfully, causing tremors to begin along the walls of her silken sheath.

She removed one of his hands from her breast and placed it over her hard clit. Once she took her hand away he began rubbing her swollen bud in a slow, tantalising rhythm. She smiled to herself, evidently he wasn't as inexperienced as he looked.

His thrusts became more and more forceful, so that she had to cling on with all her might to prevent herself from losing her balance. He increased the press-ure of his fingers on her clit so that she could feel her insides cascading and reaching a point of no return.

'I don't think I can hold out any longer.'

'That's OK,' she said. 'Neither can I. What you're doing with your cock is almost too much for a girl to take.' Then she lost consciousness, revelling luxuriantly in the great waves of sensation that broke over her. He gripped her shoulders and groaned as he too came.

'I don't want to spoil anyone's fun but we're about to come off the motorway, and frankly I'm finding it difficult to keep my eyes on the road.'

'That was great,' said Mike, as he pulled away and leaned, completely spent, against the headrest.

'Yeah, it was but I guess we should get dressed,' said Clara, her head swimming. 'We really should pick up hitchhikers more often.'

Moving over to her side of the seat she wanted to savour the fresh exhilaration of the experience for some more moments. Every time she thought that there was nothing left to try life threw up a surprise.

The atmosphere in the car was easy and light after they had dressed. Astrid switched on the radio and the rest of the journey passed in companionable silence. Mike looked shellshocked but happy. Before he got out of the car, he said, 'That was the best trip I've had in England so far.'

'Well, good luck,' said Clara and reached over to kiss him.

'Might be fortunate to pick you up again some time,' said Astrid, as they drove away and watched him stare after them, his face a mixture of astonishment and good humour.

When the car pulled up outside Clara's flat, Clara turned towards Astrid and said, 'That was just the tonic I needed.'

'See,' said Astrid, 'it's different for guys. He loved every minute of that.'

'So did I,' said Clara, leaning over to kiss her friend before getting out of the car.

Chapter Twelve

The next morning, Clara almost overslept. It had been an exhausting weekend, in so many different ways. Even when she managed to pull herself out of bed she could not summon the energy to pick out her clothes for the day. Eventually, she pulled on some sheer stockings and fastened them to a flesh-coloured suspender belt.

The image that had coloured her dreams and now still lingered was the unreal experience of lying naked on the chess board, her nude flesh flooded with pink light while Astrid pleasured her. She opened the window and took a deep breath of fresh air, hoping that it would wake her. Autumn was approaching and there was a slight chill in the air.

Still feeling lethargic she slipped on a bright red wool minidress and some high-heeled black patent boots. Looking at herself in the mirror, pinning up the tangle of dark hair, she looked dazed, like someone who had experienced something momentous.

Realising that it was nearly ten o'clock prompted Clara into action. Usually, she hated to be late at the gallery, but her limbs still felt heavy and it was with some effort that she got herself out of the front door.

On the tube she thought of Daniel. The way she had made love to him in the forest, and the way in which they had parted, leaving things unsaid and unresolved between them. She had had so much carefree fun these past months. It annoyed her that suddenly and unexpectedly he had got under her skin.

As she got off the tube at Green Park, she resolved that she would gain the upper hand over her emotions that were threatening to spiral out of control. As yet, she reasoned, Daniel was a two-dimensional character who she knew little about. He had yet to prove that he could handle an involvement with her. And yet she knew that they were kindred spirits.

At the gallery she drank her coffee and began to open her post. A heavy cloud still hung over her that she was anxious to be rid of. Her head felt as if it were stuffed with cotton wool.

When she read Mr X's short e-mail, How was your weekend? Did your fantasies become flesh? it brought forth an unfamiliar twinge of irritation. She drummed her fingers on the desk as she stared at the stark black letters against the glow of the screen, trying to verbalise the emotion. Mr X had not brought forth the familiar flutter of excitement in her stomach. She realised that she was tired, tired of his prurient curiosity.

She resolved to be proactive. Maybe it was time to finish with Mr X. Now that she had met Daniel, everything else seemed grey and flat in comparison. She would always be indebted to Mr X, because he had given her the push she needed, to bring her buried desires to the fore. But she was most indebted to him because he had led her to Daniel.

She thought about writing Mr X a curt-but-friendly farewell note. The dilemma was a tricky one, because although everything pointed towards Daniel being Mr X, she had no real proof. And by losing contact with Mr X she might also risk losing her connection to Daniel. It was not something that she could afford to make a rash decision about. She closed down her e-mail.

'Good weekend?' said Xavier, pushing open the door and letting a cold stream of air in. That was strange, thought Clara, he didn't usually enquire much about her private life. The sexual frisson had ebbed out of their relationship since they had sated their craving for each other in his office. But now, suddenly, it was there again, binding them together, a powerful attraction, based as much on sexual chemistry as intimacy and trust.

'Yes, very good indeed. I went up with Astrid to stay with Daniel Stanford.'

Xavier's eyes twinkled with excitement. 'Daniel? Are you sure? You mean, *the* Daniel Stanford?'

'Yes.'

'I thought he'd retired and was living as a recluse.' Xavier leaned on the counter conspiratorially. 'I think that a lot of us thought he'd cracked up. Not that I ever knew him personally.'

She was surprised to feel a fierce protectiveness towards Daniel. 'Well, he seemed more than sane to me.'

'Good, good,' Xavier said. Clara knew that he cared less about the fact that Daniel was of sound mind than that he might present a lucrative business opportunity. 'Is he working on anything. Still doing the nudes?'

'Um, no.' She hesitated. How much could she afford to say?

'What then?'

'It sounds stupid, I know, but he's sworn me to secrecy. His new work is very original though.'

'Do you think he might consider having a show with us?'

'It's a possibility, but don't get your hopes up.' Much as the work of art had excited her, it was quite impossible to entertain the thought that it could be shown in its present state.

'Well, please suggest it to him. And if he's amenable, set up a meeting.'

She stood up, so that her eyes were level with his. 'I'll do my best.'

He surveyed her breasts appreciatively, wrapped as they were in the soft red mohair dress.

'You know what, I really don't feel like working today.'

'What? Am I hearing this right?'

'Why don't you take the day off?' His eyes met hers and her insides started to melt.

'Thanks, but I really need to get on with some work.'

There was an awkwardness between them. All thoughts of Daniel had flown out of her head and she felt the lips of her pussy tingle in anticipation. The green eyes and dark hair were working their familiar magic. Embarrassed, she lowered her head.

Then unexpectedly, she felt his hand cup her chin and tilt it upwards.

'Don't think that I don't know what you think of me. That I'm a cold fish.'

She was inches away from him, looking into his eyes, so close to his luxuriant dark eyelashes that she could see each separate lash.

'But I've wanted you, ever since you started working here.' His voice had become urgent, and hoarse with desire.

'Why don't you lock the door so that we can talk privately.' She was surprised at how cool and collected her voice sounded. A few months ago she would have been delighted to hear these words, now only her body ached in anticipation of his touch.

He locked the door and came back to her, slipping behind the counter where she was standing. He pulled her towards him with a violent passion. Her nipples throbbed against the material of his suit as he kissed her. As his tongue explored her mouth she felt a hot sensation pulse through her and she ground her pubic bone against his erect cock.

'But anyone could see us,' she said, drawing away.

He ran his hands over her bottom and, pushing his hands under her hem, began to caress her through the filmy surface of her panties.

'I've often watched you through the window, from across the street. I've often thought how nice it would be to take you from behind.' She had heard those words before somewhere, but couldn't place who had uttered them.

She bit her lip as he pushed the panties aside with one hand so that his fingers could explore her entrance. Toying with her clit, he continued talking, his voice hypnotic, almost menacing.

'I've held myself back, not knowing if you wanted me. Even after the last time, I was unsure.'

'The time for talking is over,' she said as he slipped his fingers into her and rubbed the front wall of her pussy in tiny circles. She gasped with pleasure. 'Don't you care if someone sees us?'

He covered her neck with urgent kisses. 'Isn't that what you want?'

'This is what I want,' she said, deftly unzipping his trousers and gazing down at his rampant cock. 'No underwear,' she said. 'Very kinky.'

He drew away from her and pushed her against the counter. Bunching her dress up around her waist, he pulled his fingers out of her silken sheath and replaced them with his cock.

Supporting herself on her elbows, she let her eyes skim the street. The odd person passed by, but no one looked into the gallery. She felt the secret desire building within her, willing someone to look, knowing that the gaze would send her over the edge.

Closing her eyes she revelled in the strong sensations he was generating within her quim. He was using a corkscrew motion so that she felt a marvellous friction all through her and tilted her bottom up so that he could penetrate her deeply with the full length of his cock.

'Oh, that feels so good,' she moaned.

She stretched out her hands and her fingers curled over the edge of the counter. His hands now crept up under the front of her dress, his fingers seeking out her hard nipples inside the cups of her bra.

'Oh, Clara,' he said, his breath hot on the back of her neck, his face buried in her hair. Now his thrusts had become more forceful and he had gripped her around the waist to steady himself.

As she ground herself against him her eyes flew open and she gasped in surprise. For there, standing casually by the door, a wry smile playing around his lips, was Mark. It was clear from his expression that he liked what he saw. His eyes glowed with excitement.

Should she tell Xavier that Mark was standing there? She revelled in the delicious sensations his cock was drawing forth. There was really no point in spoiling her fun, she thought, self-indulgently. Her eyes locked into Mark's as she began to feel her climax rise up through her body, up through her legs, like water pounding over a waterfall. Helpless now, she closed her eyes again as he too came inside her. Distantly she heard her cries as the feelings welled up and crashed around her over and over again.

When eventually Xavier had recovered from his exertions he sank down in the chair, his view of Mark

213

obscured by Clara's body. She pushed her dress down and waited for the giddiness that still raced through her to pass. Turning to face him she ran her fingers through her hair.

'That was wonderful. Don't be angry now, will you?'

'Why should I be angry?' he said, sprawled back in the chair, tucking a shirt-tail into his trousers.

'Because Mark's outside.'

'Mark?' he asked. 'How long has he been there?'

'I rather think he saw more than he bargained for.'

'Oh well,' said Xavier, 'I suppose he's seen worse in his time.'

'Yes, undoubtedly.'

'Let him in.' He buttoned up his suit and zipped up his trousers.

She walked along the floor in the red dress and the patent leather boots, still feeling extremely sexy and desirable, knowing that the two men were watching her every move.

'Mark,' she said with a smile, once she had unlocked the door. 'Sorry that I didn't let you in earlier. But I was otherwise engaged.'

He leaned forward to kiss her on the cheek. 'Quite alright. I rather enjoyed the view, myself.'

'How come you're back already? I thought you'd stay at Daniel's for another couple of days.'

'Well yes, I would have, only he wasn't in the most sociable of moods after you left. In the end we all decided to drive home this morning.'

'Why was he in a bad mood?'

'Search me, you know what these artists are like. But it was good fun wasn't it?'

'Oh, absolutely.'

Xavier had come up behind her. 'Mark, great to see you. What brings you to the gallery?'

'Oh, just wanted to take Clara to lunch. That OK with you?' he said, turning to Clara.

'Mmm, yes, I have worked up quite an appetite.'

'Care to join us?' said Mark.

'No,' said Xavier despondently. Obviously Xavier was a little jealous of Mark. Well, let him have a sulk. Things were much easier with Mark, she thought. He embodied the meaning of the term 'no strings'.

They walked in the direction of the Barton Club. When they arrived and were shown to their table Clara looked around. The velvet booths were, of course, still there. But the lighting was brighter and the place was crowded and filled with chatter. No one turned to look at Clara. How different it all was from the last time she'd been here with Claus and Mark. And how long ago that now seemed!

She stretched her legs out in front of her and relaxed. She felt really good. That session with Xavier had certainly pulled her out of her exhaustion. She ate her salmon steak hungrily and sipped at some white wine.

Heaping more vegetables on her plate she noted that there was a change in Mark. She felt herself rambling on and him observing her, drinking in every little detail of her without saying very much.

'I was just thinking,' she said, 'of that time with Claus. What fun that was. Do you see much of him?'

'Yes, in fact, he's in London at the moment.'

She sipped her wine. She realised that she was a little tipsy but didn't care.

'I'll tell you what, when Daniel exhibits with us, we'll invite Claus to the opening.'

'Hang on,' said Mark. 'What did you say? That Daniel's going to exhibit?'

'Well, he hasn't exactly said so.' If only Mark knew how far off she actually was from having a firm commitment from Daniel! But she was buoyed by the Dutch courage from the wine.

'But Daniel hasn't so much as shown his new artwork

215

to anyone yet. Not even to us, his closest friends,' said Mark.

Clara prickled with anger. Mark evidently didn't include her in that group. Why was she letting herself be annoyed like this? She was enjoying proving her worth to Mark and didn't intend to stop now.

'I may not be one of the inner circle,' she said, sarcastically. 'But I have been granted the privilege of an exclusive private view of it, as you very well know.'

'Hmm,' Mark said, shaking his head. 'You don't know Daniel like I do. That piece is everything to him. Besides, he hasn't been down to London for years. You've got as much chance of dragging him down here as, well, I don't know, as of hell freezing over.'

'Leave it to me, Mark. It's in the bag. And do invite Claus. Do you think he might put a good review in one of the papers he writes for?'

Mark grinned. 'I'm sure he'd do whatever you say. But it's sheer fantasy!'

'We'll see,' she said. Their little argument had made Mark more talkative. But now that they had touched on the matter of Daniel she could think of nothing else and found it hard to keep track of what Mark was saying. She was certainly going to convince Daniel to exhibit – and do much more than that besides of a more personal nature.

'What are you smiling at?' said Mark.

'Nothing,' she said abruptly. 'Let's get the bill.' She laid her hand on Mark's leg.

'Xavier got you in the mood?' said Mark.

'Mmm, something like that.' Once they had left the restaurant they strolled along Dover Street looking for a cab. Thinking about Daniel had made her feel uncomfortably aroused. Once they got into the taxi she toyed with the idea of initiating something right there. But Mark was lost in his own thoughts again so she leaned back and closed her eyes, knowing instinctively that the afternoon would have a satisfactory ending.

When they got back to Mark's house, he led her into the corridor and she felt a wave of familiarity hit her as she glanced into the sitting room, at the pretty chandelier and comfortable low sofas.

'Make yourself comfortable,' said Mark. There was an edginess to his voice that she found a little odd. 'I've just got a couple of phone calls to make.' She followed him into the corridor and watched him walk towards the foot of the stairs, which he began to climb. 'Have a look in the fridge in the meantime. I think there's some strawberries in there. But don't eat them, I have plans for them.'

Clara was a little put out that Mark should consider some private calls to be of greater importance than her. She pulled off her coat and draped it over the banister, wondering what to do with herself. With a shrug she decided that she might as well have a look in the kitchen. Idly, she walked over to the fridge, and pulled it open. She bent over a little to investigate, feeling the hem of her dress ride up her legs. There, right at the back, she could see the pile of strawberries, glistening deep red.

She picked up the plate and began to straighten herself up. She would treat herself to just one or two, she thought, the inside of her mouth tingling with anticipation.

'Clara!' The voice sounded so harsh behind her that the heel of her boot slipped between two of the floor tiles. In the surprise of it all she dropped the plate, which smashed loudly at her feet. Swivelling round she saw Jason standing in the doorway, his hands pushed into his trouser pockets.

'You gave me one hell of a fright!' she said, looking down at the shards of china and the fruit. Red juice was seeping over the tiles. 'I've got to get this mess 'cleared up.' He came towards her as she walked over to the sink. As she reached over to get a dishcloth she felt his body pressed up close against her back. Grabbing both her arms from behind he held her firmly at the elbows.

'That was a very stupid thing to do, wasn't it?' His voice was edged with danger and she felt the familiar effect, the harsh wave of arousal and the feeling of humiliation as he pressed himself close to her.

'But it was an accident.'

'You are a bad girl, Clara.'

'I was just going to clean it up.' She felt his breath on her neck, and his hands pressing into the soft flesh above her elbow. The grip tightened and she gasped as she felt his cock hardening against her bottom.

'Bad girl,' he whispered, lifting her hair and biting her, hard, on the back of the neck.

'I don't think we should be playing this game now. I mean, Mark could come back down at any minute.'

As he turned her around to face him he laughed. 'I don't think that Mark would bat an eyelid. He'd be as appalled as I am at your behaviour. Maybe more so.'

She wondered what to do. She hated to do what Jason wanted, well, simply because she didn't like him. He had got the better of her so many times before, and she had vowed to turn the tables. And yet he also knew how much she enjoyed being humiliated, and that gave him his power over her.

She struggled against him as he gripped her wrist and led her to the kitchen table. He sat down on a chair, and with the other hand pulled up her dress and lowered her over his lap. Her hair tumbled in a dark mass, almost touching the floor, and she reached out to touch the cold tiles with her fingers.

Inch by inch he was pulling up her dress now, getting a good view of the flesh-coloured stockings.

Deftly, he unclipped her suspenders and pulled down the panties.

'Bad, bad, bad girl,' he repeated, as he brought his hand rhythmically down on her arse.

'But what if Mark comes in?'

'Shut up and be punished.' He gripped her hair and yanked her head back, then abruptly let it fall again. Her head swam. He started to spank her, just above her thighs, where her bottom curved upwards. The skin was more sensitive there and she yelped as a smarting pain began to throb under his ministrations. She wriggled, trying to get away from the hand, but he brought it down harder still.

'Let me get up!' she shouted, the tears welling up in her eyes. Just as she thought she could bear it no more he slipped his hand over the opening of her pussy. Her bottom tingled, and then the tingle turned into a buzz of pleasure all over her overheated skin. And in the middle of it all, against the hot swollen core of her, he was bringing his hand down on her pussy. The slaps were gentler, and generated a violent response in her. Each time he spanked her pussy she felt herself take one step nearer to her climax.

'This will teach you,' said Jason, starting to spank her bottom again. To her relief, she felt his fingers slide into her opening, pistoning in and out while he spanked her with the other hand.

Her head spun, it was full of blood and now she began to see darkness in front of her eyes. She almost blacked out, her body wracked with excitement now, but still able to take some more. After his long spanking of her bottom, her skin had become desensitised, and now it was she who urged, 'Harder, harder!'

He increased the rhythm of his slaps, faster and faster, at the same time slipping his fingers in and out of her tight tunnel. In a split second, her body, overloading with pleasure, buckled and she came, the tremors of pleasure rushing over her. She no longer heard the slap of his hand against her flesh. He had ceased the rough treatment. All she could hear were her own cries as her body shook and spasmed against his hand.

She lost track of time for a long while. Then she became aware of her hands, pressed against the tiled floor.

'I think you've learned your lesson,' said Jason. 'Now get up. Mark's coming down.' She scrambled up from Jason's lap. But she was unsteady in the high-heeled boots and had to lean on the table to steady herself. She heard Mark's shoes on the tiles behind her and was surprised to feel a rush of excitement pass through her as she imagined the surprise he must be feeling. No doubt he was taking in her naked bottom, with the imprints of Jason's palm reddening the cheeks.

She began to pull the dress down, and turned around coyly to look at Mark. His face was dark, with what appeared to be anger upon it. She did not know how to react. She had never seen Mark in this state before and wondered what had prompted this strange mood.

She walked over to the fridge and hung her head. Could he be angry about a broken plate? 'I can explain.'

Mark took a few steps towards her, his eyes flashing darkly. Jason, who was still sitting impassively in the chair, now sensed the chill in the atmosphere and got up.

She looked at the pile of strawberries, pulpy and mixed with fragments of white china.

As Jason brushed past Mark he said, 'Make sure she cleans that up.' Clara watched Mark's eyes follow her as she bent down to examine the mess.

The look was unequivocal. It was full of longing yet

also peculiarly frightening. She looked back at him, her gaze a mixture of desire and defiance. Dropping her eyes to the floor she was unsure how to proceed.

He walked over to her and dropped the dustpan-and-brush, which clattered to the floor.

'I was going to smear you in strawberries and cream and eat it off you, but you've foiled that plan.'

'I'm sorry,' she said weakly, beginning to shovel up the mess. Her skin still smarted from Jason's spanking, but as she felt Mark's eyes on the curve of her bottom she started turning wet.

'You've made a stain on my tiles.'

She shuffled around so that she was a short distance from his feet. Not daring to lift up her head she waited, feeling somewhat humiliated as she crouched on the floor. She was tense as she waited for what would happen. She had never seen Mark act this way before. This kind of domineering behaviour was something that she expected from Jason, but not Mark. And yet she could not remember desiring something more urgently than she did just then.

Swiftly he kicked the dustpan away from her. 'Leave that. You can't even make a good job of cleaning it up.' Unexpectedly, tears prickled in her eyes. She tried to steady herself, but her hands slipped on the remains of the crushed strawberries and she collapsed in a prone heap at his feet.

He leaned over, his face reddening with anger and, lifting her body like a rag doll, pulled off the dress and bra with a barely controlled fury.

'Take your underwear off!' he commanded.

A tear ran down her face, and at the same time her whole body ached, with an urgent need for him to take control of her and do what he liked.

Pulling off her boots, she removed her stockings and panties.

'Alright. Now put your boots back on.' As she did

221

so he pinched her chin between his fingers. 'What are you crying for? I haven't even started with you yet.'

'Oh, don't hurt me, please don't hurt me,' she moaned, dimly aware that in that instant she had become completely his and under his control. When she began to whimper he slapped her, first on the left cheek, then on the right. Her head was cloudy, he was only a red blur to her now, his eyes glinting like chips of granite.

She sank to her knees, so that her face was level with his crotch. He tipped her head up and then craned it back so that the tendons at the base of her neck ached. 'You have been bad. You're a dirty girl!' He jerked her head back a fraction more.

'I'm sorry.'

'Be quiet. How do you feel? Like you could come right now?'

She began to make a sound at the back of her throat, trying to formulate some words. But his hard grip was preventing her lips from opening.

'Now, let me see you finger yourself.' She sat down on the floor, which was cold beneath her naked bottom. She wanted to touch herself, but she was so coiled with tension and desire she feared that the slightest pressure might set off her climax. Something in Mark's eyes told her that she would have to wait until he allowed her to come. She ran her fingers lightly over her moistened pussy and bit her lip as she felt her body tremble with anticipation.

'Get on your knees and take my cock in your mouth.' He had unzipped his trousers and held his cock in one hand, already fully erect. With the other hand he grabbed the back of her hair and pulled her head backwards. Gently, he pushed the head of his cock into her open mouth, sliding it slowly into the wet tunnel made by her tongue and the roof of her mouth. She tasted his pre-cum on its tip and tightened her mouth around the girth of his cock.

He began to moan as he pushed his cock in a little further and her face was inches from his pubic hair and balls. She closed her eyes and drank in the pungent scent of his maleness.

'I thought I told you to play with yourself,' he murmured, as he began to move his cock back and forth, tentatively, moving a fraction deeper each time.

Brushing her fingertips over her clit her body buckled and spasmed. She experienced a feeling of flying, shooting up into the atmosphere, as the sensations flushed hotly all over the surface of her skin.

'I didn't tell you to come, did I? You dirty bitch,' he said, his cock still in her mouth, preventing her from replying. Both his hands were gripping her hair now.

With one hand she pulled his cock out of her mouth and swirled her tongue in rapid motions around its head. She began to tease his balls with the tip of her tongue while she rapidly worked her hand over the tip of his cock. But just as she could feel his balls tensing beneath her lips he pulled away.

'No, no, not like this. I want to see you all spread out before me. Lie down on your front.'

Confused, she lay down on the cold floor and opened her legs. Soon she felt him press one finger into her secret passage. The finger went in easily and she guessed that he had used a lubricant. She relaxed against his fingers, feeling him push another finger and then a third into her. Then he replaced his fingers with his cock, pushing it in, all the way in, and the unexpected sensation of his cock-head pressing on the underside of her clit made it engorge again.

Slipping her hand underneath her pussy she rubbed her swollen bud as she felt him move in and out of her, slowly and sensuously, prising her open.

'Do you like that, you whore?'

She did not reply, caught up in the heady waves of heat that were flowing from her pussy. He tugged at her hair again, catching it and twisting it in his fingers so that her head hurt. She was dimly aware of the coldness of the tiles, the sharp edges that were pressing against her flesh and his insistent voice.

'What are you?' His voice was faint and breathless as he thrust more rapidly. He pulled her up by the hair so that her face was clear of the tiles.

'A dirty, filthy whore. A slut. Do what you want with me. I'm nothing but a whore.' And as the debasing words came tumbling out of her mouth she felt her body tip over into her orgasm. He too jerked inside her and came as she revelled in the strength of the sensation, which almost split her body in two.

Dazed, she felt him collapse in a heavy heap over her.

Eventually she moved out from underneath him and lay across him, the tiles no longer quite so cold due to their exertions. He put an arm around her and she lay across his chest. Then a drowsy sense of exhaustion fell over her and she felt herself being pulled into sleep. And though she fought it she must have finally given in. The next thing she remembered was waking in the darkened kitchen and then of Mark leading her up the steps to bed.

Chapter Thirteen

Clara awoke, her face pressed into Mark's shoulder. She looked over at him. His eyes were closed and he was dozing peacefully.

As she leaned over to give him a kiss on the lips his eyes opened.

'Good morning,' he said. The old amiable Mark had returned.

'Last night was an eye-opener,' she said.

'Was it?'

'I didn't know you had it in you.'

'Did you enjoy it?'

'Oh yes,' she said, kissing his bicep.

'There are lots of things you don't know about me.'

'Maybe I like it that way,' she said and dozed again. She was so spent and exhausted, but happy too. When she awoke again she realised it was nearly eleven and that Mark had got up.

Languidly, she rolled over and lifted the receiver to call the gallery. Xavier answered.

'Hi, Xavier. Listen, I'm not feeling too well,' she lied. 'I don't think I'll come in today.'

'That's OK.'

'But I'll call Daniel to try and arrange a meeting next week. What day would suit you?'

'Thursday would be OK. Take it easy.'

'Thanks, I'll see you tomorrow.'

'Oh, Clara.'

'What?'

'Paul phoned.'

A chill settled over her and she gripped the phone more tightly. 'What did he want?'

'He didn't say, but he sounded a little bit hysterical.'

'OK, thanks.'

Setting down the phone she tried to forget about Paul. It was too much to bear, having him contact her unexpectedly again. What on earth could he want? She leaned back on the bed and closed her eyes. Paul's face and his piercing blue eyes swam into view and a strange but familiar longing rose up in her. But she pushed the image away and, after leafing through Mark's address book on the bedside table, dialled Daniel's number.

She was nervous, but to her surprise when he answered the phone his voice sounded clear and open.

'Hi, it's Clara.'

'Oh, hi there! Did you have a good time?'

'Mmm, yes, very interesting.'

'Look, I must apologise.'

'What for?'

'For being moody. It was childish.'

'That's alright. You're forgiven. The reason I'm phoning is, I've talked to Xavier and we're really interested in exhibiting your piece.'

'Oh, I don't know about that.'

She heard the anxiety in his voice.

'Well, would you at least consider discussing it? I was thinking maybe you could come down to the gallery next Thursday, about 11.30?'

'I don't know.'

'What, are you busy?'

'No, but I haven't been in London for years.'

'I promise I'll look after you. It probably seems more scary in your head.'

'I don't think I can.'

'Don't be silly. You claimed that you couldn't make love, but that was cured easily enough wasn't it?' She panicked. Had she over-stepped the mark? She waited tensely for his reply.

Then, to her relief, his voice broke abruptly through the silence. 'You're right. It is time. I'd like to see your gallery again.'

'You've been here before?'

'Yes, but it was a long time ago.'

'Can you do Thursday?'

'Yes, I don't see why not.'

'I look forward to it.'

As she replaced the phone a sense of power welled up in her. It was just a question of time, she sensed, until he was completely under her spell. His resistance acted as an aphrodisiac and captivating him would be a slow drawn-out pleasure. She stretched, feeling her limbs gradually awakening. Daniel had put her in a good mood. Right now, though, she would go downstairs and find out where Mark had got to.

The week passed smoothly and effortlessly. Something had definitely changed, thought Clara. The restlessness that had coursed through her these past couple of months had dissipated. Every day she toyed with writing to Mr X, but each day the urge became smaller and less important. Maybe it was simply connected with her weekend with Daniel. Since she had met him he had achieved the unthinkable, getting under her skin and filling her thoughts. It was as if her subconscious was telling her that the mystery was solved, that Daniel was Mr X and that was an end to it.

The following Wednesday, after Xavier had left the gallery, Clara made her decision. She would tell Mr X that she could no longer write to him. But her thoughts were jumbled. For a while he had fanned the flames of her imagination, pushing her to heights of pleasure that she had not imagined existed, even in her wildest dreams. She would always be grateful to him, but now, she knew, the game was over. Since meeting Daniel, the restlessness had left her, for now. But she did not doubt that when she met him again it would return, leaving her body churned up and desperate for release.

She leaned back in her chair and stretched. It was so difficult to explain. Although nothing had been said, Daniel offered her a sense of security, which differed from the type that she had had with Paul. It was a security that allowed her the freedom to be who she wanted to be. And besides that there was this inexplicable bond, that had very little need for words or explanations.

That was what it really came down to, she thought. With Mr X it had all been about words, trying to verbalise her fantasies, then making them real. Now there was no more need for words. She started to delete Mr X's e-mails, which she had saved on her machine.

'Bye bye, Mr X', she said softly as she deleted them one by one. There was simply nothing more to say. How could she say goodbye to someone she had never met?

It was Thursday. Clara sat watching Xavier, who sat on the corner of the desk, impatiently drumming his fingers on it.

'He's late,' said Xavier.

'Only by fifteen minutes,' said Clara, leaning back in the soft director's chair.

'Are you sure he's going to show up?'

228

'Yes, of course I'm sure.' She tried to put a confident face on things but now that the minutes were ticking by she was beginning to doubt that Daniel was going to come after all.

Getting up from the chair she smoothed down the camel-coloured skirt of her suit, and moved towards the door.

'I'll check to see if he isn't upstairs.' Xavier got up from the desk and started to pace slowly between the desk and the bookshelves that ran up the wall.

'I really hope he doesn't let us down.'

'I'm sure it'll be alright.'

She left the office and climbed up the stairs. Her stomach was performing back flips, but that was because of Daniel's imminent arrival. As soon as she had pushed open the door and was in the gallery she saw his face, inches away from the glass window, staring in at her.

The click of her high-heels echoed around the gallery and she felt tense. Fumbling with the key she unlocked the door.

She stepped outside. 'Why didn't you ring the bell?'

At first he appeared not to have heard her. He was staring into the gallery as if lost in some old memory.

'What? Oh, sorry.' Then unexpectedly he took a step towards her and drew her into his arms. 'I was just thinking about something.'

She smiled at the delight of having his arms around her and his face in such close proximity. 'So you made it?'

'Looks like it. You look beautiful.' He lifted her hair up and kissed the side of her neck. She felt herself melting, dissolving from the sensations his soft lips were making as he moved his kisses over her, finally meeting her mouth and urgently prising open her lips with his tongue.

After a long time she finally pulled back, and, taking

229

his hand, led him into the gallery. She held his hand all the way down the stairs. But before she opened the door to Xavier's office she dropped it abruptly. She saw a cloud draw over Daniel's face but chose to ignore it.

'Daniel,' said Xavier, 'it's such a pleasure to meet you.'

Clara drew up a chair for Daniel. Then she sat back in the swivel chair, while Xavier continued to pace the room. She had never seen Xavier this excited about anything, apart from sex, but now he rapidly outlined his plan – that Daniel exhibit with the gallery as soon as possible.

'As I think I mentioned to Clara before,' said Daniel, 'in its present form the piece isn't really suitable for public consumption. The artwork deals with questions of an adult nature and this being a mainstream gallery, I really don't see how it could fit in.'

'But you program the questions into the computer?' said Clara.

'Yes.'

'How about if we put in new questions?' Daniel looked at her suspiciously. 'Then we three could decide whether each question should have a yes or a no answer. The preview could be free, but after that we could charge people to take part. Each event would be more like a party. Each question would have a set answer, a yes or no, although no one but us and the computer would know what the correct answer was.'

She felt her heart beat rapidly in her chest. Daniel was staring back at her, his eyes wide open, trying to digest what she had just said.

'I really don't think that Daniel can just modify his questions, Clara. He's an artist, and these things just come to him, it's not for the likes of us to specify.'

But then, to her surprise Daniel held up his hand and gave a shy smile. 'No, it's alright Xavier. I think that what Clara says is worth thinking about. Until now, the artwork has only been for my own private pleasure, but clearly it needs to change if it is to be exhibited. How do you see it working?'

Heartened, she went on. 'Well, each person aims to get from one side of the chessboard to the other. Like I did, on the prototype, by second-guessing the computer.' That wasn't strictly true. In fact the computer, or rather Daniel, had anticipated her answers, but for the moment that was irrelevant.

'Yes, I can see how that could work,' said Daniel and Xavier began to nod in agreement.

'If they guessed the answers correctly, or just got them right by chance, they would become part of an exclusive club, and be invited to future events.'

'What kind of questions were you thinking of?'

'There's nothing wrong with the questions that you have now apart from the fact that we need to appeal to a wider audience. So I was thinking along the lines of general questions like, is size important? Is beauty only skin deep? That sort of thing.'

'I think it has potential.'

'And it shouldn't take you too long to program that information into the computer?' said Xavier.

'No, no problem at all.'

'What about an exhibition in three weeks time?' said Xavier, his eyes sparkling. 'We've got a slot free then haven't we, Clara?'

'Well, yes.' An artist had cancelled her show only days before. 'But could you prepare everything by then?'

'Well, it would be tight, but I guess I could.'

'And rather than building it from scratch, could the panels just be transferred to the gallery?'

'Yes, that's no problem at all. Why don't we think of some questions now, while we're all together.'

The next two hours were spent thinking of questions

that could be programmed into the computer. By the end they had more than thirty questions and the atmosphere was convivial.

'Finally,' said Xavier, 'is size important?'

His eyes rested first on Daniel and then on Clara. Was he trying to signal that he knew that something was going on between them? Clara smiled, it was really none of his business.

'It's something only a woman can really know,' she said. 'I would say yes. What about you Xavier?'

'Yes, undoubtedly, it has something to do with it.'

'Yes it is then,' said Clara, standing up and feeling unexpectedly embarrassed. Why such an innocuous question should cause her to blush she had no idea.

'I'm beginning to understand,' said Xavier. 'In this instance the player on the chessboard would have to answer yes to stay on the board.'

'Yes, indeed, although there probably won't be much argument on that one.'

Clara was tired of thinking so hard. 'Shall we all go for something to eat? I was thinking maybe of the restaurant at Harvey Nichols?'

'I'd rather not. I've got a few things to finish, but you two go on. It was great to meet you Daniel.'

Once they had climbed the stairs and had hailed a taxi in the street, Clara said, 'I just got the urge to splurge some money on a new dress. Also, I'm famished. Thanks, Daniel, for agreeing to exhibit.'

He squeezed her hand. 'No, thank you. That was a brilliant idea of yours.'

'Let's not talk about it any more now.' She leaned back in the taxi, a haze of happiness falling over her. Everything was going to be alright. And now that she had Daniel she wasn't going to let him go in a hurry.

Eventually the spell broke. They arrived at the department store and entered the bright artificial atmosphere. They took the escalator to the top of the building and wound their way through the food store to the restaurant. Luckily there was a table free. Once they were settled at the table she began to relax. She ate pasta and it was delicious, as was the tiramasu that followed, which she was now finishing the last morsels of. 'You travelled down by train then?' she said, licking the last trace of the creamy dessert from her spoon.

'Yes, it's years since I've driven. The thought of the motorway was just too terrifying to contemplate.'

Clara thought of the young American hitchhiker she had picked up the week before. The memory made her smile.

'What are you smiling about?'

He looked delicious, she thought, sitting there in his worn denim shirt. 'I'm just glad you made it to London. It wasn't too difficult was it?'

'I couldn't have done it without you.' He placed both his hands over hers and she looked down, his gaze too intense to take in for a moment.

'Let me pay the bill,' she said. 'Then let's have a look around at the clothes.'

'Oh no, I don't mind being your sexual plaything,' he said good-naturedly, 'but I draw the line at being your personal shopper.'

'Well, if you behave yourself, maybe I'll give you a reward.'

They were in very good spirits, even after Clara had tried on several outfits and Daniel had waited patiently outside the changing rooms. Clara had slipped into a sliver of a dress. After looking at herself in the mirror she had poked her head out to see if Daniel could get her a smaller size. Not finding him there she decided to find another dress herself. In her bare feet she padded over to the rack of dresses. The slippery material felt good against her naked skin.

She was just rifling through the dresses and had found the right size when she felt a hand on her neck.

A ripple of excitement ran through her. She decided not to react. She waited to see what Daniel would do next.

He traced a line all the way down her back, along her spine. As she felt his fingers begin their investigation beneath the material of the low-cut back of the dress, she swung around.

'Daniel,' she began. But the man who was standing behind her was taller and altogether more familiar. 'Paul!' She looked up at his blue eyes, which were piercing in their intensity. 'What on earth are you doing here?'

'I needed to see you.'

She turned away from him and began to fiddle with the clothes.

'Look at me,' he said and pulled her by the shoulder.

She felt angry now, angrier than she had felt in a long time. How dare he touch her, follow her and now confront her?

'Haven't you had enough yet?' she said, her brown eyes blazing defiantly.

'No, not by a long way,' he said softly.

Despite herself she felt his Irish brogue begin to charm her but she forced herself to remain in control.

'What you did, the way your friend tied me up, it was unforgivable.'

'I'll do what I damn well please. I don't have time for this nonsense. Nor do I have to explain myself.' Why was Paul making her feel as if what she had done was wrong? She fought down the desire to make amends. She must stay strong.

'Why did you take me along to that house?' His brow creased in innocent puzzlement.

She could see Daniel coming towards her, across the racks of clothes. Thank God, she thought, he's going to save the situation.

'To humiliate you, what do you think,' she answered

234

sharply and turned away from him. But to her shock and surprise he again grabbed her by the shoulders and yanked her round.

'Hey! What do you think you're doing?' She had forgotten how powerfully built he was. And despite her anger at his presence she also felt a shudder of excitement pass through her.

'Is everything alright?' It was Daniel. Cool, calm and collected. He gave Paul the once-over.

'Let go of me,' she said and reluctantly he let his arms drop to his sides.

'Ah,' said Paul, 'Daniel. How nice to see you. Your knight in shining armour, or your latest conquest?'

'He's an artist that the gallery represents.'

'Artist!' Paul threw his head back and laughed. 'A filthy depraved pervert if you ask me. Don't you see that you've got to get away from these people? I can help you to, if you'll let me.'

'Look, I've got to go.' She carried the dress over one arm and Daniel put his arm around her protectively. 'I'd appreciate it if you left me alone.'

'But I can't, you know I can't.' As she turned away her face smarted and a well of emotion built up inside her. Why was it always so hard to say these final words to Paul? After all the trouble he had caused there were still these residual vestiges of feeling, feelings she had no time to confront now.

'He's really messed up,' said Daniel, as they approached the dressing room.

She went into the cubicle and gestured to Daniel to follow.

'I don't want Paul finding me again,' she said, her voice just above a whisper.

'But surely men aren't allowed in here.'

'So, who cares?' she said, wriggling out of her clothes so that she stood there in her bra and panties, which were made of scarlet lace.

235

'Alright then.' He pulled the curtain closed behind him and turned to look at her body and its reflection in the mirror. She slipped the other dress on.

She watched him standing behind her, watched as his hands began to travel up the front of the dress, tormenting her skin through the filmy material.

'Do you think I should buy this for your preview?'

'I'm not sure. I think I'd prefer you in something a little more provocative. Like this.'

He picked up a shiny black and red corset that someone had discarded in the corner of the changing room.

'But that's underwear!'

'Worn with a tight black skirt and a jacket, it'll be just the thing. Let me help you get into it.'

Soon she had slipped out of the dress and was standing there, just in her red panties, waiting patiently as he laced her into the corset, enjoying the feeling of constriction as he tightened the laces. Would it be possible, she wondered, to make love to him, right now?

He stood back and ran his eyes appreciatively over her bosom, which spilled over the top. The corset had pulled her waist in tight and she knew that Daniel was right, it would certainly get her noticed at the private view.

'I knew it would suit you perfectly,' he said, nuzzling the back of her neck. He was rubbing against her and she could already feel his cock stirring against her bottom.

'Do you think we should?' she asked.

'Oh, definitely, most definitely.' He turned her around and began to kiss her. She could tell that he was very aroused and that he wanted her, right then. But she held back a little. She was not used to Daniel making a move on her and was uncertain as to how to respond. After all, she had done all the running up to that point.

But before she could give the matter much more thought the curtain was whisked open and they were confronted by a furious-looking shop assistant.

'What on earth is going on in here?' The woman had her grey hair scraped back in a bun and was wearing a dowdy blue uniform. 'Gentlemen are not permitted in the ladies changing rooms!'

'I'm terribly sorry. He was just trying to give me a second opinion.'

'I can see what he was trying to do!'

Clara could hardly contain herself from laughing. The woman's eyes, behind the rimless glasses, were trained directly on Daniel's cock, which was tenting the front of his trousers.

'Now get out, before I call security.'

'I'll wait for you outside the store,' said Daniel, going red and trying to inch past the angry sales assistant.

'I've never seen anything like it in my life.' She walked off in a huff.

Clara doubled up in laughter as she thought of the look on Daniel's face, like a rabbit caught in headlights. Still, she reasoned, at least they hadn't been naked. She didn't fancy being arrested for lewd conduct.

After paying for the corset she left the store and soon found Daniel.

'That was so hilarious,' said Clara. 'But it also made me feel very frustrated. What about you?' She placed a soft kiss on his mouth and slipped her hand into the neck of his shirt.

'Look, I really don't want to be a killjoy but I need to get back home. There's so much to do if we're going to have this exhibition in three weeks.'

'I know. I appreciate how seriously you're taking it. But one night off won't kill you, will it? Don't you think I've waited long enough?'

He drew back and gave her that intense, enigmatic smile.

'Surely you can wait a little while longer?' He turned away from her, his eyes already on the traffic, looking for a taxi. He was drawing away from her. Maybe it was her fault, she had pushed him too fast, too soon.

They kissed hastily and before she knew where she was he had disappeared into a taxi. She stood there forlornly, watching the stream of traffic. Despondently, she turned and walked in the direction of Knightsbridge tube. Daniel was right, she supposed, they had to focus on the exhibition.

The last few weeks had been hectic. The upstairs gallery had been closed so that Daniel's artwork could be installed. For the first few days Clara had hovered around as the panels were laid, reconstructing the mysterious human-sized chessboard that she had first encountered in Daniel's playroom. But she soon found that she was getting under the workmen's feet.

Now, as the day of the opening approached, she was spending most of her time downstairs in Xavier's office. He made himself scarce most of the time. He could see how excited and agitated she was about making the show a success. She spent her days phoning up every contact she had, trying to make sure that Daniel's show got the coverage that it deserved.

She had not seen Daniel since their aborted attempt at making love in the changing room. He had given clear instructions to the workmen installing the sculpture from his end and so far things were going smoothly.

Then, a few days before the preview she got the phone call that she had been dreading since her last meeting with Paul.

'Clara, I just wanted to say that I'm sorry for creeping up on you like that.'

'Well, Paul, I would have thought you might have better things to do with your time.'

'It's just that you persist on being spiteful.'

'Spiteful?'

'You won't talk to me, you treat me like I was dirt, when all I've ever tried to do is look out for you.'

'I've got a new life Paul, and you'll just have to accept that.'

'If you'd just agree to meet me. I can explain everything.'

'I really don't have the time.'

'Why don't you make time?'

'I don't see what you can say that will make any difference.'

'Just give me a chance. That's all I'm asking, and then I'll leave you alone.'

'When?'

'Tomorrow evening. Come to our flat?'

'Our flat? You mean your flat?'

'Whatever. How does that suit you?' His voice had suddenly become businesslike and sterile. He was beginning to scare her a little.

'I really can't, that's the evening before the preview.'

'Exactly.'

Her head had begun to ache. 'What are you talking about Paul?'

'You remember that little scene at the last preview. Suppose I chose to repeat it? I don't think your precious Daniel would be too impressed.'

'You wouldn't dare!'

'Oh yes I would. So shall we say seven o'clock?'

The risk was just not worth taking. Wearily she had acquiesced.

Now here she was, in her car, on the evening before the preview, outside the block of flats where she had once lived with Paul. As she glanced up at the red-brick building with its impressive stone balconies, she realised that this was going to be one of the toughest evenings of her life. Clutching the wheel she felt all her strength seep out of her. If only there was someone there with her, right now, just for support.

She thought of Mr X. Suddenly she longed for him, whoever he was. She let her mind wander for a while. A pang of guilt hit her when she thought of him. She had been so busy organising Daniel's opening that she had had no time to address the matter of Mr X's identity further. It was silly, she knew, to dwell on it, but it was Mr X who was partly responsible for taking her life in this unexpected and new direction. Maybe she owed it to him, to resume contact, to find out once and for all who he was.

She pulled a letter, which she had received that morning, from her bag. In it, Paul begged and pleaded to be given a hearing. Reading it again now, the emotional tug was unmistakable. Somewhere, in a primitive part of her brain, she wanted to give Paul another chance. It was difficult to accept the fact, as Astrid often told her, that Paul had become obsessive towards her, a fact which no amount of talking would ever overcome.

'If you don't turn up,' she read, 'I will have no alternative but to turn up at Daniel's private view. I won't be ignored by you or any of your new friends.' He had put her in a position where she couldn't refuse him. Everything, her relationship with Daniel and the success of the gallery, was resting on tomorrow night going without a hitch.

Stuffing the letter back into her bag she got out of the car and went up to the front door. It felt strange to ring on the intercom of a block of flats where they had lived together for almost a year. She had not been back at all since the split. Once in the hallway a strange flood of nostalgia rushed over her. They must have had some good times, she reasoned, but right now she couldn't remember any of them.

In the lift she smoothed down her short-sleeved cream dress, made of a wool and lycra mixture that clung to her curves. She had wound her hair up in a chignon, wanting to feel in control. But as soon as Paul opened the door she felt her knees turn to jelly and all her resolve leave her.

Why did Paul have to look so attractive, she thought angrily to herself. His hair had been cut recently, making him look boyish and vulnerable. The soft light in the hall accentuated all that was familiar about him – his slightly melancholy gaze and the pronounced cut of his cheekbones.

'I'm so glad you could make it.' He leaned over and kissed her on the cheek. Another burst of nostalgia hit her, the familiar smell of his aftershave, a mixture of pine and cedarwood.

'I can't stay long.' She would stay precisely as long as it took for him to say his piece, and not a moment longer.

The flat looked larger than she remembered. As he led her into the sitting room she realised that the place had been completely redecorated.

'Well, you are a changed man,' she said, standing in the centre of the room and surveying it. The expensive low sofas were a neutral brown, and the décor was subdued, the only flash of colour a picture above the fireplace. 'I don't recognise the place.' It was true, the flat had been transformed from a mass of mismatching antique pieces to this minimalist haven.

'No doubt you can afford a cleaner these days, what with you being a famous novelist and all.'

'I do have one actually. Here, let me show you the bedroom.'

She followed him into a cool oasis of sea-green

bedlinen and worn – but she could see, very expensive – Persian rugs on the floor.

'I don't understand,' she said. 'Where's all your clutter, all your books?'

He explained that the pristine walls actually had hidden cupboards behind them where he stored his mess.

'I'm very impressed by your taste.'

'Thanks, but I didn't invite you here to talk about interior decoration.'

Once she was settled back in the sitting room and sipping a glass of wine, she waited. As he settled down beside her, her pulse began to race, a reaction to his proximity. Primly she uncrossed her legs and pressed them together, trying to pretend to herself that she wasn't aware of his eyes roaming over her.

'What you and your friend did,' he said softly, 'was really low.'

She sipped at her wine nervously. 'Oh, come on, it was just a laugh. We would have untied you.'

His face was deadly serious as he continued. 'You never used to be like this. Humiliating people for your pleasure.'

'Well, a lot has changed. You've probably changed as much as I have.'

'One thing that hasn't changed is the strength of my feelings towards you. And you, you had feelings for me once. I don't understand. How could you just tie me up and leave me?' He looked down. For one terrible instant she thought he was going to cry.

'It was just a game. A prank. To shock you I suppose.'

'It did that alright. Those people you were with, weirdos, the lot of them.'

'Oh, come on Paul, let's not reduce this conversation to personal insults.' As he poured some more wine into her glass his knee brushed against hers and her

242

body reacted violently. She knew that he had seen it and she blushed deeply. 'You said you wanted to tell me something.'

'I wanted to say I'm sorry about how things were when we were together. Maybe it's me, maybe I handled things all wrong. I wasn't ready then. But I am now.'

'What are you ready for? Paul, what on earth are you talking about?'

'When we were together we talked of marriage. I couldn't offer you that kind of commitment then, but I think I'm ready for it now.'

She laughed. The very idea of monogamy, marriage and commitment, which had once been what she had wanted, now seemed an irrelevance.

'I think it's what you need.'

'I don't think so Paul.'

'These people – Daniel, Mark – they're not right for you.'

'How do you know? Besides, don't tell me that you've been living like a monk.'

He put down his glass and leaned forward. Clutching her arm he spoke with an urgency and passion that made her body respond instinctively.

'Do you think I'd ever want anyone after you? I haven't even looked at another woman. I want to spend my whole life with you.'

Before she could reply he had pulled something out of his pocket. He pressed the little box into her hand. 'Open it,' he said.

Flipping open the box she looked down at the beautiful emerald set on a band of gold. 'Oh, this is crazy! You're not asking me to marry you?'

'Yes I am. Will you marry me, Clara?'

She snapped the box shut and put it on the sofa between them. Part of her was flattered, yet another part of her was becoming scared at the strength of his feelings.

'Will you think about it?'

'No, Paul. The matter's closed.'

To her surprise, he put the box in his pocket and dropped the subject. She tried to turn the conversation on to other issues and soon they had drained the bottle of wine. He was relaxed, and they talked about old friends and dipped into past memories. As she leaned back in the sofa and kicked off her shoes she noticed that her hem had riden up a little, almost exposing the black lacy stocking tops. She noticed too that his crotch was bulging provocatively in his trousers. It would only take one fluid movement and he could lean over and kiss her.

The moment lingered between them. His head was turned in her direction, his intense blue eyes looking soulfully at her. Yes, there had been some good times. It was all coming back, the memories beginning to flow a little freer. She remembered their first kiss with a shudder of excitement. And the first time they had made love. It would be so nice to re-create that feeling again. Just one more time, before they said goodbye forever.

Paul's face inched forward. She closed her eyes, waiting expectantly for his lips to touch hers. A little drowsy from the wine she thought how wonderful it was that their differences were behind them. But then his voice cut through her reverie.

'Would you like some more wine?'

'What?' The mood was broken. 'But the bottle's empty.'

'I just thought I could pop down to the off-licence and get another.'

'Well, I don't know. I really should be going. Tomorrow's a big day.'

'Oh, come on, I won't be five minutes.' He leaned

forward and kissed her on the nose, something he had often done when they were together. That little kiss had an unexpected reaction. It made her feel as if melted ice cream were being dripped all over the surface of her skin and between her legs.

Once he had left she stretched sensuously. It was hard to believe, now, that this was the man who had followed her and bombarded her with letters. Now that she had rejected his proposal of marriage, and he had accepted that she had moved on, couldn't he give her one last perfect night to remember him by? She knew it was dangerous, emotionally dangerous, but that was why it was attractive. She would suggest it when he came back.

Slipping on her shoes she decided to have a look around the flat again. Suddenly, she was gripped by an urge to have a look at the photo albums of their shared memories. He used to keep them in the bedroom cupboard she remembered. Maybe they were still there. Once in the bedroom she surveyed the walls, trying to find out where the seamless built-in cupboards opened.

Eventually she managed to prise them open. She was hit by how strong the contrast was between the tangled pieces of clothing and piles of yellowing manuscripts and the flawless wall that concealed them.

After several minutes of looking for the photo albums she was about to give up and look in another place. But then her eyes were drawn to a stack of video tapes shoved behind some tennis rackets.

Grabbing a few she took them out in the light to get a better look at them. There were no words on the spines, simply dates. She opened the cupboard door wider so that light flooded in. Crouching down she could see that the videos had been catalogued chronologically, the earliest one dating from early last year.

Her heart started to beat hard as the realisation dawned that she had still been living with him then.

For a second she considered putting them back. But something about the anonymity of the videos drew her. She just knew she had to see what was on them. But at the same time she was also aware of how fiercely Paul guarded his privacy, and she felt apprehensive about him finding her.

With her heart pounding in her chest she took the videos into the sitting room and swiftly pushed one into the machine. The image was grainy and obviously home-made. Two figures were in a cheap motel room. The woman was middle-aged, with badly-dyed blonde hair. Paul sat on the bed beside her and handed the prostitute a wad of notes. The sex that followed was basic and unimaginative.

She stopped the tape. Glancing at a tape she had in her hand she read the date, 1st September 2000. That had been the day, the day Paul had come to the gallery and declared his undying love. With trembling hands she pushed the tape into the slot and pressed play. An almost identical scenario ensued. This time the girl was younger, but again, she was clearly a prostitute, submitting to Paul's sexual advances with a barely concealed distaste.

As the image whirred on, Clara started to feel numb. She couldn't understand why these tapes should make her feel so strange. She had experienced so much of the variety of sexual pleasure recently. Maybe her palate had become more sophisticated but she couldn't understand his motivation to record these hastily completed acts.

She got to her feet, letting the video play on. Before she let herself out of the flat, she picked up another of Paul's videos to take with her. She never knew when she might need something to defend herself against him. After what seemed like forever, she got into her car to drive home.

What she had done with Astrid was nothing compared to this, she thought to herself, as she drove through the dark street. Firstly, he had been with some of these prostitutes while they had been a couple. The thought sickened her. Then, on the very day that he had made his profession of love in the gallery he had made yet another of these weird, clinical tapes.

No, she could not bear to think of it. She turned on the radio, hoping the pop music would drown out her thoughts. But still she kept turning things round in her mind. How could someone be so hypocritical, condemning her sexual freedom while having another set of rules for himself? She shook her head sadly. Thank God that she had found the videos. What he had done was low, but she would have lowered herself to his level if she had slept with him.

When she got home she slumped on the bed. Her body felt heavy as lead. She could call someone and tell them about it. But what would that achieve? She closed her eyes, imagining the scene, as Paul returned to the empty room and saw his dark secret revealed, the video still running, a cold documentation of a fleshly transaction. There was a little satisfaction in that vision at least, she thought as she drifted off, fully clothed, into sleep.

Chapter Fourteen

Clara opened the buttons of her fitted black jacket to reveal the red and black corset. A few eyes turned towards her. She moved amongst the crowds of people that filled the gallery. She felt good, brimming with confidence. Yet, the experience with Paul the day before had shaken her up. She looked around for Daniel, but couldn't see him.

This time blue lights flooded the room, emanating from the tiles. Again the computerised voice was Daniel's and although the questions weren't sexually explicit they were still generating a great deal of interest and amusement from the people who were playing the game.

Clara was delighted that so many people had turned up to the opening, but also because the press were taking such an interest.

Xavier passed by and squeezed her hand. 'I can't tell you how pleased I am about all this. I'm just going to talk to a TV cameraman. They want it to go out tonight on the local news. How about that?'

Xavier was sucked into the throng. A familiar face pushed his way towards her.

'Clara!' He kissed her on both cheeks.

'Hi, Claus. It's great to see you. And thanks so much for the write-up in *The Times*.'

'No problem. Are you responsible for all this?' he said, gesturing around the room.

'What do you mean?'

'Well, you must have seen the headlines. "Recluse re-emerges as new art sensation." You know, that type of thing!'

'I have been surprised by the amount of coverage we've got.'

'I couldn't believe it myself, when Mark told me, that Daniel Stanford had risen from the dead! What I meant was, are you responsible for getting Daniel back in the land of the living?'

She could just see Daniel in the far corner of the room, being interviewed by a presenter for the local news slot. She felt a warm rush of love come over her. 'Oh, I don't know about that,' she said.

'Don't be modest now, you've done a marvellous job.'

As Claus moved away from her, Clara stood still for a while, watching the hive of activity around her. She felt proud of what she had achieved. She had done what she set out to do, to put the gallery on the map. And she had said goodbye to Paul, well, almost. But all that paled into insignificance compared to the fact that Daniel had overcome his fears for her.

The evening passed very quickly. Even at ten o'clock people were still taking their turn on the chessboard. She watched as the computerised voice asked a question, 'Are women more sexual than men?' The woman who was standing on a square shrieked with laughter, then turned to her friends, asking them what she should answer. All the faces were bathed in the ethereal blue light, making them look ghostly and slightly sinister. But everyone was enjoying themselves, that was the main thing. Maybe they would start to leave, Clara thought hopefully, now that the drink had almost run out.

Clara moved to the side of the gallery and caught sight of a video camera that was on the floor. She bent down to pick it up and noticed that red wine had been spilt on it.

'Oh God! My video camera!' It was Astrid. They had spoken earlier but now Astrid was a little the worse for drink, her face flushed and her eyes wide.

'It's going to get crushed with all these people. I'll put it in the office.'

Clara struggled to get through the crowds. All around her she saw familiar faces, there were Jason and Mark over in the corner. Even Eric had flown over especially! Finally she pushed through the back door and tried to get down the stairs, which were also lined with people quaffing the last dregs of Champagne.

She got into the office and stood looking around her, pleased to have a bit of peace and quiet at last. The evening had been an unqualified success. Yet she felt that she couldn't fully enjoy herself. Paul was in her thoughts again and this time she knew that she would never be rid of him unless she took decisive action. She wiped the red wine from the video with a tissue, turning over an idea that was forming in her mind.

She walked over to the bookshelf and positioned the video between two books, so that the lens was turned towards the room. Taking a few steps back, she realised that she had hidden it very well. Unless they looked carefully, no one would see the video camera waiting to film the action.

Back in the gallery Clara placed her hand on Astrid's arm.

'I suppose Daniel's told you everything?' said Astrid.

'About what?'

'So he hasn't told you! He always was a secretive one.'

'What are you talking about?'

'Well, you know, all this stuff about all your sexual fantasies mysteriously coming true?'

'You mean Daniel was behind it?'

'Yes, well, we were all in on it,' said Astrid. 'Surely you guessed that?'

'I'm sorry Astrid, I don't understand.'

'Daniel had seen you once, by chance. He'd been visiting his lawyers in London. When I saw him shortly afterwards he was in quite a state. He was quite shaken up.'

'Really? Why?'

'Well, partly by London. He said he hated everything about it. The filthy streets, the traffic. But he had also been affected by you. He wouldn't stop talking about you. He went on and on, until he began to drive us mad.'

'Oh, come on Astrid, do you really expect me to believe all this? Isn't it a bit far-fetched?'

'Look, let's just say that Daniel was very taken with you. I told him that it wouldn't be difficult to arrange a meeting, since your gallery was showing Eric's work. We wanted Daniel to come along to the private view. He said that he would. Then he changed his mind.'

'Why?'

'I don't know. But I think he was a bit scared. He'd lived this reclusive life for so many years. He couldn't cope with the idea of too much human contact.'

'So what happened?'

'We said that we would help him to meet you, if that was what he wanted. But he was determined to go about it in his own way. He said that he would approach you anonymously, as Mr X.' Clara stared at Astrid incredulously, barely believing what she was hearing. 'Then, once he made contact he phoned Eric and asked him to enact the scenario that you had fantasised about. You remember, that first time, in the basement of the gallery?'

'I could hardly forget it!' Clara could not shake the feeling of unease that was creeping up on her as the mystery unravelled.

'We thought that that would be an end to it, but then he kept giving us the information and asking us to help out.'

'I imagine it wasn't too much like hard work?' Clara said sarcastically.

'No, of course not, quite the opposite. But still, we began to give up hope of Daniel ever making a move. So in the end I invited you up to meet him.'

'I see. And what about Mark? He was in on it too, I suppose?'

'Well, yes. He said he'd help out.'

'You lot are really too much,' she said, sipping at her Champagne, trying to hide her shock at this sudden revelation.

Daniel came up to them and put his arm around her shoulders.

'It's a happy ending for both of you isn't it?' Astrid leaned over and kissed Clara on the cheek. 'Don't bother thanking me, you ungrateful pair.' Clara gazed stonily at Astrid's back, which moved away into the crowd.

'Are you alright? Did Astrid say something to upset you?' said Daniel.

'I want you, now, in my office.'

'I don't understand.'

'Just follow me.'

He looked puzzled. For a moment she thought he wasn't going to follow her but when she turned to look she saw him a few feet behind her. They walked in silence all the way to the foot of the stairs.

As she opened the door to the office she said, 'Wait there.'

Shutting the door behind her she went into the room and switched on the video camera. She knew that she was going to enjoy this part of the evening very much indeed.

He opened the door and stepped into the room.

'Close the door.'

When he had done so he took a step towards her. She had never desired him so much. Something about his wounded look made her feel very angry and very aroused at the same time.

'What's the matter?'

'Don't act the innocent with me.'

'You know, don't you?' he said softly.

'Yes, I know alright.' She was desperately trying to hold down the irrational fury which was building up.

He raised his hand to touch her face but she gave him a harsh stare and brushed it away. As he started to protest, to ask for an explanation, she retorted, 'Get undressed.'

When he had stripped down to his boxer shorts she got him to lie on the floor. Crouched down beside him, she noted with interest that his erection was already tenting the cotton of the navy shorts, but matter-of-factly she lifted his arms above his head.

First she tied his hands to the radiator, her eyes travelling over the lush dark armpits.

'All this time, you've been so concerned with what I want.' Her voice was steady, but there was a just perceptible edge of agitation in it. She pulled his boxer shorts down roughly, and his cock sprang free. Holding it deftly in her right hand she moved his foreskin back, watching as he struggled against the rope with which his wrists were bound.

'Oh, come on, don't play about. What about the guests, the party?'

'Right now that's of no importance to me.' She saw that his wrists were becoming red from rubbing against the rope. A rush of excitement was flowing through her. She revelled in the sense of power, knowing that she had him beneath her, to do whatever she pleased with.

'Stop that! Stop it this instant! When I tied you up I didn't expect you to try to escape. I think that you need to be punished, if only I didn't have the suspicion that you might end up enjoying it.' She hesitated, listening to the soft rise and fall of voices outside the door, then ran her nails lightly along the dark hair on his chest.

'What are you going to do to me?' he said, a flicker of amusement in his eyes.

She stood up and began to peel off her skirt and jacket. Soon she stood there in the satin corset, which was tied tightly to accentuate her narrow waist. She unclipped the sidefastening of her panties and threw them aside. She saw his eyes grow wide as they travelled up the black seamed stockings and came to rest at the dark triangle of her bush.

Who was Daniel, she thought, as she watched his cock thicken and swell as he gazed up at her. She widened her legs so that he could get a good glimpse of her pussy lips.

In a split second the atmosphere changed, imperceptibly. Her pussy beginning to tingle, she looked down at Daniel's taut muscular chest, with its thatch of dark hair.

'I can't wait much longer,' he said. 'You're driving me crazy.'

'How do you think I felt?' she said, looking down at him fiercely. 'First you approached me, making me get all hot and bothered in the gallery. All through that long, hot summer, tormenting me, making me want you more and more.'

'But you got what you wanted.'

'Shut up!' she commanded. 'It's only fair that we get this straight. If I hadn't organised this exhibition, if I hadn't forced you out of hiding, hadn't made you reveal your identity, you'd still be in your hiding place, wouldn't you, with all your cronies doing your bidding. Wouldn't you?'

'But it was just a game!' he protested. She squatted over him, her pussy grazing his chest, and slapped his face. She knew that maybe she had gone too far, and yet the throbbing pulse of excitement in the pit of her stomach urged her to go on.

'Yes, well, now it's time that I had my fun with you. It's about time that you discovered who was boss. She leaned forward, letting her hair fall over his face. She dragged her hair down over his chest, adrenaline pumping through her veins at the novelty of the situation. She hesitated for a second, unsure as to how to proceed, then settled herself on him and flung back her head. Leaning forward so that the corset hovered tantalisingly, inches above his face, she loosened the laces, pulling it apart so that he got a view of her full breasts and hard, dark nipples. Then with one deft movement she tossed the corset aside.

A rapid fluttering started in her pussy and because she could suddenly bear it no more she rose a little and then lowered herself down over his mouth.

'Make me come, you miserable worm.' She waited, holding her breath, and soon he began to exploratively lick between her labia, his tongue finally coming to settle on her swollen bud. She ground her pussy into his mouth, forcing him to open a little wider.

'Don't stop! I didn't tell you to stop!' The lapping began again, creating a delectable frisson. She steadied herself on her hands, revelling in the fact that at last she had him exactly where she wanted him. Soon she came, rubbing her wet pussy over his face as the tremors raced through her. Taking deep breaths she felt her head fill with tiny points of light, as she gave herself up to the spasms that were shaking her body.

When she had regained her composure she slid along the length of his body. Holding his cock in one hand she rubbed the swollen lips of her pussy along its length. He began to moan and thrust upwards, urgently trying to get his cock inside her. It was tempting to allow it, but in her new mood of control she decided on a different approach.

'Don't move! Don't think that I'm going to let you do as you please with me. No, for too long I've been a pawn in your game, a piece to be moved about on your chessboard out there,' she said with a sneer. There was no noise coming from outside the door now, she noted. Maybe the guests had left.

'You know what happened to poor old Paul, don't you? If you make another movement you might find yourself in the same predicament.' Bending down, she kissed him on the lips. 'I might leave you here all night. It's really all you deserve.'

She watched as his mouth formulated some words of protest, but then he thought better of it. She felt that he was almost, but not quite, ready to submit to her demands and the thought made her skin tingle and her throat grow dry.

His cock was growing rock hard in her hand and was lubricated from her juices. Instead of ramming her pussy down on it she positioned her secret passage over its head. With one fluid movement she had him an inch inside her. She moved another inch, the friction of his cock inside the tight passage making sweat break out in the cleft between her breasts. Soon she felt his cock thrust upwards, and sensed Daniel's impatience to be fully inside her.

'What did I tell you? Do that again and you'll really be for it!'

'I'm sorry.'

'You think I'm joking, don't you? Well, I'm not.' She stared deep into his eyes, which were now quite clouded over with desire. He no longer struggled against the ropes, and as she slid down the full length of his cock, she felt the tension of his body against her bare thighs, and then he grew limp and started to submit. Well, he could wait, she thought, trying not to reveal by her facial gestures the intense pleasure building up within her. But the need was too urgent, her arsehole widening a fraction so that she could slide his cock in and out.

'This is all you're good for,' she said breathlessly, rubbing her clit feverishly with her fingertips. She watched his eyes close, drifting away into his own private realm. 'Look at me! Look at me!' His eyes opened. 'I want you to see exactly what I'm doing to myself.'

The pleasure was building up ferociously, and yet she didn't want it to end. The raw, primeval feeling of power overwhelmed her as she rammed herself onto his cock, over and over again, her fingers brushing her clit until the pleasure was so intense she feared she might blackout.

'I wish you weren't enjoying this. You don't deserve this, any of it.' Then she lost track of her thoughts, knowing that he was thrusting up into her, and no longer caring because it felt so good. Her climax was powerful, like molten wax dripping through her insides, making her cry out with its brutal intensity.

She was aware of him moaning as he came and gradually she stopped riding him, and they stayed still for a while. Clara's face was turned to the radiator to which he was tied. Then she heard the doorknob being turned behind her and felt a tremor of fear.

Astrid opened the door. Clara swivelled round to

look at her. She was wearing a sky-blue silk dress and clutched a bottle of Champagne.

'Ah good,' she said. 'I see that you are reconciled.'

'Are we?' said Daniel.

Clara smiled. Now that she had taken out her anger on Daniel in a flood of sexual energy she felt calmer, lighter. Astrid held the bottle out in front of her and tried to pop the cork.

'Here, give me that,' said Clara, who still sat naked on Daniel.

'You didn't answer my question,' said Daniel.

'Will you two stop squabbling.'

Clara gasped as the Champagne went off with a pop and the icy liquid spilled over Daniel's chest.

'Ah!' Daniel moaned. Astrid quickly knelt down and began to lick at the fizzing liquid.

'Yes, I forgive you.' Clara took a sip of Champagne from the bottle. Astrid was still greedily licking it up, and Clara saw that her dress was wet with Champagne and clinging to her firm breasts. Glancing past Astrid's tumble of blonde curls her eyes locked with Daniel's. As her gaze moved lower she saw that he was growing erect again.

Swilling the Champagne round in her mouth she bent down and took in Daniel's cock. He gasped as the frothy liquid tingled along the length of his cock. Still keeping him in her mouth, Clara reached over to Astrid and pulled down a strap of the Champagne-soaked dress to reveal her flushed breasts. It was going to be one hell of a night.

Both Daniel and Astrid were too busy to observe the tiny red light of the video camera on the shelf at the back of the office. Clara smiled to herself. How she would enjoy sending it to Paul, with a note, 'one for your collection'. The very thought of his crestfallen face made her tingle. She hoped that he would feel shame, knowing that she had found out his true colours.

As Clara watched Astrid peel off her dress she felt a sense of satisfaction sweep over her. Clara was enjoying the kick that she was getting from the fact that she was the only one who knew that they were being filmed. She gazed down at Daniel, whose eyes were closed. He had taught her so much, but now she had learned all that he had to teach her. It was inevitable that now the roles would be reversed. She looked forward to a bright future, in which Daniel was hers, to do with as she pleased.

Visit the Black Lace website at
www.black-lace-books.com

LOOK OUT FOR THE ALL-NEW BLACK LACE BOOKS – AVAILABLE NOW!

All books priced £7.99 in the UK. Please note publication dates apply to the UK only. For other territories, please contact your retailer.

ONE BREATH AT A TIME
Gwen Masters
ISBN 978 0 352 34163 1

Kelley is a woman with a broken heart. She doesn't need another complication in her life, and certainly not another man. But when she stumbles across Tom, the things she thought she didn't want are exactly what she needs. As they fall for each other and engage on a compelling journey through dominance and submission, both lovers strive to shake away their dark pasts. But is blinding passion enough to prevent them being ripped apart?

To be published in February 2008

A GENTLEMAN'S WAGER
Madelynne Ellis
ISBN 978 0 352 33800 6

When eighteenth-century young lady Bella Rushdale finds herself fiercely attracted to handsome landowner Lucerne Marlinscar, she does not expect the rival for her affections to be another man. However, the handsome and decadent Marquis Pennerley has desired Lucerne for years and, when they are brought together at the remote Lauwine Hall for a country party on the Yorkshire Moors, he intends to claim him. This leads to a passionate struggle for dominance – at the risk of scandal – between the highly sexed Bella and the debauched aristocrat. Ultimately it will be Lucerne who will choose the outcome – and his decision is bound to upset somebody's plans.

Black Lace Booklist

Information is correct at time of printing. To avoid disappointment, check availability before ordering. Go to www.black-lace-books.com. All books are priced £7.99 unless another price is given.

BLACK LACE BOOKS WITH A CONTEMPORARY SETTING

☐ ALWAYS THE BRIDEGROOM Tesni Morgan	ISBN 978 0 352 33855 6	£6.99
☐ THE ANGELS' SHARE Maya Hess	ISBN 978 0 352 34043 6	
☐ ASKING FOR TROUBLE Kristina Lloyd	ISBN 978 0 352 33362 9	
☐ BLACK LIPSTICK KISSES Monica Belle	ISBN 978 0 352 33885 3	£6.99
☐ THE BLUE GUIDE Carrie Williams	ISBN 978 0 352 34132 7	
☐ THE BOSS Monica Belle	ISBN 978 0 352 34088 7	
☐ BOUND IN BLUE Monica Belle	ISBN 978 0 352 34012 2	
☐ CAMPAIGN HEAT Gabrielle Marcola	ISBN 978 0 352 33941 6	
☐ CAT SCRATCH FEVER Sophie Mouette	ISBN 978 0 352 34021 4	
☐ CIRCUS EXCITE Nikki Magennis	ISBN 978 0 352 34033 7	
☐ CLUB CRÈME Primula Bond	ISBN 978 0 352 33907 2	£6.99
☐ COMING ROUND THE MOUNTAIN Tabitha Flyte	ISBN 978 0 352 33873 0	£6.99
☐ CONFESSIONAL Judith Roycroft	ISBN 978 0 352 33421 3	
☐ CONTINUUM Portia Da Costa	ISBN 978 0 352 33120 5	
☐ DANGEROUS CONSEQUENCES Pamela Rochford	ISBN 978 0 352 33185 4	
☐ DARK DESIGNS Madelynne Ellis	ISBN 978 0 352 34075 7	
☐ THE DEVIL INSIDE Portia Da Costa	ISBN 978 0 352 32993 6	
☐ EDEN'S FLESH Robyn Russell	ISBN 978 0 352 33923 2	£6.99
☐ EQUAL OPPORTUNITIES Mathilde Madden	ISBN 978 0 352 34070 2	
☐ FIRE AND ICE Laura Hamilton	ISBN 978 0 352 33486 2	
☐ GOING DEEP Kimberly Dean	ISBN 978 0 352 33876 1	£6.99
☐ GONE WILD Maria Eppie	ISBN 978 0 352 33670 5	
☐ HOTBED Portia Da Costa	ISBN 978 0 352 33614 9	
☐ IN PURSUIT OF ANNA Natasha Rostova	ISBN 978 0 352 34060 3	
☐ IN THE FLESH Emma Holly	ISBN 978 0 352 34117 4	
☐ LEARNING TO LOVE IT Alison Tyler	ISBN 978 0 352 33535 7	

☐ DARKER THAN LOVE Kristina Lloyd ISBN 978 0 352 33279 0

☐ DIVINE TORMENT Janine Ashbless ISBN 978 0 352 33719 1

☐ FRENCH MANNERS Olivia Christie ISBN 978 0 352 33214 1

☐ LORD WRAXALL'S FANCY Anna Lieff Saxby ISBN 978 0 352 33080 2

☐ NICOLE'S REVENGE Lisette Allen ISBN 978 0 352 32984 4

☐ THE SENSES BEJEWELLED Cleo Cordell ISBN 978 0 352 32904 2 £6.99

☐ THE SOCIETY OF SIN Sian Lacey Taylder ISBN 978 0 352 34080 1

☐ TEMPLAR PRIZE Deanna Ashford ISBN 978 0 352 34137 2

☐ UNDRESSING THE DEVIL Angel Strand ISBN 978 0 352 33938 6

BLACK LACE BOOKS WITH A PARANORMAL THEME

☐ BRIGHT FIRE Maya Hess ISBN 978 0 352 34104 4

☐ BURNING BRIGHT Janine Ashbless ISBN 978 0 352 34085 6

☐ CRUEL ENCHANTMENT Janine Ashbless ISBN 978 0 352 33483 1

☐ FLOOD Anna Clare ISBN 978 0 352 34094 8

☐ GOTHIC BLUE Portia Da Costa ISBN 978 0 352 33075 8

☐ THE PRIDE Edie Bingham ISBN 978 0 352 33997 3

☐ THE SILVER COLLAR Mathilde Madden ISBN 978 0 352 34141 9

☐ THE TEN VISIONS Olivia Knight ISBN 978 0 352 34119 8

BLACK LACE ANTHOLOGIES

☐ BLACK LACE QUICKIES 1 Various ISBN 978 0 352 34126 6 £2.99

☐ BLACK LACE QUICKIES 2 Various ISBN 978 0 352 34127 3 £2.99

☐ BLACK LACE QUICKIES 3 Various ISBN 978 0 352 34128 0 £2.99

☐ BLACK LACE QUICKIES 4 Various ISBN 978 0 352 34129 7 £2.99

☐ BLACK LACE QUICKIES 5 Various ISBN 978 0 352 34130 3 £2.99

☐ BLACK LACE QUICKIES 6 Various ISBN 978 0 352 34133 4 £2.99

☐ BLACK LACE QUICKIES 7 Various ISBN 978 0 352 34146 4 £2.99

☐ BLACK LACE QUICKIES 8 Various ISBN 978 0 352 34147 1 £2.99

☐ MORE WICKED WORDS Various ISBN 978 0 352 33487 9 £6.99

☐ WICKED WORDS 3 Various ISBN 978 0 352 33522 7 £6.99

☐ WICKED WORDS 4 Various ISBN 978 0 352 33603 3 £6.99

☐ WICKED WORDS 5 Various ISBN 978 0 352 33642 2 £6.99

☐ WICKED WORDS 6 Various ISBN 978 0 352 33690 3 £6.99

☐ WICKED WORDS 7 Various ISBN 978 0 352 33743 6 £6.99

☐ WICKED WORDS 8 Various ISBN 978 0 352 33787 0 £6.99

To find out the latest information about Black Lace titles, check out the website: www.black-lace-books.com or send for a booklist with complete synopses by writing to:

Black Lace Booklist, Virgin Books Ltd
Thames Wharf Studios
Rainville Road
London W6 9HA

Please include an SAE of decent size. Please note only British stamps are valid.

Our privacy policy
We will not disclose information you supply us to any other parties. We will not disclose any information which identifies you personally to any person without your express consent.

From time to time we may send out information about Black Lace books and special offers. Please tick here if you do <u>not</u> wish to receive Black Lace information. ❏

Please send me the books I have ticked above.

Name ....

Address ....

....

....

....

Post Code ....

Send to: Virgin Books Cash Sales, Thames Wharf Studios, Rainville Road, London W6 9HA.

US customers: for prices and details of how to order books for delivery by mail, call 888-330-8477.

Please enclose a cheque or postal order, made payable to Virgin Books Ltd, to the value of the books you have ordered plus postage and packing costs as follows:

UK and BFPO – £1.00 for the first book, 50p for each subsequent book.

Overseas (including Republic of Ireland) – £2.00 for the first book, £1.00 for each subsequent book.

If you would prefer to pay by VISA, ACCESS/MASTERCARD, DINERS CLUB, AMEX or SWITCH, please write your card number and expiry date here:

....

Signature ....

Please allow up to 28 days for delivery.